SITTING DUCK

Prophet turned to stare northwest over the rubble heaps. He'd heard what sounded like a blackfly sort of buzzing and whistling. The buzzing and whistling grew louder.

Mean and Ugly jerked his head up. At the same time, Prophet felt a sudden, searing pain in his upper right arm.

Before he knew what was happening, thunder clapped sharply in the northeast, and Mean and Ugly bucked suddenly with an indignant whinny.

Prophet cried as, losing his reins as well as his rifle, his entire right arm on fire, he twisted around and flew straight back off the pitching dun's right hip . . .

PRAISE FOR
PETER BRANDVOLD:

"Takes off like a shot, never giving the reader a chance to set the book down."
—Douglas Hirt

THE GRAVES
AT SEVEN DEVILS

PETER BRANDVOLD

BERKLEY BOOKS, NEW YORK

THE BERKLEY PUBLISHING GROUP
Published by the Penguin Group
Penguin Group (USA) Inc.
375 Hudson Street, New York, New York 10014, USA
Penguin Group (Canada), 90 Eglinton Avenue East, Suite 700, Toronto, Ontario M4P 2Y3, Canada
(a division of Pearson Penguin Canada Inc.)
Penguin Books Ltd., 80 Strand, London WC2R 0RL, England
Penguin Group Ireland, 25 St. Stephen's Green, Dublin 2, Ireland (a division of Penguin Books Ltd.)
Penguin Group (Australia), 250 Camberwell Road, Camberwell, Victoria 3124, Australia
(a division of Pearson Australia Group Pty. Ltd.)
Penguin Books India Pvt. Ltd., 11 Community Centre, Panchsheel Park, New Delhi—110 017, India
Penguin Group (NZ), 67 Apollo Drive, Rosedale, North Shore 0632, New Zealand
(a division of Pearson New Zealand Ltd.)
Penguin Books (South Africa) (Pty.) Ltd., 24 Sturdee Avenue, Rosebank, Johannesburg 2196,
South Africa

Penguin Books Ltd., Registered Offices: 80 Strand, London WC2R 0RL, England

This is a work of fiction. Names, characters, places, and incidents either are the product of the author's imagination or are used fictitiously, and any resemblance to actual persons, living or dead, business establishments, events, or locales is entirely coincidental.

THE GRAVES AT SEVEN DEVILS

A Berkley Book / published by arrangement with the author

PRINTING HISTORY
Berkley edition / January 2009

Copyright © 2009 by Peter Brandvold.
Cover illustration by Bruce Emmett.

ISBN: 978-0-425-22547-9

BERKLEY®
Berkley Books are published by The Berkley Publishing Group,
a division of Penguin Group (USA) Inc.,
375 Hudson Street, New York, New York 10014.
BERKLEY® is a registered trademark of Penguin Group (USA) Inc.
The "B" design is a trademark of Penguin Group (USA) Inc.

PRINTED IN THE UNITED STATES OF AMERICA

10 9 8 7 6 5 4 3 2 1

*For K.G. and Frank
with much affection and a ton
of appreciation*

1

LOU PROPHET TIED his hammer-headed line-back dun, appropriately named Mean and Ugly, to a scrub willow along a narrow creek somewhere in the devil's maze of looming peaks and plunging valleys of western Colorado.

"While I'm away, Mean," the bounty hunter said, ducking his head to peer through the willows, "don't go runnin' off with any mustang fillies, hear? Pretty and frisky they might be, but they'll chew you up and spit you out like spoiled oats. I know that from exp—"

In the corner of his right eye, Prophet had seen the horse swing his head toward him too late. Mean and Ugly sunk his long, flat-edged front teeth into Prophet's right shoulder, dropping a bright red veil of pain down over the big man's eyes.

"Son of a bitch!" Prophet swung around and smashed an elbow against the dun's blaze-faced snout. "How many times I gotta tell you not to *do* that, you black-hearted cuss?"

Unfazed by the blow, Mean and Ugly bobbed his head, snorting. His white-ringed eyes blazed with mischievous satisfaction.

Sucking air through his teeth, his broad, broken-nosed face flushed with pain and exasperation, Prophet canted his head to inspect his shoulder. The horse had torn the oft-repaired tunic seam once again. A small tear, but a tear nonetheless. No blood shone, but the tall, lean, hard-bodied man in dusty, sweaty buckskins felt as though his shoulder had been laid bare to the bone.

What a horse's teeth lacked in sharpness they made up for in hardness—and Mean and Ugly's choppers were hardest of all. The horse had always had a penchant for biting, and long, hard rides ghosting outlaws tended to bore him, making him frisky and contentious and especially prone to sinking his teeth into human flesh.

Or horse flesh, for that matter. But no other horses were near. The nearest were those of the stage robbers Prophet had been following for the past two weeks and that, when he'd glassed the area from a hill a few minutes ago, he'd spotted by the cabin a good two hundred yards away. So Prophet's shoulder, carelessly offered, had proven too enticing for the dun to pass up.

Cursing again with disgust and keeping an eye on the horse, who had now dropped his head to crop bromegrass with infuriating indifference, Prophet leaned down to remove his spurs. "Don't know why I've put up with you all these years, Mean and Ugly. I must be touched. To think of all the *good* horses I've passed up!"

Truth was, Mean and Ugly was the best horse Prophet had owned. Maybe not the handsomest, but the best, toughest stayer a bounty hunter could ask for. And while he'd never admit it out loud, Prophet felt a close kinship with the hammer-headed dun. They were cut from the same cloth. Both were big, ornery, green-broke loners who lived to stomp with their tails up.

He dropped the small-roweled spurs into his saddlebags, then hung four sets of manacles from his cartridge belt, with enough space between each so they wouldn't jostle one another and give him away. Shucking his Winchester '73 from its saddle boot, the bounty hunter racked a fresh shell into the breech. He glanced at Mean and Ugly once more, adding under his breath as he began tramping off through the willows, "A horse like that is an abomination against God and all that's holy. Can't sell him, though. Wouldn't sic that cursed cayuse on my worst enemy. And he ain't *worth* a bullet!"

He spat to one side and, rubbing his still-barking shoulder, continued through the willows to the shore of the shallow, slow-moving creek rippling over rocks and around sandbars. Halting at the edge of the stream, partly concealed by branches, he squeezed his rifle and looked around.

A few crows and mountain jays milled amongst the cottonwoods on both sides of the creek. Otherwise, nothing moved. No sounds but the gurgling stream, rasping weeds, ruffling leaves, an occasional bird cry. It appeared that Emmitt Sanderson, the leader of the outlaws whom Prophet had tracked north from Alamosa, threading the broad San Luis Valley before veering west into the high country, had appointed no picket to watch the gang's back trail.

Resting the Winchester on his right shoulder but raking his cautious gaze from right to left and back again, Prophet stepped into the stream, keeping to the shallow ford as he made for the other side, the water refreshingly cool as it slid over his boots.

When he gained the other shore, he had another look around, then began climbing the slope beyond, working his way right and holding the Winchester in both hands across his chest. His wet boots slipped in the brittle, sun-cured grass.

His breath rasped, and his sweaty buckskin tunic clung to his back. He kept his shrewd bounty hunter's eyes narrowed as he swept the terrain around him.

He'd hiked a hundred yards, uphill and down, when he spied the outlaw cabin perched on the shoulder of a low bluff among sparse pines and boulders. It was a small, worn-gray log affair with a rusty tin roof. A thin ribbon of smoke issued from the chimney pipe, rising nearly straight up to the faultless vault of cerulean sky.

An old fur trapper's track.

A corral and lean-to stable lay on the cabin's near side, and inside the corral five horses milled lazily, clumped head to tail for shade and to keep the flies out of one another's faces. They were the horses Prophet had been tracking, including the stocky steeldust the outlaws had used for packing the stage loot they'd appropriated from the trails around Durango.

The gang had killed nine drivers and stage passengers in the past six months, including a young girl who'd caught a

ricochet. They were as deadly a bunch of long-coulee riders to
stalk the San Luis Valley. Prophet wouldn't begrudge himself
the bounty money he'd pocket as the four were led off to the
gallows. In fact, he'd toast their hangman and beseech Ole
Scratch to turn up the heat in their honor.

Another hunt was almost over. The bounties on this bunch
would set him up through the fall and part of the winter—if he
didn't drink and carouse it all away in one wild weekend, as
he was prone to do. As his sometime-partner Louisa Bonaventure often reminded him, he had to keep himself on a short
leash, show some horse sense. He wasn't getting any younger,
and he'd like to retire with a nest egg someday.

Prophet jogged a beeline toward the cabin, crouching and
threading a narrow crease between hills. He'd just worked his
way through a brushy hollow showing the packed-down weeds
where deer or elk had slept, when he stopped suddenly, dropped
to a knee behind a stunt cedar, and lifted his head, listening.

Beyond the camelback to his left, voices sounded, muffled
and tempered by splashing water. A woman squealed shrilly.
"Ouch, ya big ape! That *hurt*!"

Prophet squinted up the ridge. Women? Then he remembered that Sanderson's boys had all gotten hitched a while back,
including old Emmitt himself for the fourth or fifth time. Apparently they'd needed some female flesh to cook and sweep
out their hideout cabin and warm their mattress sacks.

Prophet chewed his cheek, troubled. Women and dogs were
the bane of the bounty hunting profession. Dogs would bark
and give you away while women often defended their men as
they did their children—viciously and unpredictably. And for
some reason, it was harder to shoot a woman than a man. Many
a bounty hunter—and lawman, for that matter—had been
turned toe down after hesitating with an armed female in his
pistol sights.

Prophet scrutinized the cabin once more, tapping his Winchester's stock with his gloved right thumb. Spying no one
milling about the cabin, he turned and, keeping low in case
someone was staring out a window, tramped back the way he'd
come. Following the voices and splashing water, he approached
the crest of a steep southern ridge, the voices rising from down
the other side.

Breathing hard from the tough climb, Prophet doffed his hat. He got down on hands and knees and crabbed to the brow of the ridge, snuggling up between two boulders and casting a glance into the valley below.

Lying flat, he pressed his chin to the gravelly ground as his eyes swept the broad, shallow stream angling along the base of the ridge. There were no trees between Prophet and the stream, so it wasn't hard to see that all four of the Sanderson bunch were frolicking with four women in the stream's shallow, sun-speckled water—all as naked as the day they were born.

The men's clothes were strewn with the women's along the rocky shore. Prophet spied a few rifles, revolvers, and knives with the clothes, but one of the men—a big, bald, mustached hombre whom he recognized as Horton Whipple—wore a revolver on a rawhide loop around his broad, tattooed neck. Another man, who looked like Emmitt Sanderson himself, lolled farthest left with a redheaded girl on his lap, a brace of holstered revolvers within easy reach on a nearby rock.

Even skinny-dipping, the sons of bitches kept themselves armed. But it took that kind of savvy to stay ahead of the law for five, going on six years, as this bunch had. They'd left two sheriffs and three U.S. marshals moldering in graves behind them.

Prophet considered the situation. He had two owlhoots lolling in the water on the near side of the stream, their backs facing him. Another—who appeared to be the youngest of the bunch and Emmitt's stepson, Rodney Hayes—was splashing around and playing patty-cake with a pretty, big-breasted blond out in the stream's shallow middle. The fourth man was on the far side of the creek, perched atop a half-submerged tree in the shade of a sprawling sycamore. A brunette faced him, head tipped up toward his, her arms draped over his knees. He lazily kicked the water on either side of the girl, who occasionally lowered her head to the man's crotch.

The bounty hunter pulled his head back behind his cover and backed a couple of feet down the hill, out of sight from the stream. He thumbed grit from his dimpled chin, a scowl etched across his broad, suntanned forehead.

The outlaws were too spread out for an easy takedown. If Louisa Bonaventure were here, he could bring her in from the other side of the river. Working together, they'd corral the whole group in no time. That would take the outlaws' women out of the equation, as well, for Louisa brooked no grief from other women, and she wasn't influenced by their looks, be they clothed or naked.

Since Prophet was on his own, he might have to wait until the women were out of the way and the men were grouped tighter before showing his hand. Even if it meant skulking around out here for several hours—maybe even until tomorrow. In a similar situation, he'd once had to bide his time for three days.

Like soldiering and lawdogging, bounty tracking was often a waiting game, boredom being as much a nuisance as dogs, women, and flying lead.

He hunkered down and waited, tipping his funnel-brimmed hat to shade his face. Below and behind him, the conversations continued and the water splashed. Rodney Hayes and the busty blond continued playing patty-cake, laughing and teasing each other with nauseating sweetness. After a time, one of the women took umbrage with something one of the men nearest the base of Prophet's bluff said, and a slap cracked sharply.

"Ouch," Prophet said beneath his low-canted hat brim. "That musta hurt."

A brief, indecipherable argument followed and then the man—for some reason Prophet figured it was the bald-headed Horton Whipple—begged forgiveness, insisting he'd only been joshing and that the woman had known what a prankster he was when she'd thrown in with him. The couple quieted for a few minutes, and apparently the woman softened under Whipple's charms.

After a time, her voice rose from the stream's steady rush to say, "I reckon me and the girls better get some dinner goin'. You boys must be starved!"

Prophet quickly poked his hat brim back off his forehead and turned to peer through the gap between the rocks. "At least they got their womenfolk trained." He watched the naked females head toward their clothes strewn about the near shore.

Not a bad-looking bunch, all in all, though the one who'd been frolicking and fighting with Whipple appeared to outweigh the big, bald outlaw by a good twenty pounds. Built like an apple barrel, she carried most of her weight in her hips and breasts. Prophet thought he recognized the redhead from a whorehouse up in Montana, but it was hard to tell from this distance.

The blond was a saucy-looking number with large, nicely shaped breasts and porcelain-pale skin, her face painted garishly, her hair drawn up in a loose bun. The brunette was round-faced, hippy, and small-breasted. She seemed to be speaking in a thick German accent while she and the others stumbled around the shoreline a hundred feet below Prophet, pulling on their silk stockings, pantaloons, and corsets, and shaking sand from their high-heeled shoes.

"Y'all beat a pan when the grub's on the table," ordered Emmitt Sanderson, lolling in the current not far from Whipple, only his head and toes showing above the water. He was smoking a stogie. "Me and the boys just fogged a long, hard trail, and we're gonna soak awhile."

"You just do that, Emmitt," Prophet muttered, keeping his head low, one hand on his rifle. "You just keep soakin' right there . . . let them girls get on up to the cabin and the hell out of my way. . . ." He chuckled at himself, more afraid of the unarmed women than he was of the armed outlaws.

The bounty hunter watched the girls drift up through the knee-high bromegrass and wheatgrass toward the cabin capping the hill's shoulder a hundred yards away. Spread out in a shaggy line, they chattered and laughed. The blond and the redhead had left their tops off, exposing their breasts to the sun. The blond continued clapping her hands, as though still playing patty-cake with Sanderson's stepson, while the German girl conversed with Whipple's lummox about soon needing more meat for their larder.

When they'd all drifted into the cabin, Prophet crawled backward down the rise, keeping his head low. He would tramp upstream, staying clear of the water, then circle back down to the shore to get the drop on Whipple and Sanderson.

He started to gain his knees. The sickening sound of a cocking gun hammer rose behind him. Something hard jabbed against the back of his neck, just up from his collar.

He froze, his throat drying suddenly like desert hardpan.

A nasal, raspy voice said bluntly, "One more move and you might as well go ahead and tell me what name you want scratched on your tombstone, ya big son of a bitch of a squint-eyed polecat!"

2

"COLDER'N A GRAVE digger's ass out there after that rainstorm," said Marie Antoinette Fletcher.

The pretty, blond former prostitute didn't so much step through the timber-frame jailhouse door as she blew in on a chill wind gust rife with the fresh smell of a recent desert gully washer. Holding a wicker basket only partly covered with oil-cloth in one hand, she kicked the door closed behind her.

Marie Antoinette's husband, Sheriff Tobias Fletcher, glanced up from some paperwork strewn about his cluttered desk. "Uh, Marie . . . honey . . ." He jerked his head back toward the woman's twelve-year-old son, Colter, hammering the legs back on a chair that a recent drunk prisoner had smashed against the wall.

The pretty blond, her disheveled hair tumbling about her shoulders, turned toward her husband, frowning. "What?"

"The boy."

Marie Antoinette wasn't her real name, but she'd seen no reason to change it back to Marlene Karlaufsky when she gave up the world's oldest profession to marry Fletcher. She cast her brown-eyed gaze into the shadows at the back of the small room where the boy continued to hammer the leg back onto the chair, several nails dangling from between his lips.

"What about him?" Marie Antoinette blinked. "You don't think he's heard 'grave digger's ass' before?"

"No doubt he has," said Fletcher, wincing slightly at his wife's salty tongue. "But perhaps using such . . . uh . . . *terminology* in front of him isn't setting the proper example . . ."

"Pshaw!"

Marie Antoinette set the lunch basket atop the desk, then dropped into Fletcher's lap, making his swivel chair squawk, and wrapped her arms around his neck. "I told Colter when he first started talkin' what was right and proper. Didn't I, Colter? And that, while I didn't always say and do what was right and proper myself, he sure as hell better!" She glanced around her husband at Colter Fletcher. The sheriff had legally adopted the boy a year ago, just after he and Marie Antoinette had married. "Isn't that so, my darlin' child?"

"That's right, Ma," the boy said, customarily deadpan, between hammer blows. He stopped suddenly and squinted an eye at the sheriff. "That's an advantage I have over the other fellas, Pa. *I* know from *example* what I can't do and say, while the others can only guess at it. Most of the time they guess wrong and end up with a switch across their backsides!"

"There you have it, Sheriff." As Colter continued working on the chair, Marie Antoinette planted a kiss on Fletcher's mouth and squirmed around on his lap. "My salty tongue and evil ways are my boy's advantage over the others. Hell, soon he'll be so well behaved he'll be able to skirt the seminary and head right to the pulpit!"

Fletcher chuckled as he wrapped his arms around his headstrong wife, drew her to him, and kissed her. "I don't know about that, but I reckon I see your point. Sort of, anyway. . . ."

In spite of her tongue, Fletcher had never loved a woman more than he loved Marie Antoinette. He was no saint himself, having ridden on the wrong side of the law several times when he was younger. He was pushing thirty-five now, and he couldn't argue that so far Marie Antoinette hadn't done a first-rate job raising Colter to be a respectful, hardworking young man—one whom Fletcher was proud to call his son.

He kissed her cheek and squeezed her shoulder. "So, what'd you bring us boys for lunch, Mrs. Fletcher? We'd best eat. I gotta ride out to the Double Diamond this afternoon."

"Rustlers again?" Marie Antoinette wriggled off Fletcher's lap.

" 'Fraid so. Prob'ly Injuns off the rez. If so, I might have to pay a visit to Fort Dixon."

"Dixon?" Marie Antoinette scowled as she slid the towel from the basket and began setting out plates and silverware. "That means you'll be gone overnight."

" 'Fraid so." Fletcher plucked a bread 'n' butter pickle off a glass dish and bit into it, glancing at Colter, who was putting his tools back into his toolbox. "But you got him. He'll protect you. Only twelve years old, but he'll be tall as me in another year."

"I hate it when you have to leave town."

"Don't like it much myself, honey," Fletcher said as Marie laid a thick sandwich of last night's antelope roast on a blue tin plate and set it before him, nudging aside a can of cheap cigars. "But it's the way sheriffin' works, and I can't complain. I drove cattle long enough. Dug wells, strung fence. Even mustanged down south of the border for a while."

The sheriff bit into his sandwich atop which Marie Antoinette had piled a good helping of raw green onion from the kitchen garden she tended out back of their rented frame house at the west edge of Seven Devils, Arizona Territory. She and Colter had even dug an irrigation ditch down from the creek.

"This is good, steady work. And around here about the worst you have to contend with is long-loopers and drunk soldiers from Dixon. Your occasional bandito on the run from *rurales*."

"And Mrs. Berg's hired man," said Colter as the lanky boy with a thick mop of auburn hair and brown eyes drew a chair up to the right side of Fletcher's desk.

Amos Adler was the drunk who'd busted the chair the boy had been fixing. During the week the big German was quiet as a church mouse as he worked around the big house and grounds of the widow of Seven Devils's founding father. But every Saturday night, Adler's wolf got loose, as they say, and Fletcher had to arrest the man for breaking up saloons or harassing the soiled doves over at Miss Kate's sporting parlor.

"And Amos Adler, correct," Fletcher said, playfully nudging Colter's shoulder.

"Well, you be careful, Toby," Marie Antoinette admonished as she sat down on the other side of his desk. "If anything happened to you . . ." She bit into her sandwich and regarded her husband angrily, her big, brown eyes grave. "I'd just be really bad piss-burned, that's all. . . ."

Fletcher and Colter shared a glance. They chuckled around the food in their mouths, and Marie Antoinette gave a snort and followed suit.

As they ate the sandwiches and garden vegetables, they chatted about work that needed doing around their place—the house needed a new porch, the chicken coop needed a new roof, and the stable door was off its hinges again. To help makes ends meet, Marie Antoinette sold eggs and bread around town, and she was having trouble keeping up with her growing clientele.

"It's going to be a big help to have my cousin here," she said, biting into a radish. Chewing, she glanced pensively at the remaining radish between the thumb and index finger of her right hand. "Dear Louisa . . . haven't seen her in years. Not since she was just a little tyke running about her family's place in Nebraska. . . ."

"What's her last name again, Ma?" Colter asked. He'd finished a sandwich and held his half-empty glass of milk to his lips.

"Bonaventure. Louisa Bonaventure," Marie Antoinette said. "She's a good five, six years younger than me. Not yet twenty, I don't think. My ma and her pa were brother and sister. We all lived in the same county up in Nebraska until Pa went crazy from drink, and Ma took us out to Colorado. That was long before renegades burned the Bonaventure farm, killing everyone in Louisa's family except Louisa herself."

"That's a terrible thing," Fletcher said, brushing crumbs from his vest and leaning back in his chair, hands on his thighs. "How'd she get away?"

"Don't know," Marie said. "All I know is she's been on the drift ever since. Not sure doin' what—but a young woman alone"—her eyes grew dark as she reflected on her own experience after her mother passed away from a fever—"I can imagine. Judging by her letter, she's looking forward to finally settling down." She leaned forward on her elbows and gratefully smiled at her husband across the desk. "I know how she feels."

Fletcher stood, sucking meat from between two teeth. "I'm glad you'll have family here, honey. This winter, and funds permitting, I'll see about adding a new room onto the house. In the meantime, I best shade the trail for—"

"Hey, Pa." Colter had moved to the open jailhouse door for a breath of air still fresh from the recent downpour. He was looking westward up the broad main drag. "Best come have a look at this."

"What is it, son?" Brushing crumbs from his soup-strainer mustache, the tall, lean sheriff, his longish brown hair beginning to gray at the temples, crossed to the front door. He sidled up to the boy, whose head came up to his shoulder, and followed Colter's gaze westward along the soggy, deserted main street.

The Arizona town of Seven Devils claimed a population of a little over two hundred, but since gold had grown scarce in the surrounding mountains, that figure was now stretching it. The jailhouse sat in the middle of Main Street, on the north side, but the west edge of town was only about sixty yards away. That's where the last sandstone and adobe-brick business buildings abruptly stopped and the desert took over—red rocks, creosote shrubs, mesquite, sage, and saguaros, all hemmed in by towering, craggy ridges now partly concealed by gauzy, fast-moving clouds.

The desert floor wasn't concealed, however. Fletcher's eyes had no trouble picking out the handful of riders moving down a gentle slope toward the town—about seventy yards from the town's edge and closing quickly, horses loping as they meandered around rocks and boulders and cactus snags.

A wan light filtered through the low clouds, but there was light enough to reflect off the silver trimming the horses' tack and the high-crowned hat of one of the three lead riders. It reflected also off the bandoliers crossing the chests of two of the riders, and off the silver-plated pistols holstered and thonged on the thighs of the rider farthest back.

All six were distinctive, but the last one rode a high-stepping, white Arab with a fancy black bridle and a bloodred saddle blanket peeking out from beneath the gold-trimmed saddle.

Colter glanced up at Fletcher, a sharpened matchstick protruding from the boy's lips. He squinted one eye, incredulous. "Those boys sure ain't from around here."

Fletcher shook his head as he continued staring at the approaching group, fascinated not only by their distinctive attire but by the number of revolvers, rifles, shotguns, and knives each somehow managed to cram onto himself and his horse. A man in blue army trousers and wearing a faded blue cavalry hat, with bandoliers crisscrossing his chest, even had a sword dangling off his right leg.

The hoof thuds rose as the group entered town, splashing through mud puddles and flooded wheel ruts. Their saddles squawked, bridle chains and spurs jangling.

Fletcher could now see that only five of the gang were men. The one bringing up the rear, well back from the others and riding the sleek white Arab, was a woman—a big-boned but attractive girl with copper-red hair streaming down from her funnel-brimmed straw hat. Her hair appeared highlighted with lime-green streaks, and green paint outlined her green eyes.

In front of her, in the group's middle, rode the man with the cavalry hat and the sword. Beside him rode a beefy black man with a black, gold-buttoned clawhammer coat, white shirt, gold vest, and a red sash around his waist. Two Buntline Specials were wedged behind the sash while bandoliers filled with shotgun shells crisscrossed his broad chest and a sawed-off shotgun dangled down before his bulging belly by a wide, brown lanyard.

Footsteps sounded behind Fletcher, but he didn't turn away from the street as Marie Antoinette moved onto the boardwalk to his left, saying, "What's goin' on out here, fellas?"

The three front riders drew even with the jailhouse as they continued east down the wide street, probably heading for a saloon or whorehouse. Fletcher's skeptical eyes slid back and forth across them, and he almost snorted with bemused disbelief.

The three men—tall, gangly, pale, and with long, black hair dancing about their shoulders—wore physical features so identical that, if they'd been attired in the same clothes, they would have been impossible to tell apart. They were hawk-faced and, aside from beak-like noses, almost delicate-featured, with pale skin and thin beards and narrow necks rising from bony shoulders.

They all wore checked suits of similar cuts. One wore a brown suit, the second a green suit, and the third a salmon-colored suit. They all wore collarless, pin-striped shirts beneath their shabby coats. Two wore straw sombreros while the man in the salmon-checked suit wore a black opera hat and rose-colored glasses like those favored by gamblers. They all wore high-topped, mule-eared boots adorned with a thick coating of clay-colored dust and large, Spanish-style spurs. Continuing on past the jailhouse, the look-alike in the opera hat turned a toothy grin to Fletcher and gave a courtly bow.

"Afternoon, Sheriff," he said in a thick Southern accent. Tennessee, Fletcher thought. The man's small, brown eyes slid to Marie Antoinette, giving the sheriff's wife a cool up and down as he added, "Wet one today . . ."

Then he and the two others were past the jailhouse and beginning to angle toward Carstairs's Saloon on the other side of the street, near the east edge of town.

As the black man and the man with the cavalry hat and the sword rode past the jailhouse, dismissing Fletcher with belligerent sneers, the redheaded girl behind them stopped her white Arab abruptly to cast her gaze toward Fletcher's side of the street and several buildings west.

"Hi there, little girl!"

A woman in a bonnet and shawl and a little girl with yellow sausage curls flopping to her shoulders had stopped in the street to let the riders pass. Both stood a few feet into the street, the little girl clinging to the woman's hand and regarding the female rider cautiously.

The girl atop the Arab reached up and picked a flower from behind her ear and held it out over the side of her saddle. "Come get a flower!"

The little girl with the sausage curls glanced up at her mother, then suddenly jerked her hand free and dashed into the street.

"Kayleen!" admonished the woman.

Kayleen ran to the Arab and stopped suddenly, gaining a timid air and holding both hands straight down by her sides. She shyly regarded the well-set up redhead leaning out from her saddle and gently offering the white flower between thumb and index finger.

"I just picked it out yonder," she said. "It's new and fresh as you are. Go ahead. Tuck it behind your ear. It'll bring a shine to the whole rest of your day!"

3

STANDING WITH HIS wife and stepson on the plank stoop fronting the jailhouse, Sheriff Tobias Fletcher watched the little girl—whom he recognized as Kayleen Finnegan—pluck the desert wildflower from the hand of the strange young woman with green-streaked red hair sitting atop the spry white Arabian.

Fletcher's heart was beating in his throat. Something about this group—more than just their bizarre appearance—had pricked the hair on the back of his neck, but he couldn't pinpoint what it was. Not wanting to frighten the girl needlessly, he restrained himself from stepping down off the stoop and ordering Kayleen's mother, Constance, wife of the town harness maker, to grab her daughter and skedaddle.

Instead, he stood tensely between Marie Antoinette and Colter, his right hand draped over the worn walnut grips of his old Remington .44, watching.

"Mama, look what that nice lady gave me!" Holding the white flower up to her nose, sausage curls dancing on her shoulders, Kayleen ran back toward her mother waiting a few feet from the boardwalk fronting the drug shop.

The redhead chuckled and gigged the Arab forward, making tracks after the five men in her group. Fletcher unconsciously slid his hand from the .44's grips and felt a slight cessation of pressure in his throat. As the girl and the Arab drew even with the jailhouse, the girl, who'd spied Fletcher, Marie Antoinette, and Colter before she'd given Kayleen the flower, grinned and waved as though she were passing on a train.

"Hi there, Sheriff!" She had a strangely pitched, little girl's voice coupled with a bodacious, tomboyish air that Fletcher found at once alluring and off-putting. Around her waist she wore two bone-gripped .36 Remingtons in oiled, brown-leather holsters trimmed with silver stars. Adjusting her funnel-brimmed straw hat, she slid her green-eyed gaze to Colter and then back to Fletcher and Marie Antoinette. "Strappin' young lad ya got there. By this time next year, he'll be sproutin' up tall as a fir tree. He'll do ya proud, that one. Well, see ya!"

With that, she heeled the Arab into a lope, passing the jailhouse and angling over to Norman Carstairs's two-story, adobe-brick saloon with a brush-roofed front gallery and gray smoke billowing out the chimney. The rest of the group's horses were tied to the hitchrail, swishing their tails and drawing water from the stock tank.

"That's about the looniest-looking crew of hard cases I've ever seen," Marie Antoinette said softly, staring toward the saloon and giving a jerk as though from a sudden chill.

Kitty-corner across the street, the redhead glanced back toward the jailhouse, smiling brightly as she tied the Arab to the hitchrail. She ducked under the rail and skipped up the gallery's three front steps, her spurred boots chinging softly in the heavy, post-rain silence.

"You can say that again," Fletcher said, watching the girl sashay through the saloon's batwing doors as though she owned the place. "If they weren't so well armed, I'd say they were part of some traveling burlesque show. But I never seen actors arm themselves like bandits."

Colter looked up at him, eyes bright. "You think they're here to rob the bank, Pa?"

"Don't know," Fletcher mused, nibbling his mustache as he stared toward Carstairs's place.

He'd been sheriff for a little over a year, and he'd had a relatively easy time in spite of all the outlaws reportedly holed up in the Seven Devils Range only fifty miles south of town. He'd had to turn the key on only harmless drunk prospectors and Mrs. Berg's hired man. Aside from a couple of half-breed, low-at-heel rustlers, he'd had to pull his gun on no one. He'd never shot anything with less than four legs in his life and was only fair to middling at drawing quickly.

Most of the time, while practicing his fast draw out back of the chicken coop after Marie Antoinette and Colter had gone to bed, he got the gun's fore sight hung up in his holster. He feared that if he ever had to draw down on someone, there was a good chance he'd shoot himself in the thigh or blow off his foot.

Now he swallowed down a small, dry knot in his throat as he stared across the street at the saloon and said pensively, "They could be one o' them groups from the range, but there ain't much for 'em *here*. No . . . I just don't know. . . ."

Colter was still looking up at him with that excited, boyish gleam in his eyes. "You gonna check it out, Pa? Maybe give 'em the boot, if ya have to?"

"Colter!" Marie Antoinette wrapped her hand around Fletcher's forearm. "You best steer clear of them, honey. You see how many guns they were carrying? I saw at least three on each man. Even the girl was sportin'—"

"I saw." Fletcher felt suddenly annoyed that his wife and stepson were here to witness his apprehension. He put some steel in his words as he said, "I reckon I'll check it out if I have to. But first I'm gonna look through that fresh batch of wanted dodgers I got in last week. See if any of their faces match—"

He'd just turned toward the jailhouse's open door when a man's scream rose suddenly. It was a shrill cry, filled with excruciating pain and terror.

Fletcher turned toward Carstairs's Saloon as the scream came again, even louder than before as it shot out from behind the saloon's batwing doors to career around the street, echoing off buildings. A woman shouted something that Fletcher couldn't make out, and then there rose the muffled scuffs and thuds of boots and the raw scrapes of chairs being kicked around a wooden floor. Men grunted and yelled.

The woman's voice sounded again, shriller and clearer this

time, and Fletcher recognized the squeaky, girlish voice of the redhead with the straw hat and green streaks in her hair. Only now that high voice rumbled with fury. "Goddamnit, Jack, grab his *feet* and pull him *upstairs*!"

"Christ . . ." Marie Antoinette rasped darkly as she stared across the street, one hand to her chest.

"Holy moly," Colter said. "What do you suppose they're doin'?"

A couple of storekeepers stepped out of the shops up and down the street, casting their cautious, befuddled gazes toward Carstairs's place before shuttling expectant looks toward Fletcher.

"I don't know," the sheriff said, swallowing, draping his right hand over his pistol's grips, and then starting off the porch, "but I reckon I'd best find out."

Marie Antoinette grabbed his arm. "Toby, wait."

He swung around. The fear in his wife's eyes mirrored his own, made his throat even tighter. "This is my job, honey. You and the boy go on home. I'll be along shortly to pack 'fore I head out to the Double Diamond."

Marie Antoinette's chest fell as she released Fletcher's arm. He turned away, stepped off the stoop, and, keeping his sweaty hand draped over the .44, angled across the street toward the saloon growing larger and larger before him, its roof and smoke-spewing chimney raked with low, cottony clouds the color of lightly soiled rags.

Another muffled cry rose from the saloon's second story as Fletcher tramped up between two trail-dusty horses tied to hitchracks and mounted the gallery. The girl yelled something indecipherable from somewhere back in the building's second floor, and there was more shuffling and stomping. Fletcher swallowed again and closed his hand around his Remington's grips, as much to stop the hand from shaking as to prepare for battle.

He topped out on the porch and stopped to peer over the batwings, squinting against the murky, smoky shadows within. Finally, taking a breath, he pushed through the doors and angled toward the mahogany bar running along the wall to his right. To his left and about halfway down the room, three of the strangers sat smoking and playing cards—the three identical men who'd led the gang into town.

The redheaded girl, the black man, and the man in cavalry blues were nowhere to be seen, though Fletcher could hear the girl's odd voice squealing angry orders from somewhere upstairs.

Meanwhile, amidst the girl's screams and the occasional boot scuff, a man begged and sobbed so softly now as to be nearly inaudible.

The three identical men didn't turn toward Fletcher, but only glanced at one another conspiratorially. One grinned and laughed around the fat stogie between his thin lips and shook his long hair back from his shoulder—a strangely feminine gesture.

Fletcher moved up to the bar. The owner of the place, Norman Carstairs, stood with both hands spread out atop the mahogany, a grim cast to his eyes, a dark set to his lips beneath his neatly trimmed and waxed mustache. He was a big, paunchy, balding man, with a face so seamed and gouged that it resembled a map of southern Arizona.

While the three identical riders conversed casually as they flipped cards and coins onto the table, Fletcher looked at the bartender, an unspoken question in his eyes.

Carstairs said quietly, his face implacable as he canted his head toward the narrow stairs at the rear of the room, "Three of that gang nabbed Dewey Granger away from the bar. Dragged him upstairs. That's him squealin'. His partners, Trace and Dawson, lit out the back like the devil's hounds were nippin' at their heels."

"What's it all about?" Fletcher asked.

The sheriff had kept his voice low, but apparently one of the men behind him had heard. "None o' your concern, Sheriff. Just know it's just. An eye for an eye, a tooth fer a tooth."

Fletcher turned toward the hard cases' table. They continued to play, the one on the left side of the table casually dealing a round of blackjack. A bottle and three shot glasses were on the table, as was an ashtray in which a couple of cigarettes smoldered.

Fletcher narrowed an eye. "What's that?"

The one with his back to the bar was the one wearing the salmon-checked suit and opera hat, his spectacles shoved back on his head. He half turned toward Fletcher, removing the fat stogie from his mouth and blowing a thick cloud of blue smoke at the rafters. "The dull-witted drover, Mr. Granger, had the misfortune of getting drunk one wild Saturday night over to Lord's Station and killing Miss Cora's brother, Cecil."

"Avril," corrected the man in the brown-checked suit, leaning back in his chair to leisurely study his cards. His sombrero hung down his back by a horsehair thong.

The man in the green-checked suit clucked impatiently. "Whichever brother it was, he's dead as a hammer, and Miss Cora is extracting her satisfaction from the man who killed him."

Fletcher squared his shoulders at the table and took a slow, deep breath to steady himself. "You best call Cora down here. If Mr. Granger killed someone, it'll be up to the law to decide his punishment."

Just then a long wail rose above the rafters. There was a clattering thud, as if a chair had been knocked over. The wail died abruptly, and the girl laughed.

The man in the stovepipe hat threw back his shot glass and said with a liquid sigh, his back to the sheriff, "I reckon it's too late for that." He and the others chuckled.

Fletcher had turned toward the stairs, his heart beating faster, his face hot. A man was dying upstairs while he, the sheriff, stood down here palavering with a couple of the queerest-looking cutthroats he'd ever laid eyes on.

He glanced at Carstairs, who looked as though he'd seen a ghost.

"Christ!" Fletcher moved toward the stairs.

On his right flank, there was the raking squawk of a chair turning on the rough wood puncheons. A man bellowed, "Uh-uh!"

Fletcher stopped abruptly and turned toward the queer-looking hard cases. The one with the opera hat, his chair turned toward Fletcher and his rose-colored spectacles now sitting low on his nose, held two long-barreled Smith & Wesson pistols straight out from his belly, arms just above his spread thighs. The gun hammers were cocked.

"No, suhh," he said in his molasses-thick Southern accent. "For Cora, vengeance is a religious experience, and I won't have you stompin' up there and interruptin' her moment of glory. Besides, there ain't nothin' you can do for that murderin' scalawag anyways. He done paid for *his* ticket."

Fletcher stared at the twin bores yawning at him. Rage and fear broiled within him. Sweat dribbled down his cheeks, soaking his mustache. He looked at the three long, hard, bearded faces peering at him through the room's smoky shadows. They were leering, challenging, daring him to reach for his .44.

They wanted him to. He could tell by their eyes that they would no more hesitate to kill a lawman than they would a rattlesnake along the trail. In fact, they'd enjoy it.

Angry and humiliated, his chest rising and falling sharply, his hands bunched at his sides, Fletcher glanced at Carstairs. The saloon owner peered at him skeptically over the bar.

"Tobias . . ." Carstairs swallowed and shifted his eyes toward the hard cases. "You maybe best just . . ."

Fletcher cursed and began stomping back along the bar toward the door. To his right, one of the queer-looking hard cases chuckled. As Fletcher pushed through the batwings and stepped out onto the gallery, he heard coins clink as one of the hard cases said, "Kinda thought he'd see it our way."

Rage nearly blinding him and causing the street to rise and fall around him and muffling all sound, Fletcher angled toward the jailhouse. He walked stiffly but quickly, jaws taut, eyes pinched, hands squeezed into fists. Colter and Marie Antoinette were blurred shapes standing on the jailhouse stoop before him.

"Honey, what's going on over there?" Marie Antoinette said, standing beside Colter, one arm around the boy's waist.

"I told you two to go on home!"

Fletcher brushed past them as he moved through the open jailhouse door and stomped across the hard-packed earthen floor to the gun rack on the wall opposite his cluttered desk. He fished a small key ring from his pocket and removed the padlock from the chain securing the three rifles and a rusty shotgun to the rack. He let the chain and padlock drop as he grabbed the old Greener, his clammy hands shaking as much from rage as fear.

"Toby, what're you going to do?" Marie Antoinette called from the doorway.

"My job, honey." Fletcher breeched the shotgun, moved to the desk, and opened a drawer. He set a box of shotgun shells on the desk, fumbled the box open, and grabbed one of the wads. "You and Colter go on home like I said."

"Don't go over there, Toby. I saw how well those men . . . and that *girl* . . . were armed." She paused as Fletcher thumbed the first wad into the shotgun barrel, then plucked another from the box and punched it into the shotgun's second tube. "At least find someone to help you."

"Carstairs is over there," Fletcher said, snapping the gun closed with a click and heading for the door. "He has a sawed-off under the bar."

He stopped before his wife. She looked up at him, eyes wide with fear. Her hair, mussed by the wind, hung beautifully disheveled about her slender shoulders. Her hair . . . He'd like nothing better than to take her home and run his hands through her hair.

He fought the temptation. He had a duty to perform. If he turned tail, he'd never be able to look Marie Antoinette and their son in the eye again. Nor anyone else in town, for that matter.

Odd, though, how enticing the idea was. To just go home and bury his head in a pillow and call the killing of Dewey Granger, an average ranch hand with a checkered past, justified.

Fletcher wrapped his hand around Marie Antoinette's and squeezed. "It'll be all right. Please go home so I don't have to worry about you two."

His feet were suddenly heavy as lead, but he managed to walk around her and out the door and past Colter standing on the porch, watching him. The boy no longer looked as excited at the prospect of a shooting as he had before. He looked worried.

"Pa . . ."

Fletcher hurried off the stoop and made a beeline for the saloon. "Take your ma home, Colter. I'll be along later. Go on, now. Don't make me tell you again."

4

FLETCHER MOVED WITHIN twenty yards of Carstairs's Saloon, then turned abruptly right. Holding the shotgun in both hands across his chest, his right thumb caressing each rabbit-eared hammer in turn, he turned down the gap between the saloon and Fairchild's Tonsorial Parlor, noting a couple of faces peering out the parlor's front windows at him.

He continued through the trash-strewn gap to the saloon's rear.

A rickety, unpainted staircase rose along the back wall to a door on the second story. Fletcher took the steps two at a time and slowly, quietly opened the door, relieved to find it unlocked. He looked both ways down the dim, papered hall and pricked his ears, listening.

The only noise came from the first story. The screams had ceased. The girl had stopped yelling. The second story was utterly quiet. It smelled like kerosene lanterns and musty carpet runners.

Fletcher closed the door, so it wouldn't silhouette him against the outside light. Thumbing both hammers back, he stole quietly down the hall to his left, squeezing the shotgun in both hands.

When the town had been booming, Carstairs had kept a couple of soiled doves, who'd plied their trade in the six rooms on both sides of the hall. Now the only doves in town were over at Miss Kate's place. Fletcher didn't know what Carstairs did with the rooms now, but one of the doors on the hall's right side was open.

As Fletcher approached the open room, the hair on the back of his neck pricking, he detected the coppery smell of fresh blood. The smell thickened, tightening his gut, as he sidled up to the door frame. His heart thudded, his pulse beating in his neck.

He held his breath, trying to listen above the beating of his own heart. Only the sickening blood stench and silence issued from the open door.

Fletcher bolted out from behind the wall and swung his shotgun barrel into the room, squaring his shoulders and spreading his feet. The stench hit him like a fist, and then he saw the body lying about six feet back from the door, between a dresser on the right and a bed on the left.

Dewey Granger lay on his back, arms thrust straight out from his shoulders. His denims and underwear had been pulled down around his boots. There was so much blood that Fletcher couldn't tell exactly what they'd done to him, but it looked as though he'd been carved up like a field-dressed deer.

Blood was still running out from the broad, grisly wound in his midsection and crotch and puddling on the floor around his body. Something protruded from his mouth, but Fletcher turned away before he could identify it, his guts clenching and throat contracting as though a stick dipped in fresh cow shit had been shoved down past his tonsils.

He dropped to a knee in the hall, swallowing quickly to keep from vomiting. When his stomach settled, he ran a sleeve across his sweat-soaked mustache and peered toward the stairs.

Fletcher had grown up on the frontier and had visited nearly every state and territory, even witnessed some Indian atrocities. But only once or twice, in Comanche country, had he seen a man treated the way the girl and her two cohorts had treated Dewey Granger.

Fletcher curled his upper lip. "Murderin' goddamn savages."

That they'd been so bold as to do their butchering practically in his face galled him keenly, kindling a hot fire at the base of his skull.

He rose slowly, again gripping the shotgun in both hands. Taking a deep breath, quickly brushing sweat from his face, he began moving toward the end of the hall, where the stairs dropped to the saloon's main room from which voices rose, including the screechy, contentious voice of the girl.

He stopped well back from the top of the stairs, so he wouldn't be seen from below, and peered down into the main saloon hall. No one on the stairs. He could see shadows moving ahead and left, sensed the tension of Norman Carstairs, who was probably still behind the bar, wondering if Fletcher had lit out for good like a donkey with its tail on fire.

Fletcher took another deep breath and, holding the shotgun low and angled about forty-five degrees away from his body, started down the stairs.

"Hey, Captain Sykes, why didn't you tell me you had the jack?" the girl yelled, her shrill voice echoing around the room's adobe-brick, mud-chinked walls. "*Damn* you anyways!"

Someone laughed. "Well, now, Miss Cora—that ain't exactly the way the game is played, is it?"

"Careful, Captain," said a deep voice rumbling up like an earthquake through a privy hole. "You wouldn't go sassin' Miss Cora if you was to see her doin's upstairs!" There was the slap of cards on a table. "No, suh. I think I'm gonna have nightmares tonight jus' thinkin' about it!"

As Fletcher dropped midway down the stairs, moving slowly on the balls of his boots but still making the rotten steps squawk and creak, the outlaws' table slid into view before him, about fifteen feet from the staircase. They were all gathered around it now, the girl, the black man, and the man in the cavalry blues having joined the three of a kind.

The girl was straddling the knee of one of the triplets—the one wearing the stovepipe hat—and she leaned back to kiss his cheek now as Fletcher gained the bottom of the stairs and began bringing the shotgun up, swinging it out from his belly.

The black man was expertly dealing the cards while the others snapped them up, smoking or throwing back shots or, in one case, farting. The black man wore a large diamond ring on the outside of his right glove, on his middle finger. The girl caressed the bearded cheek of the man in the stovepipe hat, then leaned forward to pick up her cards and cast a glance toward the bar.

"Hey, barkeep!" she called. "Bring us another bottle of that panther piss, will ya? It's so bad it makes me wanna blow both your eyes out the back of your head, but if it's all you got, I reckon . . ."

Her eyes found Fletcher standing and aiming the shotgun from the bottom of the stairs. She smiled brightly, weird green eyes—eyes like a cat's—flashing under the green war paint, two locks of copper-red, green-streaked hair falling down her shoulders to frame her breasts. "Hey, look who's here! It's the lawdog!"

She lowered her cards and continued to regard Fletcher as though he were the parson and she were a sweet little bride preparing for her wedding ceremony. "Come on over here and have a drink, lawdog. It's the worst hooch I've ever tasted in my nineteen-goin'-on-twenty years, and I'll prob'ly be blind by sundown, but I reckon if you live around here, you're used to it."

The others had shifted their gazes to Fletcher now, too. They looked at him with sneering amusement, like schoolboys who'd turned a turtle onto its back to see what it would do or how long it would take to die.

The look-alike in the brown-checked suit said, "Yeah, he was in here before, his panties all in a twist on account what you and Captain Sykes and Heinz were doin' upstairs."

"Oh, *really*?" the girl said, her tone and her stare hardening as she leaned back against the shoulder of the gent in the stovepipe hat. "And why shouldn't I kill my brother's killer, pray tell?"

Fletcher raised the shotgun's butt to his shoulder and aimed at the middle of the table, keeping all six faces within his field of vision. The black man had frozen in the act of dealing, looking up at Fletcher from beneath his thick brows, the whites around his dark eyes glowing in the shadows.

"Keep your hands above the table," Fletcher ordered. "You're all under arrest."

They all looked at Fletcher with indifferent expressions, as though he were only a momentary interruption in their card game—like a swamper wanting to scrub the floor beneath their table or a house girl clearing their empty glasses.

The redhead leaned back against the shoulder of the stovepipe-hatted gent once more and sneered, her smooth cheeks dimpling. "You're being silly, lawdog. Downright fool-hardy. You know who we are?"

Out the corner of his left eye, Fletcher saw the bartender, Carstairs, standing tensely behind the mahogany, staring toward Fletcher and the table.

"Norman, you still have the sawed-off under the bar?"

"Reckon."

"Pull it out, make sure it's loaded."

Carstairs stepped to one side, bent down, and came up holding the short-barreled ten-gauge with a braided rawhide cord. He breeched it, peered down the tubes, then snapped it back together.

"What do you want me to do with it?"

"Aim it. Any of these folks so much as twitches a gun toward me, cut loose with one of your wads. Consider yourself deputized."

Fletcher kept his gaze on the table, opening and closing his right hand around his own shotgun's fore stock. The outlaws continued to stare back at him with that infuriating conde-scension.

"Very slowly, one at a time," Fletcher said, "I want each of you to reach down beneath the table and, one at a time, bring your weapons up and set them on top of the table. Pistols, knives, swords—whatever you're carryin'." He glanced at the man nearest him, the triplet in the checked suit and sombrero. "Sir, we'll start with you. Nice and slow or I'll blow a hole through your back wide enough to drive a wagon through."

The girl shot a wide-eyed mocking look at the man in the green-checked suit. "Ouch! You better do as he says, Rafe."

"I reckon I'd better."

Rafe glanced back at Fletcher, deviously arching a brow as he lowered his left hand beneath the table. Fletcher watched the man unsnap the keeper thong over the hammer of the .45 holstered low on his left thigh, then with two fingers slowly lift the gun from its holster.

Fletcher held the heavy shotgun steady as he raked his gaze around the table while at the same time watching Rafe's left thumb and index finger slowly . . . ever so slowly . . . raise the .45, barrel down.

Rafe kept his gaze locked on Fletcher's eyes, a queer sort of half smile turning up the corners of his thin mouth inside the shaggy black beard. He was the most hawkish-looking of the three brothers, with an especially sharp, upturned nose and cheeks so hollow that shadows lurked within them. His eyes were small, black, and set deep within cavernous sockets. His evil leer made Fletcher's insides quiver like a nest of young rattlers, and he had to fight back the nearly overwhelming urge to drop both hammers on the hard case and watch his face disappear in a spray of blood against the far wall.

"That's high enough," Fletcher said, when Rafe had raised the gun a little above his shoulder, his evil, mocking smile still twisting his lips.

The hard case stopped raising the gun and broadened his grin.

The girl laughed suddenly, causing Fletcher to jerk the shotgun slightly.

"Lawdog's nervous!" The girl laughed harder. "Look at how his hands are shakin'."

Fletcher returned his gaze to Rafe. He hated the quake he heard in his voice as he barked, "Set the gun on the table, goddamnit! Set it down *now*!"

Running footsteps rose in the street outside the saloon, growing louder as someone approached.

"Colter, no!" Marie Antoinette called.

Boots thumped on the gallery. Fletcher felt as though his chest had been struck by a war hatchet as, in the corner of his left eye, he saw a face slide over the tops of the batwing doors and two small hands grip the door's scrolled edges.

"Don't do it, Pa! You won't make it!" Colter shouted, his voice cracking with terror. "I just seen their pictures in your off—!"

"Colter, goddamnit, I told . . . !"

Fletcher had jerked his head toward the batwings when he spied a sudden flicker of movement near the table. By the time his eyes darted back to the hard cases, Rafe's revolver was turning over in the air. The butt dropped into the hard case's hand with a soft smacking sound, and the barrel jerked toward Fletcher so quickly that the sheriff's brain was slow to comprehend what was happening until the black maw sprouted flames.

The gun's roar filled the saloon, echoing sharply off the walls. The slug careened through Fletcher's left shoulder—a little puff of dust from his shirt and then he felt as though he'd been slammed in the chest with a bung starter.

He groaned and staggered backward, trying to steady the shotgun on the table. But as if of its own volition, the fore stock swung toward the rafters at the same time that Fletcher drew back on the twin triggers.

Ka-booom!

Both shells exploded into the ceiling before and above the table, carving two pumpkin-sized gouges in the heavy rafters and throwing slivers in every direction.

Through the smoke and the dust raining from the rafters, and as he continued staggering backward, grunting and cursing, Fletcher saw the vague shapes of the killers bolt out of their chairs, moving as though they were made of little more than sinew and oil.

They reached for guns and, as chairs flew back behind them and sideways and as the girl and the two brothers on the table's left side dropped to a knee, revolvers flashed and barked, lifting an ear-numbing din.

As he spun around, dropping the shotgun, Fletcher felt two more hot chunks of lead slice through him—one through the back of his right forearm, another through his side—and then he was on the floor, screaming and rolling, his own cries rising and falling around him beneath the gun reports, as though it were someone else being shot to ribbons nearby.

Above the din of .44s and .45s triggered so quickly that the individual shots combined in one great burst of shuddering, echoing thunder, Carstairs's sawed-off boomed. There was a cow-like bellow of anguish, and as Fletcher settled on the floor on his back, he lifted his head slightly to see the barman falling against the back bar, chunks of flesh torn out of him by the outlaws' cracking revolvers, blood painting the mirror and breaking bottles behind him.

Carstairs's sawed-off bounced off the top of the front bar, in the very crater it had torn out of the mahogany when the barman had tripped both triggers. It hit the floor with a thud that was drowned by the gunfire.

Fletcher looked toward the front of the saloon just in time to see a hail of lead pepper the front of the batwings. Colter had been standing there, eyes and mouth wide as he screamed. The bullets punched him straight back, his head dropping beneath the tops of the doors, hat sailing, his boot heels rising from the porch and the soles showing as he hit the floor with a dull thud and giant dust puff.

"*Colter!*" Fletcher screamed.

No. Fletcher hadn't screamed. He'd tried, but it was Marie Antoinette's voice, growing louder as she approached the saloon.

"Colter! Oh, God—*Colter!*"

The shooting had stopped, Fletcher realized as he lay on his back staring up at the ceiling, feeling the blood leaking out of his pain-racked body. Glancing down, he saw that he'd been hit two or three more times than he'd thought. Blood poured from a wound in his lower chest as well as from his side, and there was a hole in his left thigh.

As if from far away, behind the ringing in his ears, he could hear Marie Antoinette sobbing and calling Colter's name outside on the stoop before the saloon.

"Hey," one of the renegades said. "I think we got us another female in the vicinity."

Fletcher dropped his chin to stare across the saloon. A couple of the renegades stood at the table where they'd been playing cards, thumbing fresh shells into their revolvers. Empty casings clattered around them. Three of the others—one of the triplets, the black man, and the cavalry man called Sykes—sauntered toward the batwings. Their boots thumped and their spurs chinged.

"A lawman's wife," said Sykes. "Now, there'd be a first!"

The black man laughed.

Fletcher gritted his teeth and slid his hand toward the holster on his right hip. The movement was almost unbearable, kicking up the pain in the rest of his body and nearly making him vomit.

Fletcher was dying. There was no doubt about that. But maybe he could take one or two of the crazy savages with him.

He had little feeling in his right hand, just enough to detect the walnut grip of his .44. He gritted his teeth once more and began to slide the revolver from its holster.

A boot suddenly pinned his hand to the floor. He looked up with a pained groan. The crazy redhead stared down at him with her green cat eyes, green-streaked hair wisping about her face in a breeze from the door.

"Tch, tch, tch," she clucked, shaking her head slowly.

Then she angled a bone-gripped Remington toward Fletcher's head and ratcheted back the hammer. She grinned, showing her perfect white teeth, and narrowed an eye.

Fletcher heard Marie Antoinette screaming her son's name as he watched the Remington's hammer fall.

5

"GO AHEAD," REPEATED the raspy, pinched voice behind Lou Prophet. "What name you want on your tombstone? Best tell me now . . . or drop that long gun and turn around ni-i-ice and slow. . . ."

Prophet's pulse hammered. He could hear the breeze and the stream gurgling over rocks and the voices of the Emmitt Sanderson gang rising from the other side of the hill. Turning his head to peer over his left shoulder, he saw one of the ugliest creatures he'd ever seen—human or beast—aiming a sawed-off shotgun at him, a corncob pipe dangling from a corner of the creature's mouth.

Prophet couldn't tell if the creature was human, let alone male or female. As far as species, it could be one of those part-man, part-beast concoctions glimpsed by settlers or mountain men now and then. As far as sex, this creature's wizened, stooped body in baggy denims, red flannel shirt, and knee-high deerskin moccasins owned features one could, in a pinch, call both male *and* female—namely, two large lumps pushing out the shirt in front and a distinctly mannish face complete with thin, scraggly goat beard and mustache. Long, coarse gray hair fell to its shoulders from a threadbare coonskin cap. The hips were womanishly broad, but the hands wrapped around the shotgun were thick and gnarled as overcooked sausages.

Cursing his stupidity—he knew better than to ignore his backside; he must have been distracted by the naked women—Prophet set his rifle down and turned slowly around, raising his hands shoulder high. "Who the hell are you?"

"Who am *I*?" the beast said, voice so raspy that it must have had a pound of phlegm in its throat. "Who are *you*? I'm guessin' bounty hunter since you ain't wearin' no badge and you look like you been rode hard and put up wet more times than any lawdog could hope for, women generally not favorin' your average badge toter!"

The beast laughed loudly, throwing its head back on its broad, stooped shoulders. Prophet thought that, while the beast was laughing, its colorless eyes slitted, he might have a chance at wrenching the shotgun out of its grip. But he'd taken only half a step forward when the beast snapped the shotgun barrel down suddenly, cutting off its laugh.

The shotgun exploded with a report like a cannon blast, the double-aught buck blowing a crater the size of a well cover in the weeds and gravel just left of Prophet's left boot. The blast's echo hadn't died before the beast, narrowing an eye at Prophet, lifted its chin to yell over the butte top: "Emmitt, get your horny ass up here, son!"

"What is it, Ma?" came a shout from behind and below.

"Quit askin' questions and get up here, godblastit!"

Prophet heard splashing from the river, as of men scrambling toward shore. He spit grit, which the blast had blown into his face, and eyed the creature incredulously. "You're Emmitt's *ma*?"

"That's right. Maybelle Springford Sanderson. I got more names than that, but I whittled 'em down for smoother conversation. Emmitt's pa was three, four men ago, but Emmitt and me, we stayed close." Mrs. Sanderson cast her head toward the cabin. "That's my cabin, but as long as my boy's around, my cabin is his cabin—his and his bride's."

"Especially when sonny boy comes callin' with his saddlebags bulging with stolen loot, no doubt."

"Shut up." The old woman raked a lusty gaze across Prophet's broad chest. "Big son of a bitch, ain't ya? Thought you could bring down my boy and his gang all on your lone-some, eh? I found only the one horse back yonder. Figurin' to live high on the hog when you raked up all that reward money. Ha!" The old woman threw her head back once more, wheezing a spine-raking laugh, but Prophet knew better than to try for the shotgun again. "Wasn't countin' on Emmitt's *ma* takin' ya down, *was* ya? Ha!"

"No, I sure as hell wasn't," Prophet had to admit, still hold-ing his hands up, hearing grunts and boot thuds coming from behind the butte shoulder to his left.

He cursed his carelessness once more as Mrs. Sanderson continued squinting down her gut shredder's double barrels at him. Who'd have thought Emmitt Sanderson would have a mother—much less one that had some facility with a sawed-off shotgun? Of course, anyone could have been skulking around out here, and Prophet should have kept the eyes in back of his head skinned. He had only himself to blame for the sudden fix he found himself in.

The footsteps grew as the outlaws led by Emmitt Sander-son appeared around the hill's shoulder, wet hair squashed down under shabby hats—all except for big Horton Whipple, that was, whose enormous, egg-shaped head was bald as a hunk of hard candy under his frayed brown derby.

As the men drew near, they eyed Prophet with skeptical interest. Sanderson—a scrawny little hard case with a ferrety face and jittery black eyes, a perpetual sneer on his thick lips puffy from a recent brawl—stopped beside his ma.

"Who the hell's this?" the outlaw leader asked his mother.

The other men stood spread out to his right, Horton Whip-ple towering over them. The big man hadn't donned a shirt, and there was nary an inch of skin on his muscular arms and torso that hadn't been tattooed with images of bucking horses and fire-breathing dragons and of men and women engaged in every position of fornication Prophet had even imagined and a good many he hadn't.

"We ain't got *real* good acquainted jus' yet," Mrs. Sander-son said, holding the barn blaster on Prophet though her son and the other men were all aiming six-shooters at him. "But I found his horse while I was out grubbin' fer roots—ugliest, owliest thing you ever did see, couldn't git near it—and then I tracked this ranny here, spyin' at you fellas and them worth-less squaws of yours while ya tussled in the river like savage Injuns raised without religion."

"Pervert," said Emmitt's son, Rodney Hayes, who, aside from his size and shifty, sneering eyes, didn't favor his father much in appearance. He had thin, sandy hair, a scrawny neck, pale blue eyes, and a beard growing in rough patches across his pale, pimpled cheeks. "Who the hell are you and what do you want, pervert?"

"Lou Prophet." It was Sanderson who'd spoke. He had mo-seyed up to stand five feet in front of the bounty hunter. He was a good six inches shorter than Prophet, and standing downslope from him, the top of his battered Stetson barely reached Prophet's Adam's apple. The outlaw leader tipped his head side-ways and squeezed an eye half closed as he studied Prophet's face shaded by Prophet's own dusty, funnel-brimmed Stetson. "Sure enough, this here's Lou Prophet!"

"Well, hell, Emmitt," Prophet said. "I don't remember ever havin' the pleasure of a formal introduction."

Sanderson held his cocked Schofield straight out toward Prophet's belly. With the other hand, and holding Prophet's gaze with his own, he slipped Prophet's bowie knife from the broad sheath on his left hip and tossed it into the brush. Then he removed the Colt .45 from the holster thonged low on the bounty hunter's denim-clad right thigh.

"Your reputation shadows you like the fetor of a gold-camp Chinatown." Sanderson glanced back at the other men flanking his mother. "Boys, we're in for a real treat here. This here's Lou Prophet, bounty tracker from Georgia. Not too many men slip out of his net." Sanderson laughed a jeering laugh, show-ing all his teeth. "But Ma done caught him clean—how do ya like that?"

"I like it," Horton Whipple said, glaring at Prophet as he polished his right fist against his left hand. "I like it real good."

"I was just passin' through, fellas," Prophet said, desperately fishing for any way to free himself from this bear trap. "I was thinkin' about havin' me a little soak in the river my own self." He chuckled. "Good thing I scouted it out first. We coulda had us an embarrassin' situation. Now, then, if you'll just let me col-lect my weapons, I'll—"

"A little soak, my ass," said the fourth man, whose name was Wally "Cisco" Wood, from Milestown in the Montana Territory. He was a dumb-looking, straight-nosed, straight-necked stringbean who didn't look like he'd started shaving yet, though according to the paper on him he'd killed a school-teacher and three children on a playground near Pine Bluff, Utah, when the teacher had refused him a drink of water. He stood barefoot, holding his boots and socks in one hand, his ivory-handled Smith & Wesson in the other. "Why, he's been trailin' us, boys! He knows about the bounty on our heads, and he's been trailin' us!"

"Damn, Cisco," sneered Rodney Hayes. "Nothin' gits past you, does it?"

Emmitt stood grinning up at Prophet. His two front teeth were yellow and square, with a thick layer of coffee-colored grime caked between teeth and gum. "Lou Prophet. Damn, it sure is gonna be a pleasure to kill you. Yessir!" He turned as if to step away, but then he jerked back, swinging Prophet's own Colt around, grip forward, and rammed the butt into the dead center of Prophet's belly.

The breath left Prophet's lungs in a loud *"Uhfff!"* He stumbled back up the hill, getting his boots tangled beneath him and falling hard on his butt. His hat tumbled off his shoulder. Sucking air and holding one arm across his gut, he rolled onto his right elbow and straightened his legs slightly, trying to unknot his midsection to get some air back into his lungs. Sanderson was a scrawny little bastard, but he packed a hell of a gut-stoving, rib-splintering punch.

Emmitt's mother threw her head back on her shoulders and laughed as though at the funniest joke she'd ever seen. "Good one, boy! The bigger they are the harder they fall!"

Emmitt shuffled around like a rooster, crowing along with his mother. He stepped up to Prophet once more, grabbed a handful of Prophet's sandy hair. "If you think *that* was somethin', Ma, watch thi—"

"Hold on," Horton Whipple said, grabbing Sanderson's arm as the outlaw leader was about to ram his knee against Prophet's forehead.

Emmitt frowned up at the big man, red-faced. Whipple must have stood just a few inches under seven feet. He had a big, bushy red mustache and blue eyes with what appeared to be flecks of gold steel in them.

Emmitt snarled, "Goddamnit, Whipple. I told you *never* touch me!"

Whipple stared down at Prophet. The big man looked like a bizarrely mottled mountain wall standing there, with his lewd tattoos and egg-shaped head and flat blue eyes. "He killed an old pard of mine in Missouri a few years back. I wanna shot at this four-flushin', bounty-huntin' son of a bitch." He scowled challengingly down at the pint-sized Sanderson, opening and closing his hands. "And I aim to git it."

Frowning angrily, Sanderson opened his mouth to object, then closed his mouth suddenly. The wrinkles above the bridge of his nose planed out as he shuttled his gaze between Prophet and Whipple and back again, a slow, cunning smile building on his lips.

"Why not?" Chuckling, he backed away and glanced at the other men standing in a semicircle behind him. "We might even take bets on it, eh, boys?"

His mother was grinning delightedly, three or four crooked teeth showing in her rotten gums. She'd hiked a hip on a rock and was resting the sawed-off across her denim-clad thighs. A lumpy tow sack rested on the rock behind her.

Prophet caught his breath and gained his knees as Sanderson, Hayes, and Cisco bet on the fight's outcome, including how long it would take one man to beat the other senseless, then to kill him. Scuffling around and arguing and elbowing, they handed their money to the grinning and chuckling Maybelle Sanderson, who bet five dollars just to balance things out that Prophet would knock Whipple flat on his back in five minutes.

Again she raked her lusty animal gaze across Prophet's chest and shoulders, and the bounty hunter had to suppress a shiver of revulsion. Then, when wads of greenbacks protruded from his mother's jeans pockets, Sanderson herded Prophet and Whipple down the slope about forty yards to a level area, where only wheatgrass and a few clumps of sagebrush grew, and told them to go at it.

"Hold on," Prophet said, unbuttoning his shirt cuffs. "I gotta roll my sleeves up." He took his time, darting his glance around at Whipple shadowboxing before him, grunting and snarling like a wounded grizzly, and the three other men and Mrs. Sanderson forming a rough circle around them.

How in the hell was he going to get out of this one? Even if he somehow managed to clean Whipple's clock, the others would gun him, for they each held a pistol while Mrs. Sanderson continued caressing that sawed-off like a newborn babe in her arms.

He had a fleeting notion of somehow getting Whipple into a headlock and threatening to break his neck if the others didn't give him a gun. But hell, they'd only laugh at him. Whipple meant nothing to them. His dying would only mean more stage loot for the rest of them.

Besides, Whipple had a good four inches and about thirty pounds—most of it muscle—on Prophet. The prospect of Prophet getting the giant into a headlock was as far-fetched as the hope that a gun-toting angel would ride down from Heaven to smite down the Sanderson gang in a hail of righteous lead.

Prophet rolled his right sleeve up to his biceps.

Whipple stepped toward him, holding fists up in front of his chin, eyes pinched, broad face pink with fury. "Ready for your whuppin' now, bounty man?"

Prophet raised his fists and shuffled sideways. "Tell me, Whipple, who was this fella you say I killed over Missouri way?"

The big man lunged toward Prophet, throwing a left jab. Prophet jerked his head away, and Whipple's fist only scraped the side of his chin.

"Frank Dawson."

"Dawson?" Prophet bunched his brows as he dodged another jab. "Ah, hell"—he lurched forward, feigning a blow with his right fist and landing a left jab to Whipple's hard, muscle-strapped belly, evoking a grunt from the man—"*I* didn't kill him. I was *chasin'* him and he ran out in front of a stagecoach. The team trampled him, dragged him for a good two blocks, and then the coach itself hammered him into little more than a grease splotch!"

Whipple lurched forward with surprising speed, and landed an ear-ringing roundhouse against Prophet's left cheek. The world pitched for a couple of seconds as Prophet skipped back, blinking, trying to clear his vision.

He'd thought he could rile the man into swinging wild punches, but that one had landed right where Whipple had intended. If he landed many more, Mrs. Sanderson was going to be out five singles and Prophet would soon be feeding the carp in the yonder stream.

"Yessir," Prophet said, never one to easily give up on a plan, "the undertaker's sons were scooping ole Frank outta the dust with shovels and soup ladles, and what they couldn't get the dogs finished off."

"Don't listen to him, Whip!" Emmitt shouted as the others clapped and yelled on either side of him. "He's just tryin' to get your goat!"

Whipple bunched his lips and puffed his cheeks as he stormed forward, bringing his right ham-sized fist up from his heels. Prophet ducked. The fist whistled through the air over Prophet's head. As Whipple continued wheeling sideways with the swing's momentum, Prophet bolted up and forward and slammed his own right against the man's left ear.

"Uhhn-ah!" Whipple gritted his teeth with fury and brushed at the two-inch gash angling down from the top of his ear and from which thick red blood issued. It glistened in the midday light as it dribbled down over the lobe.

"Told ya!" Mrs. Sanderson crowed, packing her pipe. "Never fight a doomed man!"

"Mercy," Prophet said, sidling around the cursing Whipple. "I bet that hurts like hell!"

Just as Prophet had hoped, the man came at him, swinging from his heart instead of his brain, and within two seconds he'd swung twice, one fist again cleaving the air over Prophet's head while the other merely grazed the bounty hunter's chin.

Prophet got inside and landed one punch to the man's right-side ribs and another to his left.

Whipple staggered backward, trying to get away. Prophet followed, keeping his own rage on a short leash, funneling all his strength to his fists, and laid a right uppercut to the big man's jaw.

Whipple hit the ground on his back.

"Come on, Whip!" Cisco cried. "I got a gold cartwheel ridin' on ya, bud!"

Prophet didn't want the man to get up again. As Whipple began pushing himself up off his back, Prophet dove on top of him, snaked his hands around the man's bull neck, and began pressing his thumbs against his rock-hard Adam's apple.

Whipple gritted his teeth and made gurgling sounds, spit bubbling out from between his lips, snot blowing from his nose. The big man wrapped his hands around Prophet's wrists, tried to pry the bounty hunter's hands from his neck. The others whooped and yelled, and Mrs. Sanderson cackled like a crazed hen, thoroughly enjoying the show. Prophet levered himself forward off his knees, tightening his grip on Whipple's neck and grinding the back of the big man's head into the ground.

"Gosh, Whip," Prophet said, stretching his lips back from his teeth, the cords standing out in his neck, "I hope the loot ole Frank was carryin' wasn't part yours. That was one helluva lot of dinero!"

Whipple managed to pry Prophet's grip loose enough to rasp, "We planned . . . that job . . . for four months . . . you son of a bitch!"

"Doesn't that piss-burn ya?" Prophet inwardly cursed as the big man continued to pry the bounty hunter's death grip loose. "Hell, you coulda lived in Mexico for *years* on all that gold!"

Whipple took a deep breath, pinched his eyes, and arched his back as he heaved straight up against Prophet's weight. "Kill . . . you . . . b-b-bastard!"

As Prophet's hands began rising from the big man's sweat-slick neck, he realized the folly of his ways. That his plan had backfired was literally hammered home when Whipple slammed his right knee into the bounty hunter's groin.

Prophet groaned. His hands slipped off the big man's neck and a half second later he found himself on his back, his balls burning and throbbing, his gut churning with nausea. He tried to lift his own right fist, but Whipple, straddling Prophet now, rammed two vision-dulling right jabs against Prophet's left cheek.

Prophet fell slack as his lights went out briefly. When his

lids fluttered open again, he saw Whipple, still on top of him, reaching down toward his right boot. The hand came up again, and a savage smile took shape on Whipple's chapped lips as he held a wide-bladed, horn-handled bowie knife out for Prophet's inspection, as though it were a weapon the bounty hunter might want to buy or trade for.

The others were shouting and whooping and dancing in circles around Whipple and Prophet, kicking up dust and flinging pebbles and grit at Prophet's face.

"Kill him, Whip!" Rodney Hayes shouted. "Kill him dead!"

"Go ahead and send him to Jesus, Whip," Emmitt Sanderson said. "The girls prob'ly done got our lunch ready, and I'm starvin'!"

"Damn." Mrs. Sanderson shook her head as she puffed her pipe. "That's five greenbacks I'll never see again."

Whipple's eyes slightly crossed as he stared down at Prophet. "See that?" he growled, turning the knife this way and that, letting the sun catch it. "That blade's so sharp it'll trim the hair on a frog's cock."

The man suddenly drew the knife back, bunching his lips and slanting the blade toward Prophet. "Won't be no job o' work to cut your *throat*!"

Prophet kicked his legs and tried to lift his arms, but it was no use. The big man had him pinned to the ground. He could only watch in horror as Whipple loosed a bearlike roar and slashed the blade toward Prophet's neck.

6

LOU PROPHET WAS about to shake hands with the Devil himself—Ole Scratch, as he was called—with whom Prophet had a special bond. The two would meet at last and, as per the agreement they had made when Prophet had survived the War of Northern Aggression and wanted only to live, drink, and carouse to his heart's content for the remainder of his days, the bounty hunter would begin his long, eternal stint shoveling coal in Hell.

Damn. He'd thought he'd have another few years on this side of the sod to stomp with his tail up.

Regretting the pact he'd made, the bounty hunter squeezed his eyes closed and gritted his teeth. He no longer felt the throbbing ache in his groin as he awaited the slash of Whipple's knife that would no doubt cleave his head from his shoulders.

Something wet sprayed across his cheek.

Prophet opened his eyes as a rifle cracked somewhere off in the hills to his right. Whipple straddled him, holding both his knife hand and his free hand chest high. The hands were quivering, the knife flashing in the sunlight. Whipple's head was tipped against his right shoulder, and oddly twisted.

There was a round hole on the left side of his head, just

above his ear—a hole about the size of a sewing thimble. Blood dribbled from the hole to form a small river down the side of the big man's bald head. The other side of his skull had opened like a smashed melon, and blood and brains and large chunks of bone ran down his right shoulder and arm to puddle on the ground beside Prophet's hip.

The big man's chest heaved once and his eyes rolled back in his head. His lower jaw dropped. He groaned as he dropped the knife and began to sag toward the ground.

Prophet was trying to figure out who'd fired the shot, as were the other men standing around him and staring down at Whipple with looks of incredulity and horror. Mrs. Sanderson was the first to recover from the shock. She bolted up from the rock she'd been sitting on, glanced around quickly, then lurched toward Prophet, bringing up her double-bore sawed-off.

"He's got a partner!" she bellowed like a chicken snagged in an eagle's claws.

She jerked as though with a start as a hole opened in the front of her man's flannel shirt, spitting a thick gob of blood across Prophet. The bullet that had torn into her back and out her chest careened between her son and the stringbean called Cisco to spang off a rock behind them. The rifle report followed a half second later, flatting out from the scattered pines on the low northern slope. Mrs. Sanderson's arms fell to her sides as she dropped the barn blaster, staggered forward, twisted around, and tumbled onto her back across Prophet's lower legs, dead.

"Ma!" Emmitt Sanderson cried, leaping toward his mother.

He didn't make it. A bullet took him through the high center of his chest. He flew backward, arms flailing straight out from his shoulders, as the other two men screamed and leaped around, raising their revolvers and trying to get a bead on the shooter.

There were four more rifle shots, booming reports spaced split seconds apart and echoing around the valley like thunderclaps. Prophet, on his back as before with Horton Whipple still straddling him, stared up in disbelief as Cisco and Rodney Hayes danced bizarre death jigs above and around him, screaming as bullets plunked through their chests and bellies, tearing out chunks of flesh, blood, and viscera and splashing the weeds and rocks around them with several shades of red.

Finally, both men were down, Cisco lying off to Prophet's left while Rodney lay straight out from his boots, belly down, one arm curled beneath him. He shook, farted, sighed, and lay still.

Prophet looked up the long, gentle slope on his right. A man with a rifle stepped out from behind a lone boulder and swung into the saddle of a brown-and-white pinto pony. All Prophet could think was that another outlaw—possibly one double-crossed by these four and their mother—had come to even the score. How the bushwhacker knew Prophet wasn't a member of the gang, Prophet couldn't say.

He was just glad to not be shaking hands with El Diablo.

As the rider trotted the pinto down the hill, weaving around cedars and junipers, Prophet heaved aside Whipple's heavy carcass. Mrs. Sanderson lay sprawled across his shins, staring toward him with a fist-sized hole in her forehead and her tobacco-stained tongue lolling out the side of her mouth.

Prophet lifted his back, pulled his right leg out from beneath the dead woman, planted his boot against her face, and gave her an unceremonious shove. She rolled off his other boot to tumble facedown in the weeds with a postmortem gurgle.

Prophet grimaced as he rolled onto his right elbow. His crotch resumed burning and his balls felt as though they'd swollen up twice their normal size. He turned to watch the rider approach on his pinto.

Her pinto.

The young woman's long, straw-colored hair bounced across her shoulders and down the striped serape that couldn't quite conceal the two matronly lumps beneath.

As she came closer, her face grew gradually clearer. Prophet would have recognized the heart-shaped bone structure, bee-stung lips, pug nose, and wide-set, crystalline hazel eyes anywhere—all shaded by a man's flat-brimmed black hat trimmed with a snakeskin band. It was a face so teeming with peaches-and-cream sweetness and persnickety schoolgirl charm that no one but Prophet would have believed the girl behind it was capable of playing hooky from school, much less gunning down a passel of pistol-packing varmints from a hundred yards uphill without one wasted bullet.

"Louisa, don't you beat all?" Prophet gave an angry chuff and slapped the ground as the girl drew the pinto up before him. "Just when I was about to get the upper hand on that lummox, you start shootin' away like Billy the Kid. If you think you're gettin' any of the bounty money, you got another *think* comin'."

Prophet gained his feet, moving gingerly, his balls still throbbing, and looked up at Louisa, not yet twenty years old but sitting her saddle with customary self-assuredness, the breeze playing with her hair. "Besides, they were all wanted *alive*. They ain't any good to me *dead*!"

"I think," the girl said, leaning forward on her saddle horn, the barrel of her Sharps still smoking faintly, "that you should be kissing my boots instead of berating me. That oaf was about to cut your head clean off your shoulders. They would have thrown your uncouth, mangy, smelly carcass in the nearest ravine and neither I nor anyone else would have known what happened to you."

Prophet leaned down to scoop his hat from a weed tuft. He dusted it off and set it on his head, glancing around at the dead men and Mrs. Sanderson already attracting flies. Horton Whipple's bowie knife glistened in the sun near his left shoulder, beneath which blood from his ruined head was puddling and congealing.

"I had a chance." Absently rubbing his neck, Prophet turned back to Louisa. His chagrin pained him worse than the groining he'd taken from Horton Whipple. Not only had he let an old woman sneak up on him from behind, but a young one—one who'd been bounty hunting fewer years than Prophet had been wearing the same longhandles—had had to save his ass. "Where in the hell did you come from, anyway? I thought you were up north."

They'd met a couple of years ago, when Louisa, only seventeen at the time, had taken off after the bunch that had burned her Nebraska farmstead and murdered her family. She and Prophet had hunted the kill-crazy renegades led by Handsome Dave Duvall from Minnesota to northern Dakota Territory, and together they'd sent each man to the spirits in a haze of gun smoke and dust.

Prophet had figured that Duvall's demise would mark the end of Louisa's vengeance trail. But long after Duvall and his gang were moldering in their graves, she, in the grip of some curious obsession for righting the world's wrongs and evening up the odds for those who couldn't do it themselves, had continued ghosting the outlaw trail, collecting bounties not so much for the money but to finance her continued tracking.

Louisa specialized in stalking men who killed or injured women or children, but she didn't discriminate. Any outlaw was fair game, and she wasn't on any man's trail long before the poor bastard was soiling his trousers and begging for mercy.

But when it came to killers and renegades, Louisa showed no mercy.

She and Prophet worked together only occasionally. But being too stubborn to stand each other for long, they spent more time apart than together. Otherwise, they'd have spent more time arguing than bounty tracking.

Besides—though neither had made a formal declaration— they were in love with each other, and love had no place in the bounty hunting business.

"You carve a wide swath, Lou," Louisa said, sliding the Sharps into her saddle boot. "I accidentally cut your trail in Denver where I ran into your old pal Hooch Mullaney, who said that when you'd finally gotten out of the local lockup for busting up the Drovers Saloon and Pleasure Parlor during a typical inebriated brawl, you headed south for the winter. In Pueblo I learned from a deputy sheriff that you'd gotten word a gang of stage robbers was running sharp-horned and high-tailed through the country north of Durango, and you intended to collect the bounty to fuel your winter—a winter that you no doubt intend to spend in the arms of some dark-skinned harlot in some rank perdition south of the border."

Prophet grinned up at her. "Why, you been followin' me. Needin' a *real* man to curl your toes, are ya?"

Louisa blinked coolly, but her smooth-skinned cheeks flushed ever so slightly. "Hardly. And I'd rather follow a bobcat into a rattlesnake den. It just so happens our trails crossed several times below Denver—I, too, am headed south—and I had a premonition you were about to get yourself into hotter water than even you were accustomed to." She raked her haughty, self-satisfied gaze around the bodies of the dead Sanderson bunch, as if to prove the validity of her portent. "I cut Mean and Ugly's trail yesterday. Who woundn't recognize that scrub horse's shabble-footed, knock-kneed gait?"

"Jesus Christ, now she's insultin' my horse."

As Prophet turned to gather his weapons, Louisa said behind him, "Your entourage?"

He stopped and swung back around. "What?"

Prophet followed Louisa's gaze westward, where the outlaw cabin sat on the hill shoulder, smoke billowing from its chimney pipe. The four women—vague, long-haired, colorfully clad figures from this distance—stood in the dooryard, staring toward their dead husbands and Mrs. Sanderson. They all seemed to be holding pots or pans while Horton Whipple's hefty gal was shoving a ramrod down the barrel of an old Kentucky rifle, awkwardly holding the barrel between her fat, bare knees.

"Shit."

"What?"

"The women."

Louisa snickered. "You think they'll whip you to death with their garter belts?"

Prophet swung around to regard the unlikely bounty hunter and sharpshooter once more and jerked his arm toward the hill. "The loot the gang stole from their last holdup around Durango is probably in that damn cabin. To get it, I'm gonna have to run that petticoat gauntlet."

Louisa stared at him skeptically, as if she weren't sure she'd heard him correctly, then rolled her eyes. "Lord!" Gigging the pinto westward, she called behind her, "Stay here and pull yourself together, for heaven's sakes. My God, this is embarrassing!"

Louisa made short work of the women.

As soon as she'd galloped within range of the hefty gal's old blunderbuss, Louisa cut loose with the twin, silver-plated Colt revolvers she kept holstered beneath her serape. The fat gal didn't have time to snap off a shot before Louisa's slugs tore into the dust and brush at the women's feet, and all four scattered like chickens from a rampaging fox.

The fat gal bellowed raucously, threw the blunderbuss away as though it were a Mojave green rattler, and ran for cover at the cabin's rear. Louisa pulled the pinto up in front of the cabin, leaped down from the saddle, and strode through the open front door.

She wasn't inside for over a minute before she reappeared, a pair of saddlebags draped over her shoulder. Swinging lithely atop the pinto, she reined the horse around and headed him back downhill to where Prophet waited, feeling even more foolish than before.

He'd returned his bowie and his Colt to their sheaths, and held his Winchester over his shoulder.

Louisa glanced at the saddlebags draped over her own bags behind her saddle and bedroll. "Are those what you're looking for?"

Prophet unfastened the flap over the right bag and peered inside where eight or nine stout wads of greenbacks resided. He sighed.

"Now, I suppose you'd like a ride back to your cayuse?"

Prophet's face warmed. "If it wouldn't be too much trouble."

7

PROPHET'S PRIDE BURNING as hot as his groin, he rode silently behind Louisa. He winced against the horse's jostling movements as they headed back to where he'd tied Mean and Ugly in the willows near the small branch stream. Louisa said nothing either, and Prophet was too absorbed in his own shame to notice her pensive silence.

As they approached Mean and Ugly, who shook his head and nickered an insult at Louisa's clean-lined pinto, Prophet slid off the pinto's rear and, holding his rifle in one hand and grabbing the outlaws' saddlebags with the other, said, "I'm gonna find a place to hole up for the rest of the day. I'm wore out, hungry, and in bad need of a drink." He slid the rifle into his saddle boot and glanced at Louisa, who sat the pinto, staring off pensively. "You might as well camp with me."

She gave him one of her wrinkle-nosed looks. "So you can curl my toes for me?"

"It's plain you're needin' it."

"Ha!" She reined the pinto around. "I'll cook my own steak and boil my own coffee, thank you."

He grabbed Mean and Ugly's reins off the scrub willow and stared after her, frowning. "Where you headed?"

Louisa stopped the horse and glanced at Prophet over her shoulder. "Seven Devils in the Arizona Territory. Know it?"

"Nope."

"I'm settling down, Lou. I'm giving up bounty hunting to live with family. Raise chickens and sew dresses and such."

"I'll believe that when I see it."

"You're welcome to visit as long as you bathe first." She heeled the horse into a trot through the brush and splashed into the stream, and Prophet stood listening as she crossed the stream and thumped up the low rise beyond, heading south.

Prophet continued to stand, feeling a strange tightness in his throat. "Well, hell, I guess I won't be visiting, then."

He turned to Mean and Ugly staring at him skeptically. "Imagine that? Her telling me when to bathe when we're not even married. Christ! Who needs women anyways?" He tightened Mean's saddle cinch and swung into the leather. "That's the beauty of pleasure girls, Mean. They don't boss you around, and if they do, you leave and find another the *next* night!"

Prophet swung the horse around and, glancing after Louisa, who was cresting a ridge on the far side of the creek, chuffed again angrily and gigged the dun downstream. Soon, following the meandering creek, he found a secluded canyon flanked by a sandstone ridge, with the shallow stream nearby and a scattering of cottonwoods and junipers to screen his smoke.

He swung down from Mean and Ugly, unsaddled the horse, rubbed him down, and hobbled him near the creek to graze and draw water at his leisure.

It didn't take Prophet long to set up camp. He was an old hand at it. Having left home at fourteen to fight for the Confederacy in the War for Southern Independence, he'd slept out in the open for nearly half his life, and aside from the occasional whorehouse, he preferred it that way.

He gathered wood for a fire, though he wouldn't start the fire until later, when the sun was setting and the mountain air was cooling. He set out his bedroll and his saddlebags, hiding the outlaws' loot in a notch at the base of the sandstone ridge, then arranged his cooking gear. After indulging in a couple shots of good Kentucky bourbon from his half-empty bottle, he stripped down to his longhandles and socks. He scrubbed the blood from his buckskin tunic and his faded blue denims in the creek as, wary of another shoulder nip, he kept an eye on Mean and Ugly grazing nearby.

When the clothes were as clean as they were going to get, he returned to his camp and draped the tunic and jeans over rocks to dry. Hanging, the buckskin would no doubt dry hard as adobe, but he didn't feel like wearing it wet.

After another shot from his bottle, he heard Louisa's voice again in his head. He wasn't sure if it was because of what she'd said, or because he was tired of his own trail smell, but he fished around in his saddlebags for a soap sliver.

Tramping out to the creek, he found a hole a couple of feet deep under the far bank. He shucked out of his longhandles, sank gingerly into the water—the swelling in his oysters had gone down, but they were still tender—and soaked himself in the cool, refreshing stream murmuring between the low banks, magpies and squirrels chittering in the branches around him. Then he stood and ran the soap over every inch of his scarred, rugged, slab-chested frame.

He flopped down again to rinse off the soap. When he'd scrubbed out his longhandles, he tramped naked back to camp, chilled by the cooling afternoon breeze but feeling pounds lighter having shed the sweat, grime, trail dust, and blood smell. And the cool water had soothed his battered crotch.

Feeling better all around, he built a fire, hung the longhandles over a rock near the fledgling flames, then lay back in a patch of wan sunlight flickering through a towering aspen, and sighed and closed his eyes.

It had been a long, hard ride after the Sanderson bunch, and he'd found no picnic at the end of the trail. If it hadn't been for Louisa . . .

Louisa. Damn her hide.

Sleep drew him down. He slept deeply, soothed by the canyon's gradually thickening shadows and by the freshening breeze rustling the leaves over his head.

He didn't know how much time had passed before Mean's warning whinny jerked his head up. He grabbed his Colt from the holster propped beside him, thumbing the hammer back and aiming straight out before him. At the same time, he pulled his saddlebags across his waist, partly covering himself. His pulse quickened.

Had someone spied the extra pair of saddlebags he'd been carrying and followed him? Or were Utes on the prowl, looking for white men's scalps to show off to their squaws around the fire tonight?

The shadows had thickened between dwindling light shafts angling through the trees and between the canyon's high walls. From his left, along the stream, the slow clomps of a single horse sounded, crunching old leaves and dry grass. A figure appeared, moving through the trees and behind a thin brush wall.

To Prophet's right, Mean and Ugly whinnied again shrilly, as he always did at the approach of strangers. But the rider approaching now was no stranger, Prophet saw, as the rich blond curls jostled across Louisa's shoulders, under the brim of her black hat. Her face was a pale, heart-shaped smudge in the tree shadows.

Swaying easily with the pinto's movement, she turned the horse from the creek and headed straight for Prophet sitting naked beside the fire that had burned itself out while he'd slept. He depressed the Colt's hammer and raised the barrel.

Louisa drew rein before him, letting her gaze sweep his scarred, deep-chested, saddle-worn body lounging there in the brown grass, wearing only a pair of saddlebags and with a few pennies of sunlight glowing across his sun-cured, fresh-scrubbed skin.

Prophet curled his upper lip at her. "That was one fast ride to Arizona and back. That pinto got wings I can't see?"

She didn't say anything, just swung down from the pinto and silently led the horse off into the brush away from the dead fire. Prophet sat staring after her. Then he heard the squawk of tack in the brush and knew she was unsaddling her mount. He threw aside the saddlebags—he was as comfortable naked around Louisa as he was alone—then lay back in the splotchy, fading sunlight, smiling contentedly.

Only a few minutes later, he heard her footsteps but didn't open his eyes until she was standing over him. "You had a bath."

Prophet opened his eyes to see her lifting her serape over

her head, blond curls rising and then flopping back down to her shoulders as she dropped the woolen poncho in the grass and began unbuttoning her plaid shirt. Her face was flushed, a cool, lusty cast to her eyes. Her chest rose and fell sharply.

Prophet feigned a yawn, crossed his ankles, and hooked his arms behind his head. No point in looking overly eager after she'd insulted him. "I started counting the days since Christmas and figured I was a day or two overdue."

He stared up at her as she removed the shirt, then reached down, crossing her arms, and lifted her camisole up and over her head to drop it in the grass with the poncho and shirt. Her deep breasts—pale and upturned, with tender rosebud nipples—jostled as she moved, kicking out of her boots, then unbuttoning and dropping her wool riding skirt. She stared back at Prophet, who could no longer feign disinterest. He could hear her sharp, desperate breaths as she removed her riding socks and pantaloons and stood before him naked, legs spread, cupping her breasts in her hands with tooth-gnashing allure.

"I'm sorry I insulted your bathing habits, Lou."

Prophet tried to speak, but his throat had pinched closed. He cleared it, ran his eyes down her small but willowy frame—she wasn't much over five feet two—somehow unblemished and unscarred despite how many badmen she'd ridden down and kicked out with her twin Colts and a shovel. With her clear eyes and waiflike charm, she could have been a city girl—the daughter of a successful grocer or mercantile proprietor with enough money to keep her in tight corsets and piano lessons, with occasional strolls arm in arm with her well-bred beau through the park at sundown.

"I reckon I can overlook it if you get down here real quick."

She knelt before him and threw her arms around his neck. He wrapped his own arms around her waist, pulled her taut against him, and kissed her hungrily, relishing the feel of the girl once more, the smell of her, the taste of her tongue, the silky feel of her ripe, full lips under his.

Her breasts pushed flat against his chest, the nipples pebbling. She sighed and shuddered as she ran her hands brusquely through his hair and returned his penetrating kiss.

Prophet held her for a long time, kissing her, running his right hand down her arm, across the swell of her hip to the long curve of her thigh, sculpted and tightened by all the miles she'd stretched out behind her. Then he gentled her onto the ground, and she spread her legs, sighing deeply as he positioned himself between her knees and, mindful of his injured groin, eased himself down.

"Oh, Lou," she groaned.

They made love desperately, hungrily, and then again more slowly, with Louisa on top, rising and falling on her haunches, full breasts sloping out from her chest as she rocked. They shuddered together in a fury of spent love, and Louisa leaned forward to squeeze the hard slabs of his chest. She sandwiched his face between her hands and nibbled his right ear.

"That felt *good*," she breathed.

At length, she lifted her head and peered into his eyes, her own hazel eyes slightly crossing as the skin above the bridge of her nose wrinkled with beseeching. "Come with me to Arizona, Lou. Let's start a new life together."

Prophet lifted his head, frowning. "Together? What the hell's come over you?"

"Don't get your shorts in a twist." Louisa stretched her body out atop his, like a cat stretching on a window ledge. She hooked her feet around his shins and rubbed her cheek against his chest. "I'm not proposing we get married and raise kids and join a church, and all that other stuff you're so afraid of. I just think you should give some thought to settling down. We could do it together."

"I have thought about it," Prophet said, slowly running his hands down her slender, naked back. "Decided against it. Now, that don't mean you shouldn't. I been tellin' you since I first met you that bounty hunting is no job for a girl. You need to settle down, get hitched to a nice boy, raise some kids, and join a church. But me?" He chuckled as he stared at the slowly fading sky. "Hell, this is all I know."

"It doesn't have to be."

".You can't teach an old dog new tricks nor a skunk not to spray. Besides, I got that agreement—"

"Oh, I know about your blasphemous contract with 'Ole

Scratch.'" Louisa rested her chin on his breastbone and absently caressed his arms, which he'd crossed behind his head. "That demon doesn't need you shoveling coal throughout eternity any more than you need to spend the rest of your life bounty hunting just so you can drink and carouse to your heart's content. You're not getting any younger. And that incident with the old lady—"

"Whoa, now!" Prophet looked down at her. "That was an isolated mistake. I had distractions."

"I saw the distractions, and they didn't look all that distracting, if you ask me."

"Nobody asked you. Forget it. I got a contract with Scratch, and I aim to keep it. But like I said, I'm glad you're settling down. What family you got down there?"

"A cousin. I heard about Marlene through another cousin I ran into up in Dakota last fall. Marlene Karlaufsky *was* her name. I think her married name's Fletcher or some such. She and I were close as girls back in Nebraska, before her father pulled up stakes and moved the family to Denver. I wrote her a letter down in Arizona, just trying to reestablish contact with her, trying to find out how she was. She wrote back inviting me to go live with her and her husband and her boy."

Louisa gently twisted one of Prophet's chest hairs, keeping her chin planted on his breastbone, and nibbled her lower lip. "At first, I didn't cotton to the idea. But then I got to thinking, why not? I've been tracking badmen for nearly three years now, and it hasn't brought my folks back. And it hasn't done anything to silence their voices I hear in my head every night before I go to sleep. Maybe it never will."

Prophet sighed. "What's your cousin do down there in Seven Devils?"

"Raises chickens and takes in sewing. She said I could work for her a year or two, earn some money. Then maybe I'll open a shop of some kind."

"Hell," Prophet said, chuckling, suppressing a sudden pang of jealousy and lonesomeness. "You go down there and settle down, Louisa girl, you'll be married inside of a year."

She rolled her eyes up at him. "You think so?"

"I'd bet the plow horse on it."

"If you drifted down there with me, you maybe could deputy for Marlene's husband. He's the town sheriff."

"I wore a badge once . . . for the last time." It had been an awful mistake, and Prophet wasn't sure how he'd come to represent the law in that little Wyoming town, but he'd woken up one morning with a thunderous hangover in bed with a pretty, painted harpy to find a badge pinned to his shirt and the whole town congratulating him on his new employ. "Them badges might be only a half ounce of cheap tin, but they weigh a ton."

"You could bartend or help out in the livery barn. . . ."

"Well, hell, I'm sure I could shovel shit off the street, too." Prophet eased Louisa off his shoulder and grabbed his long-handles, which the high mountain air had nearly dried. "But I think I'll keep doin' what I know best, thank you very much, Miss Bonaventure."

"Oh, Lou!"

Prophet had stuffed one leg into his longhandles. He glanced at her and froze, an ice pick of raw desire tickling his loins.

She lay belly down in the short, wiry grass, kicking her feet up over her round, firm bottom. Her tender pink nipples caressed the ground, and her fingers tore absently at the grass. Her hair caressed her pale, delicate shoulders. "At least ride down to Seven Devils with me, won't you? I've been lonely and—I'll admit it—hungry for your attentions."

She met his stare and lifted her mouth corners slightly, eyes slitting devilishly, her bee-stung lips seeming to swell. She crossed her ankles and curled her toes. "We'll have a good time, Lou. I promise."

8

MARIE ANTOINETTE FLETCHER, lying spread-eagle atop a bed on the second floor of the only whorehouse in Seven Devils, struggled against the torn strips of bedsheet tying her wrists and ankles to the bed's four mahogany posts.

It was to this room the men and the girl who'd killed her family had taken her, a couple of them carrying her, kicking and screaming, over their shoulders. When they'd gotten to the room, they'd slapped her until her cheeks and lips burned and her ears rang, and then they'd tied her to the bed and begun taking turns, while she heard above the ringing in her ears and the squawk of the bedsprings the screams and wails of the other women in the building being similarly abused.

She'd heard the screech and witchlike cackle of the young, demonic redhead with the green streaks in her hair—someone had called her "Cora"—a couple of rooms down the hall. And there had been one sudden gunshot that seemed to jerk the walls and make the rafters sag and that, when the echo had died, had caused Cora to laugh even harder while one of the working girls pleaded and begged for mercy.

Now the man called Captain Sykes climbed off her, grinning down at her through his close-cropped red beard. He slapped her naked thigh and spoke with a Yankee twang. "Thanks, milady. I feel much better now. Been a while, don't ya know." He winked, then turned and rolled off the bed to begin gathering his clothes.

"When you ride with the Three of a Kind Gang," he continued thickly, blinking his red-rimmed eyes as if to clear them as he reached for his longhandles, "you don't get much time for pleasures of the flesh."

While he had toiled on top of her, Marie Antoinette had loosened the knot in the strip of cloth tying her right hand to the bedpost. She was sure that one fierce jerk would free the hand entirely. As the red-bearded man stumbled around drunkenly, gathering his clothes from the floor right of the bed, she eyed the small-caliber revolver he'd dropped when he'd first staggered into the room from downstairs and began shucking out of his clothes.

She was sure he hadn't realized he'd dropped the gun, which seemed to have fallen from an inside pocket of his long, black greatcoat and rolled across the red Moroccan throw rug to half conceal itself beneath the nightstand beside the bed. In his drunken state, he might not notice it down there. Marie Antoinette was counting on that. The only thing that mitigated the horror of the past hour—having seen her son and her husband both gunned down before she'd been hauled off to the whorehouse and repeatedly beaten and violated—had been the prospect of getting her hands on that gun.

Unconsciously, she'd buried her shock and incomprehensible misery beneath a razor-edged blade of raw fury, which she'd so far contained. She hoped she could continue to contain it until the drunken lieutenant had left, and she could free the other ties and grab the weapon.

Marie Antoinette, who had once worked in this very house of ill repute before she'd married Fletcher, had been around guns enough to know that the revolver was only a five-shot. A backup pistol. That mattered little. The point was, it was a gun, and with it she could kill at least five of the six savages who'd murdered her boy and her husband.

"Ah, shit!" Sykes barked as, pulling on his trousers, he lost his balance, stumbled sideways, and fell to the floor with a loud thud. "Shit!" Then he chuckled and glanced up at Marie Antoinette staring down at him, expressionless. "That wasn't very damn graceful. Please accept my apologies, milady!"

Marie Antoinette's eyes flicked toward the gun, the ivory handle of which protruded two inches out from beneath the nightstand. Sykes's left elbow lay atop the rug only two feet from the gun. Marie Antoinette tightened her jaws nervously.

Don't look at the gun, she silently ordered the man. *Do not look at the gun. . . .*

As though defying her, Sykes turned his head toward the nightstand, his chin down, heavy-lidded eyes angled toward the floor.

Marie Antoinette bit her lower lip. *Shit, shit, shit!*

But then he raked a heavy hand across his face, turned to his left, and pushed himself up off the floor. "There we go!" He stood and inhaled deeply, glancing once more at Marie Antoinette and holding up his hands, palms out. "Quite the feat, wouldn't you say? Now, if I can only stay upright long enough to finish gatherin' my damn clothes. Who in the hell threw them around like this, anyway? *You?*"

He laughed again as he reached down to continue pulling up his pants. "No, I reckon you couldn't have done it, could ya?"

Marie Antoinette lay as if on pins and needles as the man stumbled around, dressing. She prayed he wouldn't see the gun or feel it missing from his coat.

When he'd finally pulled on his greatcoat, plopped his blue cavalry hat on his head backward, and staggered toward the door, she glanced once more at the gun.

It still lay beneath the nightstand.

"Never did the mattress dance with a lawman's wife before," Sykes drawled. He winked as he reached for the door handle. "Next time, you might put forth a little more effort."

With that, he fumbled the door open and stumbled into it before staggering out, leaving the door standing wide behind him. Sykes's boots scuffed along the hall while the drunkenly jubilant voices of the other renegades rose from the parlor below, as did the occasional angry admonition of the whorehouse madam, Miss Kate.

As Sykes's foot thuds dwindled into the distance, Sykes now humming loudly, Marie Antoinette bunched her lips and gave her right wrist a vicious tug. The knot gave with a tearing sound and a faint wooden crack.

Panting anxiously, Marie Antoinette swung around and tore at the left-hand knot with her right thumb and index finger. That knot was tighter than the other, but she worked at it desperately, gritting her teeth and ignoring the ache and burn in her nails, which she cracked and tore as she worked open the knot.

She kept her ears pricked for more approaching renegades. Thank God they all seemed to be singing and dancing in the downstairs parlor with a couple of Miss Kate's unfortunate working girls.

Finally, Marie Antoinette's left hand fell free. She wasted no time, using both hands, going to work on her ankles, listening intently to the sounds from below and the murmurs from a room down the hall, and casting quick, tense looks at the door standing open before her. She half expected at any moment to spy another gang member approaching the room.

When she had her second ankle free of the post, she scrambled off the bed so quickly that she nearly fell. Catching herself, she reached down, scooped up the revolver, and set it atop the nightstand. Then she grabbed her dress, which the savages had torn off her, and donned it as best she could, with half the back buttons missing.

Picking up the gun, holding it in both hands straight out before her, gritting her teeth against the pain of her rage hammering away at her skull—were her son and husband really dead or had this all been some hideous nightmare?—she moved to the door. She drew the pistol's hammer straight back with her right thumb and, swallowing, her chest rising and falling heavily, edged a cautious look into the hall.

Finding it empty, she turned right and began stepping slowly, barefoot, toward the top of the stairs at the hall's far end. She'd been so intent on the gun that she hadn't realized that her lips were smashed and at that one eye was swelling up, but now she felt the blood running down her chin. She blinked to keep the blood from a cut brow from her right eye.

Her heart throbbed. She ground her teeth with fury. The gun in her hands quivered. She didn't know exactly how she'd go about it, but, by God, she was going to drill as many of those savages as she could before they killed her.

A latch clicked a few feet ahead. A door on the left side of the hall opened a few feet and a girl screamed, "You bastard!" a half second before she poked her head through the gap between the door and the wall. It was one of the doxies, who called herself Nola Kentucky. A dark brown hand grabbed Nola's right arm, and the doxie's horrified green eyes found Marie Antoinette in the hall.

Her mouth shot wide as she cried, "Marie, hel—"

The scream trailed off as she was jerked back into the room, the door opening wide behind her.

"I didn't say you was *dismissed*!" a man's deep, resonant voiced thundered.

Marie Antoinette took two steps forward and turned toward the open door. The black man from the outlaw gang—Marie Antoinette had heard him called Heinz—had his back to her as he moved into the room, toward Nola Kentucky who lay sprawled on the floor, staring up at him and sobbing. The black man was dressed only in wash-worn balbriggans, a feather-trimmed hat, and boots from which the striped red tops of heavy wool socks protruded.

"Don't you know who I *am*?" he barked as he moved toward her, fists balled at his sides. "I'm Rosco Heinz, and no girl runs out on *me* less'n—"

He must have heard or seen Marie Antoinette out the corner of his left eye, for he turned quickly, both eyes widening and chin jutting angrily. Marie Antoinette raised the pistol in both hands, taking hasty aim at the man's scarred ebony face, and squeezed the revolver's trigger.

Pop!

The man had flinched sideways, and the bullet had drawn a thin, red line across his right cheek before it zinged past his right ear to hammer through a window behind him with a tinny clatter.

"Son of a bitch!" Marie Antoinette quickly cocked the gun once more and, slitting her eyes against the explosion, squeezed off another shot.

The black man dove onto the bed to his left, and Marie's second shot sparked off the brass frame with an ear-numbing clang. Marie fired again as the man, moving with the fluidity and speed of an attacking panther, bounced off the bed's far side and disappeared between the bed and the wall, hitting the floor with a loud thud and a pinched curse.

Marie's third shot plunked into the wainscoted wall.

"I'll kill *all* of you murdering sons of *bitches!*" Marie shrieked as she bounded into the room and raised the gun once more.

The feather-trimmed crown of the man's black hat stuck up above the bed. Marie drew a bead on it and pulled the trigger. The gun's hammer clicked benignly against the firing pin.

Marie screamed with fury and flung the gun as hard as she could, knocking the man's hat off as his hand snaked up toward a long-barreled revolver jutting from a holster hanging from a bedpost above his head. As the man cursed again and grabbed the gun, Marie swung toward the door, catching a glimpse of Nola Kentucky, dressed in only a torn slip, scrambling under the bed as she screamed for Miss Kate.

Voices rose from below in anger, and boots thumped on the stairs.

"No!" Marie Antoinette heard herself wail—enraged and frustrated by the fact that the gun she'd endured so much to get her hands on had been holding only three bullets. And that all those bullets had hit nothing but glass, brass, and wood.

Hearing the shouts and boot thumps growing louder—and the crazy redhead shouting, "What in the hell are you *doin'* up there, Rosco?"—Marie Antoinette wheeled and ran back down the hall, bare feet slapping the carpet runner, arms scissoring at her sides.

She'd wanted to kill at least five of the gang members. She killed none of them. She hadn't even *wounded* one of them. What she would do now, she had no idea.

There was a vague, panic-muddled thought, as she turned at the end of the hall and headed for the outside door, that her death now would be pointless. If she could find a horse, she could ride to the next town west of Seven Devils—Mescalero—and fetch its lawman.

The floor beneath her bare feet shook as the gang members gained the second-story hall behind her.

She opened the door and ran out onto the top of the outside stairs. She started down, missed a step, fell, and rolled four steps before grabbing the rail and pulling herself back to her feet. Mildly surprised that she hadn't been injured—in fact, she hadn't felt a thing except a slight scrape on her left knee—she continued to the bottom of the stairs and swung left down the alley behind the whorehouse.

She ran toward the rear of Wayne Day's livery barn, casting a quick glance back toward the top of the stairs behind her. One of the three identical men—the one in the stovepipe hat and rose-colored glasses—aimed a pistol at her, squinting an eye as he sighted down the barrel.

Marie Antoinette groaned and continued running down the alley as the pistol popped three times, chewing up sand and gravel behind her bare feet. One slug barked into the rear corner of the livery barn as she darted back behind it.

At the far side of the barn she paused to peer left, over the livery barn's corral toward the street. No saddled horses anywhere. Only a couple of unsaddled mounts stood in the corral, shading each other and regarding her with mild, dark-eyed interest as they ground hay between their jaws.

"Shit! *Goddamnit!*" Marie Antoinette hadn't realized she'd screamed as loudly as she had. Her voice echoed shrilly. She cursed again, more softly, and peered behind her, catching a glimpse of men running down the whorehouse's outside staircase, hearing the thunder of boot heels and the ching of spurs.

"Oh, Christ," she sobbed as she wheeled right and began running as fast as she could into the rocks and chaparral north of town. There were few cabins in this direction, only a couple of abandoned mine shafts, and a chicken coop or two. Few places to hide. She'd continue running into the desert and hope that the outlaws were too drunk to pursue her.

"Which way'd she go?" the redheaded girl's voice sounded behind her.

"Behind the barn!" a man returned, his voice thick from drink.

There was a clattering sound, as though someone fell down the stairs.

"Bitch damn near blew my head off!"

Marie Antoinette sucked air in and out of her lungs as she ran, weaving around junipers and mesquite shrubs and cracked boulders. The blood mixed with sweat in her eyes, and burned. She sleeved it away quickly and, only barely registering the sharp slashes of the thorns and gravel beneath her bare feet, continued running, pulling away from the edge of town and entering the open desert.

If she stumbled onto a good place to hide, she could hole up there until the outlaws tired of drinking and tearing up the whorehouse and assaulting the girls and rode on back to where they'd come from. The slight optimism she felt dropped suddenly out of her, like a rock tossed down a deep, dark well, when in her mind's eye she saw her son being blown back from the saloon doors and out into the street, the several bullet holes in Colter's chest sprouting rich red blood.

As Marie Antoinette had run to the boy and dropped to her knees, he had time only to roll his eyes up to hers, as though he were about to ask her a question, before he gave a ragged, final sigh, and his chest fell still.

The memory stopped Marie Antoinette cold, and her knees buckled. She dropped to the sand and gravel and sobbed into her hands.

Colter.

Toby.

Foot thuds and spur chings rose behind her. It was like a cold slap to the face. She whipped her head around.

Without realizing, she'd climbed a considerable rise stippled with rocks, saguaros, and mesquite shrubs. The men and the girl were moving up the slope behind her, spread out in a ragged parallel line. All except the girl were in various states of semi-dress and running heavy-footed and weaving slightly. Sykes seemed to be the drunkest; he was bringing up the rear—hatless, a bloody gash on his forehead and a hole torn in his trouser knee. He'd no doubt been the one who'd tumbled down the whorehouse's outside steps.

"There she is!" shouted the crazy redhead with bizarre cheer.

Marie Antoinette scrambled to her feet and continued running up the rise. There were more rocks and shrubs. She could hear herself sobbing as she ran, her left knee weakening. Glancing down, she saw a large patch of sand-crusted blood on her dress over the knee. She'd done more damage than she'd thought when she'd fallen down those outside steps herself, and now she could feel the bone-deep, aching burn.

She sobbed louder as the knee barked and she heard the footsteps growing louder behind her. The rise steepened. A gun cracked. The slug spanged off a rock just right of Marie Antoinette's bare right foot.

"Hold your fire, Rosco!" one of the men admonished.

"Hold this, Rafe! That bitch done tried to perforate my hide!"

"Wouldn't be the first time a girl tried to turn you under, Rosco," said the redhead. "Doubt it'll be the last, neither."

A couple of the others chuckled, but Marie Antoinette didn't hear. She found herself at the top of the rise, peering down the other side. She'd never wandered this far north of town and didn't know the terrain. But what she found herself staring down at was not a slope like the one she'd just climbed, but a deep, rocky ravine choked with cactus and wiry brush poking out from cracks between the red, brick-like rock lining both sides of the canyon.

The bottom of the cut was a good two hundred feet straight down, with a narrow, glassy blue stream snaking along the bottom. A scrawny, gray coyote had been drinking from the stream. Now it stood staring up at Marie Antoinette warily, lapping water from its jaws.

Behind Marie Antoinette, Sykes laughed thickly, and the coyote wheeled and loped away upstream, disappearing behind a thumb in the canyon's jagged wall. "What's the matter, girl? Come to the end of the line?"

Marie Antoinette's back crawled and her stomach dropped. Her eyes searched for a route into the canyon. Finding none, she glanced behind her once more. All six of the gang members were within twenty yards and closing, all grinning except Sykes, who held his cocked revolver straight out before him. His lips were bunched with fury.

The redhead glanced at Sykes. "Sykes, put that hogleg away. Look at her. She's injured." The redhead had turned back to Marie Antoinette and frowned as she moved slowly straight up the rise, holding out her hand.

"Come on, precious. Let's get you cleaned up." The big-boned girl's green eyes roamed with keen interest across Marie Antoinette's body, which was only partly concealed by the torn dress. She smiled. "Come on now. I won't hurt you. I won't let these animals hurt you no more, neither."

Marie Antoinette stood atop a flat rock at the very lip of the ravine, facing the killers. She backed closer to the edge as she stared at the men and the girl moving toward her, the girl's eyes raking her body with the same lust as that in the drunk-bleary eyes of the men.

One of the three look-alikes puffed a fat cigar and blinked his deep-set dark eyes. "Sure 'nough. Now that we're done with her, Cora, she's all yours." He grinned around the cigar. His chest was bare—pale and thin with a scrap of black hair along his breastbone. "She'll clean up right purty."

"Shut up, Billy Earl!" Cora waggled her fingers at Marie Antoinette. "Come on, honey. Let's go back to the whorehouse and get you in a hot tub." She smiled broadly, showing all her large, white teeth, her cheeks dimpling with schoolgirl charm. "What do you say?"

A chill of revulsion and horror rippled through Marie Antoinette. She glanced over her shoulder at the canyon yawning below. She turned back to the girl and the men who'd stopped ten feet away from her and set her jaw defiantly.

"I hope all you crazy bastards burn in hell."

Then she turned, stepped out into the air over the canyon, and dropped like a stone.

9

LOU PROPHET STARED at his comely partner.

Statue-still, Louisa sat her pinto pony forty yards ahead and right of him on the far side of the narrow, high-walled canyon painted ochre by the west-angling sun. A moment ago, a covey of quail had exploded out of a mesquite snag about a hundred yards straight ahead of her. She'd reined the pony to an instant stop, raising her carbine in one hand from her saddlebow. She sat straight-backed now, tensely looking around and listening.

What had spooked the quail? It might have been her presence they'd detected. But it might have been Apaches, too, or banditos, white marauders, possibly a bobcat. All brand of danger stalked this wild, remote, devil's playground of deep-cut canyons, pedestal rocks, and tabletop mesas, which loomed lemon-colored in the brassy distance.

Prophet had a better angle, so he knew that it was only a small Sonoran deer that had spooked the quail where they'd no doubt been foraging mesquite beans. As the doe stepped out from the shade of the canyon to drink at a runout spring, Prophet continued staring at Louisa.

He was amazed at how keen her senses were, how trail savvy she'd become in only the three short years she'd been riding roughshod across the frontier, stalking outlaws. He'd taught her a few things, but most she'd learned herself, instinctively knowing that in order to hunt without becoming the hunted she needed to keep her eyes and ears open always, to question every sound and movement, and to read the sign around her. It required patience, concentration, single-mindedness, and the constant willingness to kill if necessary. Such traits were rare, and few bounty hunters lived to become journeymen.

Prophet had known male bounty trackers and even lawmen who could have learned by watching Louisa.

Of course, Louisa had her rare, off-putting beauty and girlish sensuality going for her. It wasn't easy for a man—even the most depraved border bandit—to drop the hammer on such a harmless-looking creature. And it was that reluctance that often caused would-be killers to give up their ghosts in a mind-numbing storm of lead.

Louisa registered no gray areas when taking the measure of a man. And she never, ever hesitated. Once those lustrous, seemingly innocent hazel eyes began to narrow, lines forming above the bridge of her small, perfect nose, her prey was wolf bait.

They didn't even have time to piss their pants.

Louisa studied the deer, its head down about fifty yards ahead of her, and she cast a peeved glance toward Prophet. She knew he'd seen the deer and had been waiting for her reaction to the startled quail.

Prophet grinned, reached into his shirt pocket for a tobacco braid, and bit off a hunk. Ahead and right of him, Louisa gigged the pinto forward, and Prophet sat chewing, resting Mean and Ugly, and feeling his grin fade.

He was going to miss that girl. He'd wanted her to quit the trail and settle down for a long time, but he was going to miss her just the same. Leaving her in Seven Devils was going to be hard, and he didn't look forward to it. Jealousy gnawed at him. Like he'd told her, she'd no doubt be married inside of a year.

She'd choose a good man, but that man would not be Prophet—he'd made that clear to her as well as to himself; it just wasn't in the cards for either of them—and he'd have to ride without her from here on in, knowing their trails would likely never cross again . . . knowing she'd settled down with another man.

Probably have kids with that man. Raise a family.

They'd had a good trip down from western Colorado—riding through some of the most spectacularly lonely, beautiful country Prophet had ever trod. They'd camped, talked, argued some, swum in ravines after desert gully washers, and made love in the moonlight. Last night they'd even frolicked in a waterfall, the saguaros around them casting bizarre shadows amongst the rocks and the velvet ridges trimmed with starlight.

But now, two weeks south of Alamosa, they were near the end of their trail. According to a map an old prospector had drawn for them in Tucson, Seven Devils should lie just over the next saddleback ridge to the west, about a hundred miles north of the Mexican border.

Prophet spat a tobacco quid on a rock and heeled Mean forward. He caught up to Louisa ten minutes later, where the trail narrowed as it angled through cabin-sized boulders, climbing the ridge toward the faultless, cobalt eastern sky.

"Louisa, I wanna tell you something," he said as their horses moved side by side. "As long as you've been roughshoddin' it, it's gonna be hard for you to settle down at first. But I want you to give it some time. . . ."

He let his voice trail off. Mean and Ugly's ears had suddenly perked. The horse lifted his snout now, too, working his nostrils. Louisa's pinto continued ahead as usual, plodding along, but Mean had been hoofing around with a manhunter on his back for nearly ten years, and the horse's senses were as keen as those of any Apache mustang.

Louisa had seen Mean's reaction. She kept her voice low as she turned her head from right to left and back again. "What is it?"

Prophet slipped his Winchester from the scabbard beneath his left knee and cocked it one-handed, holding the reins high in his left. "Smells somethin'."

He looked at the rocky ridges on either side of the trail, and at those ahead and behind, watching for Apache smoke signals. The Indian reserves in this part of Arizona Territory were merely way stations for rampaging Apache. The braves would head to the agency for free government beef before rid-ing out in search of another white ranch to burn or a village to ransack. There was little the badly undermanned cavalry could do about it.

Prophet and Louisa had come upon a doomed cavalry pa-trol only a half day back. Chiricahua arrows had protruded from the hacked, scattered remains of the soldiers and horses, with only a few patches of blue uniform showing amidst the red.

As Prophet and Louisa neared the crest of the saddleback ridge, the girl's pinto gave a sudden whinny, then shook its head, rattling its bridle chains. Whatever Mean had sensed, the pinto picked it up now, too. Prophet held up his hand and dropped out of his saddle. Ground-tying the horse, he hefted his Winchester and moved slowly up the rutted wagon trail, lifting his head to steal a look over the rise.

Louisa came up beside him as he stopped ten feet from the crest of the ridge to stare down the other side. Beyond another, lower hill lay a broad valley studded with saguaros and chapar-ral. In the middle of the valley, three-quarters of a mile away, stretched what looked like a vast, oblong cloud shadow.

Prophet glanced at the sky. There were no clouds. And there were no near ridges to cast shadows down the middle of the valley. The nearest ridge lay a good thirty miles to the south—a hulking blue-and-copper formation, capped by the seven devil-shaped spires, which had lent the town its name.

"What is it?" Louisa said, shading her eyes with a gloved hand.

Prophet turned and started back down the hill. "Gonna fetch my glasses."

When he'd grabbed his field glasses from his saddlebags, he returned to where Louisa was standing about ten feet from the hillcrest. He lifted the glasses and adjusted the focus until the vast dark shape swam into focus beyond the second hill.

The dark oblong, cleaved by the trail, was pocked with mounds of burned debris. The burn extended a good hundred yards around the mounds of what, Prophet realized as he stared through the glasses, the hair on the back of his neck standing on end, was all that remained of a town.

Prophet lowered the glasses and turned to Louisa. She

regarded him skeptically, anxiety growing in her eyes as she read the dread in his own features. She began to reach for the glasses, then, dropping her hand, looked down at the oblong of scorched earth again, moving her eyes slowly from left to right and back again, desperately scrutinizing the black mass.

Finally, she wheeled and began striding back down the ridge toward the horses.

"Hold up."

Prophet grabbed her arm, but she pulled it free and continued on down to the pinto, grabbing the ground-tied reins in one hand, the apple with the other. As she swung into the leather, Prophet strode toward her. Keeping his voice down—whoever burned the town, Indians most likely, might still be around—he rasped, "You ain't goin' down there till we've scouted it out."

"Giddup," she ordered the horse, grinding her heels into the pinto's flanks and barreling up the rise.

As she approached, Prophet lunged for the pinto's bridle, but Louisa, sensing it coming, swerved sharply off the trail. She shot past Prophet like a cannonball, the horse blowing, hooves clomping loudly on the hard-packed trail.

Prophet swung toward her, scowling, as she crested the rise and dropped out of sight down the other side.

"Louisa!" he barked louder than he intended, taking back all his earlier judgments about the girl. The fool filly was likely to ride straight into a Chiricahua war party—probably the same ones who'd butchered the cavalry patrol they'd stumbled on earlier.

Cursing, Prophet ran down the ridge to where Mean stood eyeing him warily. "Remember what I said about fillies, Mean. Don't forget it!"

He dropped the field glasses back into his saddlebags, swung into the saddle, and spurred the reluctant, nickering dun up and over the rise, squinting against Louisa's sifting dust while eyeing the chaparral for Chiricahua pickets. He held his Winchester in one hand as the hammer-headed dun ate up the trail. Mean snorted and shook his head. Prophet wasn't sure if the horse was reacting to the acrid smell of the charred timber wafting on the hot, dry breeze or to the smell of Apaches— or both.

Mean didn't discriminate when it came to Indians. He hated them all.

He and the horse rounded a short curve and galloped between two brush-sheathed boulders standing on either side of the trail. Prophet pulled back on the reins. Just ahead, at the edge of the brick-and-wood rubble rising beyond the scorched chaparral, Louisa sat her stopped pinto, staring at a small wooden sign on the trail's right side.

SEVEN DEVILS, ARIZONA TERRITORY had been painted on the post-and-plank sign, which angled slightly back and off trail. Five bullets had been drilled through the painted letters, nearly cleaving the plank in two.

Prophet shifted his gaze from the plank to Louisa. "Hold your damn horses, girl. We're gonna ride in there slow."

Louisa cut her angry eyes at him and opened her mouth to give a tart reply. Closing her mouth, she let it go, pressed her heels to the pinto's flanks, and continued forward at a slow walk.

Prophet gigged Mean and Ugly along beside her, the owl-eyed dun snorting and tossing his head.

A few yards beyond the post, on the right side of the trail, hunched a pile of charred logs, a scorched tin roof angling down across what remained of a porch rail, a brick chimney lying broken on the near side. Stretched out along the other side of the street, to Prophet's left, humped the demolished remains of a good half dozen business buildings, a couple of shingles—one announcing a hotel, another a harness shop—still partly legible.

A couple of buildings, forlorn and skull-like, remained standing. Most had been reduced to coal-black ash and splintered logs the texture of charcoal. Here and there, wisps of gray smoke lifted.

Raking her gaze from left to right across the cinder-dusted street, Louisa said, "Apaches?"

"Don't think so."

She glanced at him, frowning.

"No bodies—Injun or white," Prophet said, keeping his Winchester's butt pressed to his right thigh, his index finger curled against the trigger. "No arrows. No dead women or babies. Not even a dead horse in the street. Hell, I don't even see a dead dog."

"What, then?"

"Wildfire, maybe, but it doesn't look like it came in from the country." Prophet jerked with a start as a chunk of wood dropped from a burned-out sagging porch and landed in the street with a crunching thud. "Whatever it was, it didn't come as no surprise. Don't smell no bodies. They musta all got out."

Louisa didn't appear overly comforted by Prophet's comment. As she and Prophet walked their horses down the middle of the street, approaching the town's center, she continued looking around fearfully, wondering what had become of her cousin in the midst of this destruction—a whole town burned to the ground.

They were fifty yards from the west end of town when Louisa drifted back behind Prophet, then turned the pinto toward the street's left side. She drew up before a charred log hovel with chunks of only two walls standing, the sod roof lying in a heap beyond the fallen, half-burned timber door. As Prophet turned Mean toward Louisa, he saw the blackened strap-iron bars of three jail cells standing at the back of what apparently had been the jailhouse.

Prophet followed Louisa's gaze down to a charred shingle protruding from beneath the jailhouse's fallen porch roof. It was a red plank, about three feet long. A tumbleweed had blown onto it, suspended by rubble from the roof.

Louisa swung out of her saddle and stooped to pull the shingle out from beneath the tumbleweed and rubble. She scrubbed ashes from the front of the shingle, then held it up for Prophet to read what remained of COUNTY SHERIFF.

"Marlene's husband was sheriff," she said grimly, glancing again at the burned hulk of the jailhouse.

"No reason to think he's in there," Prophet said, sheathing his rifle. "He and your cousin might've pulled out with the rest of the folks. Might be holed up outside town somewhere, waiting for a cavalry patrol. We'll find 'em."

Frowning suddenly, Prophet turned to stare northwest over the rubble heaps. He'd heard what sounded like a blackfly sort of buzzing and whistling. The buzzing and whistling grew louder.

Mean and Ugly jerked his head up. At the same time, Prophet felt a sudden, searing pain in his upper right arm.

Before he knew what was happening, thunder clapped sharply in the northeast, and Mean and Ugly bucked suddenly with an indignant whinny.

"Shit!" Prophet cried as, losing his reins as well as his rifle, his entire right arm on fire, he twisted around and flew straight back off the pitching dun's right hip.

10

THE GROUND SHOT up to slam against Prophet's back, snapping his jaws together with an audible clack and ramming the breath from his lungs with an enormous *"Ufff!"* of expelled air.

"Lou!" Louisa yelled beneath the rifle's echoing crack as well as Mean and Ugly's angry screams and hoof thuds as the hot-blooded beast tore westward down the burned-out town's main street, his reins bouncing along behind him.

Prophet groaned and tried to suck air into his battered lungs with little success. Another large-caliber slug blasted dirt, ashes, and dried horse dung into his face from the street beside him. He blinked grit from his eyes and tried another breath, managing half a lungful.

Running footsteps sounded, and he looked up to see Louisa sprint into the street and drop to a knee beside him. "Lou, dangit, get your lazy ass *up!*"

She squeezed off two thundering shots with the .45 leaping in her right hand, aiming in the general direction from which the sniper had fired. Tugging on his left arm, she yelled again, "Get up! Get up!"

"I'm tryin', for chrissakes!" Clutching his upper right arm and wincing against the grit the bullet had blown into his eyes,

Prophet glanced after both horses now galloping into the western distance, Prophet's Winchester '73 snugged down in Mean and Ugly's saddle boot.

Prophet cursed—he really could have used the rifle about now—and climbed to his feet as Louisa triggered two more shots toward the sniper. Still clutching his arm, feeling the slick blood ooze from the wound beneath his palm, he ran with Louisa back to the front of the burned-out jailhouse. They dropped to knees behind the ruined front wall, edging looks over the fire-blackened logs toward a hill rising northwest of town.

"You see him?" Prophet grunted as another shot thundered, the slug thumping into the hard ground just off the end of the boardwalk fronting the jailhouse.

"Saw the smoke puff on the hill. Appears to be a cemetery up there."

"Sniper shootin' from a cemetery," Prophet grouched, wrapping his red neckerchief around the bloody path the bullet had carved along the back of his arm. "Seems downright disrespectful if you ask me."

"No one's asking you." Louisa squeezed off another shot. "How's your arm?"

"Just a scratch."

"That's what you always say."

"Still kickin', ain't I?"

The heavy-caliber rifle hammered another shot into the side of the jailhouse with a thundering crack, splinters flying. It made the entire ruined hulk shudder.

Palming his Colt .45 and thumbing the hammer back, Prophet looked up the hill. Sure enough, crude crosses and gravestones sprouted from the hill's sage-and-rock-mottled shoulder, near a single, gnarled cottonwood tree. A small work wagon, the mule hitched to it looking around nervously, was parked in the middle of the graveyard, near a spindly Mexican pinyon.

Smoke puffed from around the back of the wagon. Prophet thought he could see the crown of a hat poking above the wagon's far rear wheel.

"You work your way to the bottom of the rise he's on," Prophet said, staring over the ruins of the jailhouse and the burned-out building next door. "Keep feeding him lead. I'm gonna try workin' my way around behind him."

"You tend your arm. I'll go."

"The fall from my consarned horse hurts worse than my arm." Prophet scrambled west along the front of the jailhouse wall. "Keep him busy, but keep your head down, girl!"

Louisa snapped off another shot over the jailhouse, squinting down the barrel of her .45. "Any more orders?"

"Yeah—keep an eye skinned for more shooters. Could be more than one of those bushwhackin' sons o' bitches!"

As the rifle cracked once more, the heavy slug barking into the jailhouse, Prophet bolted out from the jailhouse's front wall and across a ten-foot gap to the front of the next burned-out hulk west.

Colt in his hand, gritting his teeth against the ache in his arm as well as his ribs and battered back, he made his way about fifty yards west along the street, then tramped north between a near-leveled livery barn and a brick derelict with a sign announcing FRAUGENFURST BUTCHER'S still attached to the wall above the door. At the side of the building was another shingle telling anyone interested that Doc Murphy's office was at the top of the outside stairs, though what remained of the stairs wouldn't have held a rat.

Prophet paused at the back of the butcher shop and doctor's office, and stared into the trash-littered alley beyond. Louisa's .45s popped intermittently while the big-caliber rifle belched about every five or six seconds.

Whoever the shooter was, he knew how to handle a long gun. Prophet knew of no Apaches who'd bother with a single-shot Big Fifty or anything similar. They'd sell their children plus a couple of squaws for a repeating Winchester or Henry .44-40.

As Louisa squeezed off a couple of angry rounds, Prophet bolted out from behind the jailhouse and, swerving left and keeping his head down, plunged into the brush and boulders beyond the alley. He turned around a partly burned chicken coop and cut into a narrow, winding ravine littered with rusted tin cans and yellowed newspapers. He followed the ravine into the slope, leaping rocks and sage shrubs and ducking under mesquite branches.

To his right and above, the bushwhacker continued slinging fifty-caliber slugs toward Louisa—one round about every ten seconds now—while Louisa baited the man with her .45s. As Prophet climbed out of the ravine, heading straight up the hill's steep west slope, he kept an eye out for more gunmen, and he hoped Louisa was doing the same. The burning of the town— if it wasn't an accident—had been the work of more than one man.

The bounty hunter nearly stepped on a rattlesnake shading itself in the lee of a chair-sized boulder. Hearing the rattle and feeling the tap of the head striking his right spur with a soft ching, he sucked a breath through his teeth and felt a chill in his loins as he continued climbing the rocky hill.

Gaining the crest, now flanking the rifleman, he worked his way back toward the thundering cracks, downslope through widely scattered cedars, cottonwoods, and pinyons. Soon, crouching, he gained the cemetery—a couple of dozen crudely chiseled stones and wood crosses fronting rock-mounded graves. There must have been a rattlesnake nest nearby, because he spied several more of the bloodcurdling serpents shading themselves in the shade angling out from the graves and shrubs.

Prophet wended his way through the dry, sun-blasted bone-yard. The barks of the heavy rifle now sounded like blasts of a single Napoleon cannon down the hill before him, the echo of each shot screeching off across the valley, answered by Louisa's angry, slightly higher-pitched Colts.

Prophet paused between a cracked boulder and a large, fra-grant juniper. He dropped to a knee and peered down the slope, over a dozen rocky graves.

The wagon sat down the slope, thirty yards away. The shooter—a big man in baggy, torn coveralls and a straw sombrero—was hunkered behind the wagon's rear wheel, his back to the upslope. The big, gray mule in the traces flinched at each blast of the rifle in the man's thick arms and also at each pill Louisa drilled into the rocks downslope of the wagon.

Prophet straightened, waved his rifle. Louisa should be able to see him from this angle. When her return fire had ceased, he started down the slope, crouching and working his way around the graves. He kept his cocked Colt aimed at the beefy shooter pressing his rifle's stock to his shoulder and expertly ejecting and feeding shells into the chamber.

He was a purposeful shooter but gave little heed to his backside. Prophet moved right up behind him. When he was twenty feet from the wagon, the shooter cursed and pulled his head away from the Sharps, glaring down at it and jerking up and down on the trigger guard cocking mechanism.

Prophet leaned forward and pressed his Colt's barrel against the back of the man's thick, sunburned neck beneath a line of wiry, straw-colored hair. The man jerked with a start, then froze as Prophet said, "That's the problem with the Big Fifty, I hear. You shoot too many rounds at one time, the breechblock tends to gum up on ya . . . you fork-tailed son of a bitch!"

Instantly, the man threw his left hand up and thrust the big rifle out to his right. "Don't shoot!" His voice cracked slightly as he repeated, "Please don't shoot me, mister! Please don't! Ah, *Jesus*!"

Prophet switched his Colt to his left hand and grabbed the Sharps Big Fifty with his right. He stepped straight back. "Turn the hell around. You so much as flinch at a blowfly, I'll blow your bushwhackin' brains out your eyeballs."

"Please don't shoot!"

The man rose, turning slowly toward Prophet. The bounty hunter scowled, flabbergasted to see a young man standing before him—a big corn-fed younker, around nineteen, with a fleshy, round, clean-shaven face with farm-boy-wholesome eyes and sloping, yoke-like shoulders. There were weepy burns on the kid's broad cheeks, and a deep gash on his chin.

His light blue eyes were genuinely horrified, and he stretched both his meaty paws, which were also marked with deep burns and scrapes, high above his sombrero-capped head. Sweat streaked the dirt on his face. The skin above his nose furrowed slightly, and his lips stretched away from his big, white, gapped teeth as he studied Prophet, eyes quickly sweeping the big bounty hunter's six-foot-three-inch frame sheathed in a buckskin tunic and faded denims.

"Well, damn," the kid said uncertainly. "You're . . . you're not one o' them . . ."

"One o' who?"

"One o' the fork-tailed devils who burned the town." The kid glanced at the fire-blackened town spread out below the hill as though there might be some question about which town he was talking about. "I seen the girl . . . the blond girl . . . and figured you was . . ."

Prophet lowered his .45 slightly. "We've done got that far. I'd appreciate it if you would finish your thought, son. My bullet-burned arm and my barking ribs have got me feelin' none too friendly or patient."

The kid licked his thick lips, which couldn't quite cover his big teeth, and continued staring at Prophet as though the big bounty hunter were a particularly puzzling math problem. "The Three of a Kind Gang."

"Who the hell's the Three of a Kind Gang?" Prophet said, impatience hardening his jaws.

The kid's eyes widened at the anger in Prophet's tone, and he shuffled his square-toed boots nervously and glanced at the cocked Colt's maw. "Them're the ones that burned the town. I thought . . . I thought you and the girl were two of the gang—you know—come back to raise more hell. I see now how I was wrong . . . shoulda known you wasn't one, but, shit, I reckon I'm jumpy seein' as how I lived here an' all!"

He glanced backward down the slope, toward where Louisa had been keeping him busy with his buffalo rifle. She was moving upslope toward him and Prophet now, both guns aimed from her belly. "They gotta redhead ridin' with 'em. From a distance, that one there looks like the one ridin' with the Three of a Kind Gang, when the sun shines in her hair . . . and when I reckon the one doin' the lookin's a damn jackass."

The kid turned to Prophet once more. "I mean, you see, them *hard cases* burned my uncle Alphonse up in his livery barn. I was just trying to set things right, I reckon."

Louisa glanced at Prophet while keeping her Colts aimed at the kid. She wore a skeptical expression. "This the bush-whacker?"

"We ain't been properly introduced." Prophet depressed his Colt's hammer and lowered the gun to his side. "How 'bout it, kid? You got a name?"

The kid started to lower his hands but stopped when he saw that Louisa still had her Colts aimed at a faded red patch in the blue coveralls stretched across his bulging belly. "I'm Hans. Kleinsasser. Big Hans, they call me." He licked his lips again nervously and continued. "I'm from over near Fredericksburg way, in Texas. We was farmers before Uncle Alphonse decided to try his hand at buffalo huntin', but we ended up fightin' as many Comanche as skinnin' buffalo up on the Panhandle, and . . ." His tongue flicked across his lips again as he glanced miserably at Louisa. "Miss, you sure are makin' me nervous holdin' them Colts on me like that."

He grinned, sliding his blue eyes between Prophet and Louisa and running a hammy hand across his paunch. "I know it's a pretty big target an' all, but jeepers, I sure would hate to have a hole in it. That's where I pack away my burritos of an evenin'!"

He chuckled huskily.

Prophet looked at Louisa. "Pull your horns in, Miss Oakley. I reckon Hans here made an honest mistake." Prophet held the Big Fifty out to the kid, butt first. "You learn to shoot that on the Pandhandle?"

"Yessir," Hans said, flushing as he took the octagonal-barreled long gun in his big hands, scrubbing dust from the fore stock. "Uncle Alphonse taught me."

"He taught you pretty damn well."

The kid glanced at Prophet's arm around which a red neckerchief was knotted tight. "I sure hope I didn't hurt you too bad, mister . . ."

"Prophet. That's Louisa. I'll live." Prophet glanced at the town. "Why'd this Three of a Kind Gang burn Seven Devils, Hans?"

"Pure devilishness, I reckon." Hans sagged back on the wagon's open tailgate and shook his head, glancing once more at the town with pained disbelief in his eyes. "They rode in near on a week ago. I was workin' in the backroom of Carstairs's Saloon, arranging barrels and doin' some general cleanin' for Mr. Carstairs, when they came in and took a driftin' cow waddie named Dewey Granger upstairs and killed him slow. Lord Jesus, did poor Dewey scream! I mean, I reckon he had it comin' cause he killed the girl's brother over to Lordsburg, but jumpin' Jehoshaphat, they sure didn't do it quick!"

"They burned the whole town because some drifter killed a man?"

"No, I reckon they burned the town cause after they killed the sheriff and the sheriff's boy, they got drunk and crazy-wild and just went pure rabid-dog-ass mean and crazy!"

Louisa stared at him. "They killed the sheriff?"

"Yes, ma'am. And his boy. And then they killed his wife after . . ."

The kid let his voice trail off as Louisa jerked back suddenly, as though she'd been drilled through the heart with the kid's Big Fifty, her lower jaw sagging, eyes snapping wide. As her knees buckled, Prophet lunged for her and wrapped his arms around her shoulders, easing her down to the ground. "Easy, girl."

Louisa dipped her chin and shook her head. Prophet felt her body convulse, but she took a deep breath and gathered herself. Dry-eyed but stricken, she looked up at Big Hans. "Are you sure they killed the sheriff's wife?"

Big Hans looked as though he'd been dealt a glancing blow by an executioner's ax. He'd doffed his hat as if in respect to the girl's sudden grief and stood looking down at her, red-faced and hang-jawed. He nodded dully and glanced at Prophet.

"Mrs. Fletcher was Louisa's cousin," Prophet said, on one knee beside Louisa. "Louisa was on her way here to live with the family."

"You're sure?" Louisa asked the kid, more forcefully.

"I seen her run out the back of Miss Kate's place," Big Hans said as though confessing a grave sin. "I'd been sort of stayin' out of sight and keepin' an eye on the gang, tryin' to get a handle on what they might do. Uncle Alphonse's nerves been shot since a Coyotero raid up around Apache Pass took his scalp and one eye, and he was holed up in the hayloft of our livery barn with a bottle. Most of the townsfolk done locked themselves in their shacks."

Louisa's voice was deep and slightly quivering, teeming with barely restrained emotion. "What was Miss Kate's place?"

Big Hans colored. He glanced from Prophet to Louisa and back to Prophet again as he said, "H-house of ill repute, I'm sorry to say, miss. They'd taken her over there after they shot the sheriff and the boy."

Big Hans kept his eyes on Prophet and shook his head as though the memories were darts being fired into the back of his stout neck. "There was some awful screamin' comin' from over there. Then, like I said, Mrs. Fletcher went runnin' out the back with the whole gang on her heels like a pack o' hungry wolves. I never did ever see such a thing. Damn near peed my pants, if you'll forgive the expression, miss."

Louisa said, "Did you see them kill her?"

"No, ma'am. I was holed up in the saloon over yonder. I seen 'em run out after Mrs. Fletcher, but"—Big Hans shook his head grimly—"it was only the gang that came back later."

Big Hans glanced at Prophet guiltily. "I found her later at the bottom of Crow Gulch." He turned his head toward the cottonwood standing upslope and east, its sun-silvered leaves rustling in the hot breeze, its lightning-scarred trunk making soft splintering sounds. "I buried her over there . . . with the sheriff and her boy."

11

LOUISA TURNED TOWARD the three graves shaded by the cottonwood. Slowly, resisting Prophet's help, she gained her feet and began walking up the slope toward the tree.

Prophet watched her for a time, his heart gripped by a tight fist. The girl had come here to settle down with family. But there was no more family.

No more *here*.

How much did she have to endure?

Prophet doffed his hat, sleeved sweat from his forehead, and walked a few feet down the slope, propped a boot on a rock, and stared out over the burned town. Inky shadows bled out from the ruined hulks as the sun angled down in the west, turning the country around the town the color of a newly minted penny. Several hawks circled lazily, on the scout for carrion amongst the charred ruins.

He hooked his thumbs behind his cartridge-studded shell belt and glanced over his shoulder at Big Hans standing behind him. "The rest of the townsfolk make it out alive?"

Big Hans nodded as he thumbed an iron tie ring on the side of the wagon box. "About half the town packed up the night the gang was raisin' holy hob over to Miss Kate's. The others pulled out the next mornin', when the gang plundered both mercantiles for kerosene, and started runnin' and riding around, dousin' all the buildings."

The kid paused for nearly a minute, breath rattling up from his throat. He continued as Prophet stared out over the town. "I was so busy trying to get the horses out of the barn that I forgot about Uncle Alphonse until flames pret' near engulfed the place. I climbed into the loft but I couldn't get to him. The smoke was too thick."

The kid shook his head and heaved a ragged sigh.

Prophet turned to face him. "Don't flog yourself, boy. Few men could keep their heads in a dustup like that one."

"I let him die," the big younker said, scraping at the ground with a square-toed boot. He canted his head toward a fresh grave a few yards downslope of the wagon. A rusty-bladed pick lay over the grave. "That's him over there. I came up here to pile more rocks on him. Heard coyotes up here last night, diggin' away and mewlin' like devils."

"Where'd the rest of the townsfolk go?"

"Some headed east to Wagon Tongue. Others headed west to Fort McCarthy. They were gonna send a cavalry patrol out after the gang, but I ain't seen hide nor hair of 'em yet."

Prophet remembered the massacred patrol he and Louisa had stumbled upon, and shucked his Colt .45 from its low-slung, thonged-down holster. "The patrol didn't make it."

Behind him, Big Hans said, "Chiricahuas?"

Prophet nodded as he shook the spent brass from the Colt's wheel.

"They been burnin' ranches off in the boonies," Hans said.

"When I first saw the burn, I figured it was the work of Injuns."

Big Hans said, "You wouldn't figure on white folks to do such a thing to other white folks—would you, Mr. Prophet?"

"I would." Louisa was striding over from the direction of the three graves lined up beneath the cottonwood. "I've witnessed such deviltry before. I'll no doubt witness more again before my time's up on this wretched vale of bloody tears."

"Shit," Prophet muttered as he thumbed fresh brass into the Colt's cylinder.

He'd heard this tone before from the high-blooded queen of holy vengeance, and it filled him with his own dark dread. Not for the men she hunted, but for Louisa herself. One of her few weaknesses as a bounty tracker was lighting out half-cocked, letting emotion cloud her judgment.

Louisa stopped in front of Hans, her eyes like flint, blond curls blowing back from her shoulders. Her cheeks were ashen. "Which direction did the butchers head?"

Big Hans opened his mouth to speak, but Prophet cut him off. "We're not heading after 'em today, Louisa."

Jerking her head around, she turned those flinty hazel orbs on him, and he felt his oysters tighten. "Maybe *we* aren't, but *I* am."

Prophet snapped another curse through gritted teeth, twirled his loaded Colt on his finger, and dropped it into its holster with a resolute snick of oiled steel against oiled leather. He stepped in front of his high-blooded partner and clamped his hands on her shoulders.

"Louisa, damnit, I'm sorry as hell about your cousin. But our horses are beat. If we headed out now, our mounts'd drop within two miles, and we'd be the main entertainment in some Chiricahua camp by sundown." He shook his head and parried her fiery gaze with his own. "We'll rest the horses tonight and head out after the gang first thing in the mornin'."

Louisa narrowed her eyes and opened her mouth, but she uttered only one syllable before her eyes softened slightly, her resolve weakening, and she turned back to the cottonwood tree. She studied the tree for a time, as if searching for something hidden there.

Just above a whisper, she said, nodding, "All right. First thing in the morning, Lou."

She strode down the slope toward the town, head down, shoulders slumped. Her slitted riding skirt buffeted about her legs, her twin, pearl-gripped Colts jutting from the cross-draw holsters riding high on her hips, only partly concealed by her striped brown poncho. The ache and fury was like a red aura around her.

She was a walking, low-rumbling volcano.

As Prophet stared after Louisa, feeling sick enough to vomit, Big Hans cleared his throat behind him. "You two really ridin' after that bunch, Mr. Prophet?"

"Sure as shit in a Texas dust storm, Hans."

The kid let a pensive moment stretch. "You have experience trackin' kill-hungry desperadoes, do ya?"

"Bounty huntin's our profession—mine and Louisa's," Prophet said.

Hans pitched his voice with surprise as he stared after the girl dropping gradually out of sight down the sage-and-pinyon-stippled slope. "Hers, too?"

"Especially hers."

"You don't say. . . ."

The horses were as trail beat as a couple of Texas plugs after a long drive to Montana, so it didn't take Prophet and Louisa long to run them down. When they'd adjusted their saddles and bridles, tightening the latigos, they mounted up.

The clatter of a wagon rose on the trail to the east, and Prophet swung his head around to see Big Hans heading toward him, sitting slope-shouldered and splay-kneed on the lurching wagon's driver's seat, reins in his hands, elbows on his thighs. Picks and shovels bristled from the box behind him as the old, beefy mule gave a contentious hee-haw and shook its dark brown mane.

As the wagon approached Prophet and Louisa sitting their mounts on either side of the trail, the big blond younker pulled back on the reins and spat to one side. "I'm bunkin' with a friend of Uncle Alphonse's," the kid said, glancing skeptically at Louisa once more, as if still trying to reconcile the bounty hunting profession to such a pretty, innocent, fragile-looking girl. "He's got a cabin about a mile from here. He's a good cook, and he loves company."

Prophet glanced at Louisa. "I could do with a meal and a roof over my head."

"I gotta warn you, though," Hans said. "Buster—that's his name, Buster Davis—he favors odd critters, has a foul mouth, and imbibes to his own detriment." The kid's eyes brightened, and he wagged his head and patted his bulging belly. "But he more than makes up for his faults with his cookin'. The man can throw together an antelope stew even better than my aunt Agnes could, God rest her soul."

"That seals it for me," Prophet said, putting his horse up to the wagon box.

"It won't take us out of the way of the killers' trail, will it?" Louisa asked Hans.

"No, ma'am. In fact, it'll practically put ya right on it!"

Without further ado, Louisa gigged her horse up to the wagon. Prophet wrapped his own reins around his saddle horn, stepped off Mean and Ugly and into the cluttered wagon box. He extended his hand to Louisa, who wrapped her own reins around her apple. The horses would follow of their volition. Taking Prophet's hand, she dropped easily into the box beside him.

"There's room up here," Hans said over his shoulder, sliding his butt to the wooden seat's left side.

"No, thanks." Prophet rearranged the picks and shovels and sagged down against the box's right side panel. "I'll stretch out back here."

"Me, too," Louisa said, kicking a crowbar out of the way and sitting down against the left side of the box, removing her hat and shaking her hair across her shoulders.

Hans glanced over his shoulder again. "Ready?"

"Ready to get shed of that smell of burned town," Prophet said. "I reckon!"

Hans shook the reins across the mule's broad back. The beast gave a typically mulish hee-haw and began moving forward, jerking the wagon along the uneven terrain. With Mean and Ugly and Louisa's pinto following close behind, they headed straight west, back the way Prophet and Louisa had come to this country only a couple of hours earlier but what, after all that happened, seemed like days.

Prophet watched her sitting on the other side of the wagon box, leaning back against the side panel, her arms crossed on her chest. She'd stretched her legs out beside his and stared down at the wagon's splintered floor with a dark, pensive expression.

A few hours ago she'd been about to settle down, Prophet thought. Now she was back on the outlaw trail.

On the trail of what might very well prove to be the tough-est, wiliest killers she and Prophet had ever shadowed.

She might not come back from it.

Prophet glanced at Big Hans's broad, slumped back. "You know which direction those owlhoots headed, do you, kid?"

Big Hans lifted his chin as he turned the wagon off the road and headed south along a faint wagon trace. It was a rough ride, and the wagon clattered like dice in a well-shaken cup. Prophet stretched his arms out across the top of the side panel, holding himself as steady as possible.

"See them devils up yonder?" Hans yelled over his shoul-der, his voice quaking with the wagon's pitch and jounce.

Prophet stretched his neck for a look above the mesquites, Mexican pinyons, and boulders at the seven statue-like forma-tions rising from the hazy range before him, a good fifty or sixty miles south. "The Seven Devils?"

"Yessir." Big Hans winced as the wagon's left front wheel bounced off a rock with a crash, making the hub squawk. "I heard one of 'em say when they was leavin', with the town burnin' behind 'em and all us folks scramblin' around like headless chickens, that they was gonna have to stay up in the Seven Devils a good, long time after what they just done."

Louisa stared at the hazy formations with grim interest. "They border Mexico, don't they—the Seven Devils?"

"Yes, ma'am. And they're haunted by half the border toughs in Arizona Territory and northern Mexico. The Arizona Rangers call it a snake-infested devils' lair. Over the past cou-pla years, most lawmen and bounty hunters been givin' it a wide berth. Several U.S. marshals and even a coupla cavalry patrols went in and never came out again. Hell, all that showed up of one partic'lar marshal was his head. Whoever killed him sent it to his wife up Tucson way—in a box delivered by the U.S. mail!"

Wincing, Prophet looked at Louisa. "I bet that's one gift she won't never forget."

Louisa recrossed her ankles and said with customary wry-ness, "It's probably on her mantel."

Big Hans coaxed the mule around a thick mesquite and catclaw snag, cursing under his breath. When he had the wagon going relatively smoothly again, he said, "No, sir—I don't think I'd venture into that snake pit, if I was you—there only bein' two of ya, an' all."

Louisa turned to Prophet. "Two might have better luck than a whole patrol. Not so much noise and dust."

"But there's so many banditos out there, and so much ground to cover," Big Hans said darkly, "that it's gonna be nigh on impossible to track the group you're after." He glanced over his shoulder again, his right blue eye momentarily locking on Prophet. "Without someone who knows the country, that is. Without a *guide*."

Prophet was about to ask the kid if he knew of such a person but stopped when an agonized yell rose in the southern distance, straight out from the wagon now threading a rocky, sycamore-sheathed arroyo.

Hans drew back on the reins. "Whoa!" He stared out over the sycamores and saguaros, lemon-colored dust billowing up around the wagon box. "What the hell was *that*?"

The scream rose again, shriller this time.

"Someone ain't too happy about somethin'," Prophet said, keeping his voice low, head up, as he stared through the brush.

A man's muffled voice rose, small with distance but crisp and clear on the dry, desert air. "Ah, ya mangy yalla heathens—leave me be, ya sons o' fuckin' bitches!"

Big Hans's entire bulky body tensed and he rose half out of his seat. *"Buster!"*

As if in response to the kid's exclamation, a shrill Indian-like whoop rose, followed by another more muffled one.

"Dawg-eatin' carrion snipe!" the man screamed, the last words dwindling as his voice pinched with sobbing grief.

Big Hans lurched to his feet. "The Chiricowies're after Buster!"

Prophet swung himself up and over the wagon's tailgate and into the saddle of Mean and Ugly, the horse shaking its head and rippling its withers warily. Louisa leaped onto her pinto. Shucking his Winchester from his saddle boot, Prophet gigged Mean past the wagon, heading up the arroyo.

"Doesn't sound like they're after him!" Ahead of the mule, and with Louisa following close behind, Prophet put Mean into a ground-eating lope. "Sounds like they done got him!"

12

PROPHET AND MEAN and Ugly flew up the winding arroyo, Prophet ducking cottonwood and post oak branches leaning out from both sides of the cut. He could hear the drum of Louisa's hooves behind him, the snorts of the pinto, and the continuing cries and curse-laced harangue of Buster Davis.

That the man was being tormented by Apaches was verified by the tensing of Mean and Ugly's muscles beneath Prophet's saddle, and the horse's terror-filled snorts and knickers and the whites of his rolled-back eyes. Following the shouts, yells, and occasional spine-tingling yowls, Prophet put Mean up a game trail, and he and the horse shot up the bank, barreling through berry thickets and catclaw with a crackling rustle of trampled brush, and then leveled out on a rocky slope.

Prophet checked Mean down to a skidding halt as Louisa bolted out of the draw behind him and stopped the pinto off his right stirrup. Both horses whinnied sharply and Prophet held Mean's reins taut in his left hand as he raised his Winchester in his right.

Forty yards away at the base of a low, sage-stippled knoll, a half dozen Apaches—clad in smoked deer-hide breech cloths, moccasins, traditional red bandannas, and colored armbands—

were doing some bizarre torture dance around a bulky, red-haired, red-bearded gent they'd staked out spread-eagle on the ground, not far from a smoldering cook fire.

Several stone jugs were strewn about the rocks and catclaw. One Apache, standing on the white man's far side, was tipping back a brown bottle while throwing his free arm behind him in quivering ecstasy. As the others, jerking their heads toward Prophet and Louisa, bellowed surprised, guttural war cries, the drinking brave jerked his bottle down, his own black eyes flashing wickedly in the late day's saffron light.

As though they'd all been connected by the same invisible rope, four of the six braves lunged into instant sprints toward the interlopers, howling and screaming, coarse black hair jouncing across their shoulders, plucking knives or war hatchets from the buffeting sashes around their waists.

Prophet planted his Winchester's barrel on his left forearm and lined up his sights, shouting, "Ah, shit—aim true, girl!"

"I *always* aim true!" Louisa retorted as Prophet drew a bead on the screaming brave breaking toward him, a step ahead of the others and swinging a hide-wrapped hatchet behind his left shoulder.

Prophet's Winchester leaped and belched. The slug took the brave through his throat, just below his chin, snapping his head back on his shoulders and instantly cutting off his tooth-gnashing scream.

As the three others continued sprinting toward Prophet and Louisa, undeterred despite their comrade's death crumple, Louisa leveled a silver-plated Colt straight out from her right shoulder. As she drilled one of the three braves lunging toward her, within ten yards and closing, Prophet levered a fresh round into his Winchester's breech.

The brave on the other side of the fire grabbed a carbine from across a rock. As he wheeled and leaped the staked-out white man, raising the repeater to his shoulder, Prophet drew a bead on his chest.

Crack!

The bullet took the brave high around his left shoulder. Triggering his own long gun skyward, he screamed and flew straight back across the white man, who stared toward Prophet, his gritted teeth forming a white line through his thick, red beard.

"*Kill* the rock-worshippin' heathen mule fuckers!"

Prophet had only vaguely heard the man's shrill demand beneath the screams of the two other Apaches closing on him and Louisa. As he seated another round in his Winchester's breech one-handed, Mean screamed, bucked, and wheeled sideways.

At the same time, one of the two approaching Apaches, knife flashing in his right fist, eyes sparking like agates at the bottom of a sunlit stream, catapulted himself off his moccasined heels and flew up toward Prophet like a russet-colored, black-capped missile launched by a Stone Age catapult.

Prophet swung his rifle toward the flying brave. The brave's left arm flung the barrel aside, and then the man's head and shoulder rammed into Prophet's belly, jarring the wind from the bounty hunter's lungs. Releasing Mean's reins and reaching for but missing the saddle horn, Prophet flew down the dun's left side with the brave wrapped around him like a knife-wielding boa constrictor.

The brave's raucous shrieks were muffled by Prophet's buckskin-clad belly as the bounty hunter hit the ground on his back with another *"Uhfff!"* of displaced air. His already battered back screamed in torment. Looking up, he found the round-faced, crooked-nosed brave's head a foot from his, glaring down at him, lips bunched. Prophet's left hand was wrapped around the brave's right wrist, the point of the knife jutting from the brave's hand pricking Prophet's throat like the lingering nip of a bumblebee.

"Yeeeeee-eyyyyyyyyy!" the brave shrieked, slitting his fierce eyes and rising up on his moccasined toes for leverage, driving the knife downward.

At six-three, 210 pounds, the bounty hunter had a good seven inches and nearly fifty pounds on the war-painted demon, so he managed to lift the kid's clenched fist up and away from his jaw with relative ease until the blood-speckled knife tip rose into his line of vision.

Then, gritting his teeth and driving his right heel into the ground, he bulled the brave onto his back. The brave kicked and thrashed, howling so loud that Prophet thought his eardrums would burst. The younker's eyes widened as Prophet grabbed the kid's knife wrist in both his big, gloved hands and, lunging down, swept the knife tip across the brave's throat twice. He drew two straight lines across the cinnamon, tendon-ribbed neck, and dark red blood gushed as though it had been looking for a way out for days.

Two muffled pistol shots sounded nearby, and someone grunted.

The hand of the brave beneath Prophet opened, and Prophet, rising onto his knees, snatched the knife away, then glanced to his left.

Louisa was on her side, half lying, half sitting, legs curled beneath her. The other brave who'd been running toward them was on his knees before her, a strange, ironic look in his eyes, which had snapped as wide as two dollops of fresh cow plop. The brave's hands were wrapped around both of Louisa's slender wrists. Her own hands were filled with her silver-plated .45s, the barrels of which were rammed up against the brave's bloody chest.

Thick, black smoke, fetid with the smell of burned cordite and fresh blood, wafted from the brave's ruined chest. Keeping his hands wrapped around Louisa's, the brave convulsed once, eyelids fluttering as he glanced down at the smoking pistols.

Louisa gritted her teeth. "Let go of my guns, you black-hearted cur!"

She jerked the Colts back from the brave's loosening grip. Then, with another snarl, she smashed the right Colt across the side of the Indian's head, and he flopped onto his back with a groan.

"Nice shootin'," Prophet grunted as he gained his feet, wincing at the stiffness in his back and the saber pokes of sharp pains in his ribs.

This had been one tough day on his body.

Standing and thumbing her bloody Colts' hammers back, Louise sniffed, "Even you could have made those shots, Lou."

"Don't get sassy."

He turned toward the staked-out white man whom he assumed was Buster Davis. The prospector lifted his head to stare at the Apache whom Prophet had shot in the upper left chest, and who was now pushing up off the white man's belly as he gained his knees, grunting and groaning, blood splashing down to the prospector's ragged duck shirt.

"Ah, ya red demon," Davis snarled, flexing his knees as if to shed himself of vermin. "Get off me, you damn coyote!"

At the same time, the sixth brave—taller than the others and with a long, jagged scar running from his left temple across his nose to his right jaw—was reeling drunkenly, tripping over rocks and sagebrush, trying to get his feet beneath him. He was laughing as though at the funniest joke he'd ever heard while fumbling with the Sharps carbine in his hands, working the trigger guard cocking mechanism as though his fingers were smeared with butter.

The carbine's rear stock had been carved with the letters U.S. CAV.

Gaining her feet and holding her pistols straight down by her sides, Louisa stalked the scar-faced brave, her shoulders straight, brows mantled, jaws jutting. Prophet angled toward the wounded brave, who was staggering off in the direction of a two-story, brush-roofed shack, lean-to stable, and corral that looked little larger than a shoe box beneath the vast, red, wave-shaped monolith looming above it.

"Filthy goddamn lobo *heathen*!" Buster Davis yowled.

Prophet jogged toward the wounded Indian heading now toward a cleft in the stone monolith behind the shack. When he'd narrowed the gap between him and the brave to twenty feet, Prophet stopped, snapped his rifle to his shoulder, and yelled, "Don't make me shoot you in the back, you son of a bitch!"

He couldn't let the wounded brave flee and possibly summon more of his ilk. He'd shoot him in the back if he had to.

Unexpectedly, the brave wheeled, flashing a horrified look over his shoulder while fumbling a knife from a beaded scabbard on his hip. Prophet drilled him through the center of his chest, and he flew back, pinwheeling and falling over a boulder with a scream and a thud.

Prophet ejected the spent shell. "Thanks, *amigo*."

To his right, a revolver barked. Prophet turned to see the drunk brave, down on his knees in front of Louisa, jerk his head straight back on his shoulders. A neat, round hole had been tattooed through his forehead. Four feet away, smoke wafted around Louisa's extended right-hand Colt, another tendril dribbling from its barrel.

As the brave sagged back on his heels, Louisa raised her left-hand Colt and squinted steely-eyed along the barrel. The Colt leaped in Louisa's clenched fist, belching smoke and flames.

The brave's head jerked a second time as another hole appeared three inches left of the first.

As the brave continued sagging straight back on his heels, Louisa drilled a round through his breastbone, then lowered the right Colt to bring up the left one again smoothly, automatically, and as emotionlessly as any cold-steel artist Prophet had ever seen.

She ratcheted the hammer back, aimed again, and fired.

His brows arched skeptically, Prophet watched her. She wasn't shooting the Apache over and over again. In her mind, she was drilling a round through each face of the Three of a Kind Gang, maybe hearing them beg for their lives and scream, then watching them fall—bloody, dusty, and dead.

When the brave lay in the sage before her, she holstered one Colt, then quickly raking her eyes around the clearing to make sure all the attackers were disposed of, flipped open the Colt's loading gate. She shook out the spent brass, which thumped and pinged to the ground around her boots, and began replacing them with cartridges from the leather loops on her shell belt.

The prospector's head was turned toward her, eyes wide with awe, furred lips parted. Prophet moved toward the man, lowering his Winchester and sliding his bowie from the sheath behind his left hip.

As Prophet sawed through the leather tying the man's left wrist to a buried stake, he looked him over. He was cut and bruised, his duck shirt and baggy denims torn. His left ear had been slashed, and there was a long knife cut above his right eye. But he looked as though he'd live. "You all right, friend?"

The man turned his head slowly from Louisa, his shaggy, red-gray brows furrowed, a wary light in his eyes. "My, my, my," Davis said as a wagon clattered and a mule hee-hawed in the distance, the sounds growing louder as Big Hans approached from the west. "Where'd ya find *her*?"

Prophet cut through the leather binding the man's right wrist, then reached toward the man's right ankle. "Nebraska."

The burly prospector sat up, rubbing his wrists and turning his head to regard Louisa, who stood grimly reloading her second Colt once more. "I coulda used her 'bout an hour ago when those heathens jumped my diggin's. They was about to hack off my eyelids and sundry other parts when you two rode in. . . ."

"Buster!" Hans drew the wagon up beside Prophet and Davis.

As the wagon lurched and creaked and the mule hee-hawed at the smell of blood, the big blond leaped heavily from the driver's seat, the springs giving a raucous squawk of released tension. He bolted over to where Davis was sitting up and drawing his untied ankles in. "What the hell happened, Buster? I thought you made peace with ole Three-Toe!"

"I reckon that was last month's agreement," the prospector said, fishing a handkerchief from his pocket and dabbing at his bloody ear from which, Prophet now saw, the lobe had been hacked away.

Davis swept his green-eyed gaze from Louisa to Prophet and back again. "Who's these Injun killers and"—the paunchy, middle-aged gent wheezed a laugh as he continued dabbing at what was left of his ear—"do ya work for free?"

"This is Lou Prophet and Louisa Bonaventure," Big Hans said. He spread his lips back from his big teeth, grinning. "We're goin' after the Three of a Kind Gang, and we're gonna clean their clocks just like these Chiricowies here!"

13

"PLEASED TO MAKE your acquaintance, Davis." Prophet shook the burly prospector's big, skinned-up hand and glanced at Big Hans still grinning at him. "But I don't know's we made any plans—the boy and me and Louisa—to ride together after the Three of a Kind Gang."

As Louisa walked off, apparently in search of her and Prophet's horses, both of whom had vamoosed when the Apaches had charged, Big Hans said, "We was just gettin' to that when Buster yelled."

Holding the handkerchief to his ear, Davis looked at the kid skeptically. "I thought you didn't wanna have nuthin' to do with them mountains again, Hans."

"That was before that gang burned the town, Buster. Criminy-craw, they killed Uncle Alphonse, and I stood around like a dog cowerin' under a boardwalk!"

"Wait a minute," Prophet said, on one knee beside the big blond. "I know how you feel about your uncle an' all, but, son, you said yourself them mountains are crawlin' with fork-tailed demons. You ain't got no business—"

"Sure I do! They killed my uncle, burned my town. And I know them mountains better'n anyone around. Better'n Buster here even." Big Hans glanced around at the dead Apaches lying as though they'd fallen from the sky. "Just as good as these Chiricowies here, matter of bonded fact!"

"How?"

"That's a bonded fact." Buster Davis began pushing himself up off the ground, and the kid rose and grabbed his shoulder to help him. "For nigh on two years, him and ole Alphonse chased about every vein in the Seven Devils. The north slopes of the Seven Devils anyway."

"A good chunk of the Mexican side, too," Big Hans put in.

Prophet draped Davis's right arm around his neck. "I reckon this conversation can wait till later. That ear of yours needs tendin'."

Prophet and Big Hans helped the prospector, who was still fairly weak on his legs after the beating the Apaches had given him, over to the gray-weathered shack. Davis grunted and groaned and winced, stepping lightly on his right foot. "That scar-faced demon—drunk on *my* hooch!—whacked my knee good with the blunt end of a war hatchet. I'm just glad you and that girl of yours blew their wicks for me, Prophet. Wish I coulda kicked one off my own self. I'd go to my grave grinnin' about it—I'll tell you that!"

Mounting the shack's gallery, the posts trimmed with elk and deer horns, and several bobcat pelts nailed to the cabin's front wall, Prophet kicked the half-open door wide. Something moved in the musty shadows before him, and as his eyes picked the black-and-white varmint out of the cabin's gloom, he lurched back and sucked a startled breath.

"Kee-*rist*, Davis—you gotta *skunk* in here!"

As if in response, the critter glared through the doweled back of the chair it was standing on and gave a raucous chitter, reaching between the dowels to slash a little, black-clawed paw at Prophet.

"Oh, now you show your mangy carcass, eh, Curtis?" Davis growled. "When them Apaches was ransacking my digs, lookin' for my notorious hooch, I bet you was cowerin' under the stove. Weren't you? Ha!"

Prophet glanced at Davis as he and Hans continued guiding the man into the cabin, most of the crude furnishings of which had been either smashed or scattered as if by a heavy wind. "I take it you know each other?"

"Yeah, Curtis adopted me when I first moved in." Davis grunted as Prophet and Big Hans deposited the prospector into a chair near the overturned kitchen table beside a sheet-iron woodstove. "Come and goes as he pleases, but he usually *pleases* around supper time!"

The skunk scolded the newcomers, then dropped down and, chittering and holding its tail up, scuttled off under a plank-board cabinet against the far wall.

"Mind your manners, Curtis," Davis groused as Prophet tipped the man's head to one side, inspecting his bloody ear. "Sorry, there, Mr. Prophet. Aside from your occasional Chiricowy and bobcat, we don't get many visitors."

The lobe was hanging by what looked like a bloody thread, blood dribbling darkly from the ragged cut.

Grimacing at the prospector's ear over Prophet's shoulder, Big Hans said, "You got any doctorin' skills, Mr. Prophet?"

"No, but I reckon I can sew a lobe back onto an ear. Won't guarantee it won't fall off in a day or two, but I'll do my best with needle and catgut."

Outside, slow hoof clomps rose, and Prophet glanced out the open door to see Louisa leading both horses into the yard, Mean eyeing the pinto owlishly.

"Louisa, bring in my saddlebags!" The bounty hunter glanced at Big Hans. "Kid, start a fire and boil some water. Then you best head out, load them Apaches into your wagon, and haul 'em a good ways away. Throw some dirt and rocks on 'em, just enough to keep the smell down. I heard tell Apaches could smell their own dead from five miles away."

"You've done some traveling in these parts, Prophet," Davis said. "I've heard that my own self."

"I've traveled in most parts. Been welcome in damn few."

"They're bounty trackers, Buster." Big Hans had opened the stove door and was rummaging around in the wood box built from several Magic black-powder crates for kindling— old newspapers and pinecones. "Both him and Miss Louisa."

Just then, Louisa stepped through the door, Prophet's saddlebags draped over her shoulder. Davis turned to her, his earlobe dangling like a grisly ornament. Whistling with appreciation, he gave the girl the thrice-over.

"Bounty tracker—you don't say! Well, I could tell by the way she dispatched them 'Paches she wasn't no Sunday-school teacher."

With characteristic indifference to flattery, Louisa picked the table up off the floor with one hand, then dropped the saddlebags onto it, puffing dust. Kicking a tin coffee cup across the earthen floor, she moved over beside Prophet, who was easing the lobe back into place beneath the ear.

"How bad?"

"He'll live. Dig out my whiskey bottle."

"Ah, Christ," Davis said. "I'd just as soon you hacked the damn thing off."

Prophet chuckled dryly. "I'd still have to sterilize it, less'n you want your whole head to turn black."

When Louisa had pulled the bottle out of the saddlebags, as well as Prophet's small canvas pouch of needle and thread, the bounty hunter popped the cork with his teeth and, keeping Davis's earlobe in position with the thumb and index finger of his right hand, offered the bottle to the prospector with the other.

"There you go, Davis. Have you a good pull. You're gonna need it."

Bunching his cheeks, carving deep dimples inside his shaggy, sweat-damp beard, Davis tipped the bottle back a couple of times, making the bubble in the bottle rise and fall with a loud chug. Finally, sighing and smacking his lips, his green eyes watering, he returned the bottle to Prophet.

Prophet said, "Ready?"

Davis growled, then tipped his head to one side, his torn, bloody ear facing the low rafters. "No."

Prophet tipped the bottle over the man's ear.

"Yeee-*owwww*!" Davis bellowed, his face blanching and his shoulders quivering as the whiskey hit his ear.

Curtis poked his black, white-striped head out from beneath the cupboard and chittered like a rabid squirrel.

By the time Prophet had finished sewing Buster Davis's ear back together, albeit raggedly, the prospector was feeling little pain and had even taken to humming several parts of several saloon songs including "Little Brown Jug," "Clap-Carryin' Kate," and "Whiskey Jack and Old Leonard." Occasionally, he'd slap the table and howl, keeping time.

Curtis scratched and sniffed about the cabin, adding a few cackling chitters to a chorus or two.

Prophet began sharing the bottle with the man after he'd effected his last stitch and started cleaning the blood from the man's ear with hot water and whiskey. When he'd finished, Louisa had thrown a meal together—beans and antelope steaks from the carcass she'd found hanging in the lean-to stable and which the Apaches had left alone, distracted by the prospector's hooch and preferring mule meat anyway.

The three of them dug in, eating at the crude plank table, Prophet and Buster Davis washing the food down with whiskey while Louisa, who'd killed nearly fifty men in her short career but disapproved of spirituous liquors, drank coffee. When Big Hans returned, tired and sweaty from hauling away the dead Apaches and hazing away their horses, she filled him a bowl, and he sat up to table with the rest.

Outside, good dark fell. The little cabin, which had a loft and two cots and was cluttered with tack and every mining implement imaginable, became filled with inky shadows jostling and shifting when a freshening breeze pushed through the open door to nudge the room's single hurricane lantern hanging from a ceiling beam.

When Louisa finished her meal, she slid her plate and cup toward Prophet. "I cooked. You can clean."

She hauled her pistols out of her holsters, set them on the table, and reached into the saddlebags draped over her chair for a cloth and a tin of Hambly's gun oil. Prophet curled his lip at her. Setting his half-rolled quirley down on the table before him, he slid his chair back, stood, and began stacking bowls and cups.

Buster Davis chuckled as he fed Curtis, who'd crawled onto his lap midway through the meal, some bits of crusty bread. "Reckon a girl who can shoot like that could have a man dancin' quite a jig around her."

"She thinks so," Prophet growled.

Big Hans shoveled his last bite of beans and meat into his mouth and dropped his spoon in his bowl. Rising, doffing his hat, and heading for the door, he said, "I got me a fast mustang in the corral. I'm gonna tend his hooves and grain him, get him ready for tomorrow."

Balancing dishes in both hands as he headed for a washtub, Prophet glanced at the kid. "Hold on there, Junior. You might be good with that buffalo gun, but it ain't buffalo we'll be goin' after."

Big Hans wheeled at the open door, a grieved look on his big, fleshy, sunburned face, his blue eyes flashing fervently beneath his shading hat brim. "Look here, Mr. Prophet, I know them mountains like the back o' my hand. There ain't no way in hell you're gonna find that bunch of killers without my help. Besides . . ." He frowned and looked around as though searching for words. "Besides, I want a shot at 'em. The one I didn't take when they were burnin' up the town. . . ."

He lifted his injured, defiant gaze to Prophet.

Prophet held the kid's eyes and glanced at Davis. The prospector stared over his shoulder at Big Hans for a good five seconds before he turned to Prophet with an arched brow.

Prophet looked at Louisa. She was letting the bullets fall from the wheel of one of her Colts. They clinked to the table and wobbled in half circles.

"Well, Miss Pistolera," Prophet grunted at the self-absorbed girl. "Don't you got an opinion?"

Louisa hiked a shoulder as she slipped the cylinder free of the Colt's barrel and set it on the table with the still-dancing cartridges. "It's his neck. And I don't care to go fishing without knowing where the fish are feeding."

Still balancing the dishes in his hands, Prophet thought it over. Finally he looked back at the kid staring at him expectantly from the door, the starlit desert yawning behind him, a coyote yipping somewhere in the buttes south of the cabin.

Standing on Buster Davis's right thigh, Curtis sniffed the table edge and growled deep in his throat.

"Tend your horse, kid," Prophet growled and dropped the dishes in the washtub with a tinny clatter.

When Prophet had finished the dishes, and while Louisa continued to quietly clean her Colt and her rifle at the kitchen table, the bounty hunter sat on the stoop with Buster Davis and Big Hans. They chatted quietly, keeping their ears peeled for threat.

It was doubtful that more Chiricahuas would show up tonight, as Apaches didn't like to travel after dark, much less fight, but you never let your guard down in Apache country unless you wanted to risk being slow-roasted over a hot fire or buried chin deep in a honey-slathered anthill.

"I reckon I'll find a place to bed down out here," Prophet said, rising from his porch chair and tossing the last of his coffee over the rail.

Big Hans stretched. "We gonna take turns keepin' watch, Mr. Prophet?"

"Y'all get a good night's sleep. I'll stay out here. I've never been able to sleep through an entire night in 'Pache country anyways."

Prophet set his cup on the porch rail, stuck his lit quirley between his teeth, grabbed his saddle, bedroll, and rifle from where they'd been leaning against the cabin wall, and headed into the silent, night-cloaked yard. Not a breath of breeze. Hearing the others take their ablutions and retreat to their cots—Louisa would bed down inside—Prophet moseyed around the yard, looking and listening, all his years of bounty tracking having given him catlike vision and hearing.

There was still plenty of blood around from the Apaches he and Louisa had beefed. But no one skulking about.

Prophet climbed a flat-topped hill south of the cabin, with a good view of the surrounding terrain. He found a clear place amongst the brush and rocks and spread his saddle and bedroll. Leaning back against his saddle, he crossed his arms and ankles, took a deep breath and a long gander around the knoll and the cabin below. As he did, the cabin lamp sputtered out, and the night seemed to settle even deeper, the stars brightening, the intermittent coyote and distant bobcat screams growing crisper.

It was so quiet he could hear a pebble roll down the slide rock littering the side of the steep, velvet-black, wave-shaped monolith looming in the north. Doubtless, gravity had dislodged the rock, for not even an Apache would try to descend the monolith's steep wall.

Prophet yawned and closed his eyes.

He wasn't sure how long he'd dozed when there was the sound of a boot heel clipping a stone. He lifted his head and set his hand on the walnut grip of his .45, heartbeat quickening. He let the hand settle there when Louisa said softly but clearly in the cool, quiet desert air, "Don't start throwing lead, Lou. It's me."

Prophet slid his hand off the gun butt. Damn. He'd hoped she'd get a good night's sleep. But she hardly ever slept well, the screams of her butchered family haunting her dreams. Now she was probably nettled by those of her long-lost cousin, murdered by the Three of a Kind Gang.

He turned his head to watch her silhouette take shape in the inky darkness as she meandered up the slope around the spindly branches of the creosote, yucca, and dwarf pinyons. As she gained the crest of the butte, she stopped and turned her head, looking around.

Prophet said, "Here."

Holding a blanket across her shoulders, she moved toward him, her boots crunching gravel and the short, brown grass growing between the shrubs and rocks.

"How'd you know I was here?"

"I was watching you from the porch." She stood beside him, looking down. Her hair hung down, framing her round, pale face. Between her boot tops and the blanket, her legs were bare. "I wanted to know where you were."

Prophet reached up and squeezed her hand, gently pulling her down to him. When she knelt to his left, holding the blanket closed at her throat, he smoothed her hair back from her face. "Couldn't sleep?"

"Dreams."

Prophet wrapped his arms around her and drew her to him tightly. She pressed her cheek to his chest and slid her hands up his back, dug her fingers into his shoulder blades. Prophet could feel her hot breasts swelling against him. He pushed her away and looked down. The blanket hung open. She wore nothing beneath it.

Other than her boots, not a stitch.

Suddenly, she flung the blanket away, pulled him toward her once more, and kissed him hungrily, moaning softly, running her hands up the back of his head. She nudged his hat off and ran her fingers through his close-cropped hair.

He felt the heat of her body in his arms. Her grasping,

clutching, desperate need. She pushed against him harder, groaning almost savagely, and Prophet's loins reacted—full, heavy, and prickling with unfettered desire.

Again, he pushed her away. "Hold on."

Quickly, he shucked out of his shirt as she knelt naked before him, starlight dancing in her eyes, shadows limning her breasts, which stood up proudly on her chest, the nipples pebbled and erect. He could hear her breath rasping hotly, expectantly beneath his own.

When he'd removed his shirt, she flung it away from him, and then he stood to kick out of his boots, jeans, and balbriggans, stumbling around and nearly falling until his clothes lay strewn about him, and he stood naked before her, the cool air pushing against him, increasing his desire and the almost painful drumming in his loins.

"Make them stop, Lou," she whispered, leaning toward him and wrapping her arms around his legs. "Make it all go away!"

She closed her mouth over his jutting member.

Prophet gritted his teeth and ground his feet into the earth as her head rose and fell quickly.

Finally, she pulled back. Twisting around, she sank onto his bedroll. Looking up at him stonily, her breasts rising and falling sharply, her flat belly pale in the starlight, she lifted her arms and reached toward him.

Prophet knelt between her spread knees. As he dropped forward, propping himself on his outstretched arms, elbows locked, she lifted her head to close her mouth over his. Sucking at his lips, probing with her tongue, she wrapped her legs around his back and dug her fingers into his shoulders.

Prophet thrust against her.

She threw her head back and groaned throatily. From far away, the exclamation could have been mistaken for the mating call of a mad, lonely panther.

"Uhh-ah . . . Louuu!"

14

THE GIRL KNOWN as Cora swept a lock of her green-streaked red hair from her eye and scanned the barren yard in front of her.

She rode her cream Arabian at the head of the Three of a Kind Gang, which was named after the identical triplet brothers who'd started it—Rafe, Billy Earl, and Custer Flute—because she'd gotten tired of eating the others' dust and of listening to Captain Sykes endlessly passing wind. The ex-cavalry officer, who'd taken one Sioux tomahawk blow to his head too many, was rather infamous for his troublesome digestion, especially when he was trying to digest beans, though one would think an ex-cavalry man would have gotten used to beans a long time ago.

Cora drew back on the Arab's reins and, holding her wind-blown hair back from her eyes with a gloved hand, frowned incredulously at the porch of the old mission-style building sitting like a couple of sun-faded adobe salt boxes wedged together amidst the sage and creosote. A pedestal rock loomed behind and above, making the nondescript old house appear even smaller, even more insignificant here on the cactus-studded, sun-blasted canyon deep in the Seven Devils Range.

But it wasn't the adobe house itself or the formations behind it that interested Cora. Her narrowed, disbelieving gaze held steady on the man sitting under the house's brush arbor—a strawberry-blond, mustached gent with a black, flat-brimmed hat and with a bare-breasted girl on his knee.

"Well, I'll be ding-dong-damned," said Rafe Flute, poking his low-crowned sombrero off his head, his long black hair blowing around his face in the dusty breeze. He rode up beside Cora and cut his eyes at her, grinning mockingly. "Is that who I think it is?"

Cora clucked the stallion ahead, her heart thudding in her chest as she drew close enough to see that the blond man was the very man she'd feared he was, with his ruddy, handsome face from which two piercing blue eyes stared out like blue fire from beneath the brim of his dusty, black Stetson.

"Hello, darlin'!" greeted Jay Squires, resting both his hands on the thighs of the young, bare-breasted Apache girl straddling his left thigh. He bounced the knee up and down, and the girl's brown, pointed breasts jiggled. Squires laughed his characteristic rakish laugh. "Fancy us meetin' up out here in the middle of this devil's wide-open asshole!"

Before Cora could say anything, Billy Earl Flute rode up, his shabby black opera hat denting in the desert wind, and placed his right hand on the butt of one of his several pistols. "Cora, you want me to drill this squirrel right here and now, you give me the word, girl!"

Jay Squires laughed. "Billy Earl, how many times do I gotta tell you—that hat and them rose-colored glasses don't so much make you look mysterious as downright tin-horned stupid."

"Listen, you son of a—"

"Hold on, Billy Earl," Cora said, holding out her hand and keeping her befuddled gaze on the handsome man she'd once been so in love with that just hearing his name had tied—*still* tied!—her innards in knots. "I wanna hear what he has to say."

No, she didn't. Not really. She wanted to swing her horse and head for the high rocks, holding her ears closed lest she should hear the siren cry of his masculine, intoxicating voice. But she couldn't kill him. Not yet. She wanted to feast her eyes on the rake's handsome countenance for just a little while . . . as long as he was here, sitting suddenly before her like some heart-shredding specter out of a past she'd tried so hard to forget.

"You always was a bighearted gal," Squires told her, his tan, handsome cheeks dimpling with a grin, white teeth flashing beneath his strawberry-blond mustache.

Cora hardened her jaws and narrowed her eyes. "What the hell are you doin' here, Jay? I told you when I left you in Oregon that if I ever saw you again, I'd unleash the wolf inside me, and you'd suffer for it bad!"

"Hold on, hold on!" Squires chuckled again as he held his hands up, palms out, on either side of the half-naked Apache girl, who regarded the strangers as though they were nothing more than a small dust devil that had swirled out of the desert. "You're the one who did the shootin' back there, if you remember."

"I shot that bitch because I told her to keep her hands off you." Cora leaned forward in her saddle, jutting her dimpled chin like a weapon. "People just have to understand that if they don't mind what I say, I'm going to get angry, and the devil take the hindmost!"

"Wait, wait, wait," Squires said, that infuriating, toothy grin in place, complete with dimples deep enough to hide thimbles in. "You cheated on me first! Remember the little mulatto bathhouse girl?"

"You said it excited you!"

"It excited me when I was there to *watch*. Not when I just walked in and there you two were, goin' at it like two shewolves in a mud puddle!"

Behind Cora, Sykes laughed and farted.

"Shut up!" Cora said, turning a shriveling look on the man. Beside Sykes, Rosco Heinz saw the look the girl gave Sykes, and the black man let his own amused grin fade.

Cora turned back toward Squires and spoke with barely controlled fury. "You know she meant nothing to me. It was late and I was drunk and she'd been makin' eyes at me all evenin', said she felt we was bonded an' such." She shook her head suddenly, annoyed at herself for letting him lure her into an argument. "I asked you what the *hell* you're doin' here. Don't try to tell me it's just a coincidence that I find you trampin' around down here in my very own territory."

"*Your* territory," Squires grunted. "Christ! You're as goddamn self-centered crazy as you ever were." His eyes brushed the men beside and behind him. "At least you found the right gang!"

"Well, that'll be enough of that," Rafe said, dragging a Colt Navy from a shoulder holster and thumbing back the hammer.

A rifle boomed behind him, and Cora and the other men all jerked with a start as a bullet clanged and sparked off a copper bell hanging beneath the brush arbor, just ahead and right of Custer. The Apache girl whimpered and ducked, slapping her hands to her ears. The clang set Cora's ears to ringing. As the echo flatted out toward the bald, surrounding ridges, she looked over her right shoulder.

A tall, broad-shouldered Mexican in a short, brush-scarred, fancily stitched charro jacket stood inside an otherwise empty corral grown up with weeds. Aiming a rifle across the corral's top slat of bleached ironwood, he ejected the spent shell with a menacing jerk, then rammed a fresh cartridge into the breech.

The bearlike man wore a straw sombrero that shaded his face though Cora could just make out the whites of his eyes as he leaned over his rifle, which was aimed at the middle of her group.

"That there is Chulo Alameda," said Jayco Squires. "He's big, mean, and stupid . . . and he can blow the eye out of an eagle at four hundred yards." He winked. "Rafe, I'd holster that hogleg, 'cause losin' your head wouldn't do that silly getup of yours any good at all."

Custer turned back toward Jay, grinning at him winningly, and depressed the revolver's hammer as he raised the barrel.

"What's your game, Jay?" Cora narrowed an eye and leaned forward on her saddle horn. "If you came to get me back, you can forget it. I'm so far away from you that it took me near on a minute to recollect your name."

Squires chuckled again and canted his head toward the adobe's two stout wooden doors standing open to his left. The half-naked girl stared with the eyes of a frightened doe toward Chulo Alameda aiming his rifle from the corral. "Why don't you and your boys come on in and have a drink on me? I got a proposition for you."

Cora arched a brow skeptically. "Proposition?"

"Oh, don't worry. I ain't gonna try to get into your drawers. Little Alvina here's been treatin' me just fine the past few days." Squires hugged the girl to him and kissed the back of her bare shoulder. "Ain't you, Alvina?"

The girl said nothing as she stared, wrinkling her forehead, at the big man aiming the rifle from the corral.

"Come on in," Squires said, shoving the girl off his knee and rising to his lean six feet two and adjusting the black hat on his head. He wasn't wearing his two matched Remingtons. In fact, he wore only his underwear shirt, unbuttoned halfway down his hairy chest, under a shabby suit coat. The tweed trousers were shoved down into the tops of his beaded moccasin boots.

That was just like Jay, Cora thought. He trusted his charm even more than his gun savvy. And, on that off chance his winning smile and sparkling eyes didn't work, he had the big bear with the Winchester on the other side of the yard.

Cora looked around at her group, all of whom regarded her curiously. She knew Squires better than they did. Could they trust him?

"I reckon we *did* stop for a drink," Cora said, swinging down from her saddle. "Might as well listen to the cheatin' son of a bitch flap his gums awhile, if it'll make him feel better."

The others swung out of their saddles, tack squawking, the horses blowing and shaking their dusty manes. Cora looped her reins over the hitchrack and glanced toward the porch.

Squires had already disappeared inside, his self-satisfied chuckles floating softly out the darkened, fly-woven doorway behind him. Cora's gut tightened with anger while her loins puttied with the memory of the better times she'd shared with Jay Squires—a Baptist minister's son from Missouri and one of the best train robbers and safecrackers in all the West.

And the best lover Cora had ever shared the sheets with.

Her gaze caught on the Apache girl standing stiffly and staring toward the corral. The girl covered her breasts with an arm and, grunting fearfully, wheeled and bolted through the saloon's open doors, her bare feet slapping the flagstone tiles.

Cora turned to see Chulo Alameda sauntering toward the house, his rifle on his shoulder now, a pistol held low by his side. The big, bearded face beneath the straw sombrero was bearlike and menacing in its lack of expression.

Cora curled her lip at the man, then turned and headed into the saloon, flanked by the Flute brothers and Sykes and Heinz. The latter two hung back near the door to cover the group's flank; there might be more gunmen than Chulo Alameda outside, and they could be planning an ambush.

Cora strode across the flagstone of the dim room toward Squires. The handsome outlaw had flopped down behind a long, rectangular table with two other Americans—one a middle-aged gent and a young stringbean nearly as tall and thin as the Flute boys though not nearly as well attired. Both the stringbean and the middle-aged gent wore the nondescript clothes—brush-torn and sweat-stained—of the nomadic yanqui outlaw.

Cora chuckled inwardly. Squires had fallen on hard times.

"Come on in and meet my friends," Squires said, canting his head toward the two men on his left. They sat behind plates littered with the remains of a recent meal and two half-empty beer mugs.

Squires popped the cork on a bottle and yelled at the bartender, Rudolpho Salinas, standing behind the plank-board bar along the room's right wall, to bring glasses for Squires's friends. As the gray-haired Mexican did as he'd been told, sweating nervously and raking his eyes across the newcomers, Cora heard spurs ching on the stone flags behind her. She glanced over her shoulder.

Chulo Alameda ducked through the door as he entered the saloon, eyeing Sykes and Heinz, who stood now with their backs to the bar, rifles ready. They both looked the bearish Mexican up and down, eyes flickering apprehensively.

Alameda had three big knives strapped to his bulky frame and two long-barreled Colt revolvers. His Winchester appeared no larger than a bung starter in his massive arms and hands, and his bearded face, framed by two thin braids hanging down from under his frayed sombrero, was a veritable cutting board of savage, knotted knife scars.

Even more formidable than his looks was his stench.

"Christ!" Cora exclaimed, wincing as the rotten odor washed over her. "You ever wipe your *ass*?"

Either the big Mexican understood no English or he had an

uncommonly thick skin, for he merely gave an animal grunt, sauntered over to the bar, and stood facing the room while regarding Sykes and Heinz with bleak menace.

As the bartender heeled it back to safety behind the bar, Squires poured drinks from his whiskey bottle and clucked with admonishment. "Cora, my dear, it's a real tragedy how little your mother taught you about proper manners."

"Never knew my mother," Cora said. "And who are you to teach *anyone* about manners, you murdering swine." As Squires squeezed the cork back into the bottle and lounged in his chair, chuckling without mirth, Cora said as she turned a chair backward and straddled it, "Now, why don't you tell me about this so-called *proposition*? Not that I care, or I'm even interested in any damn thing you have to say except, possibly, 'good-bye,' but I just know you won't let me sit and drink in silence until you've flapped your jaws awhile."

Squires regarded the girl sitting across from him with a mock swoon. "God, how I've missed you!"

"How could you not, swine?"

"Could you two save the lovey-dovey stuff for later?" said Custer Flute. He and his brothers had pulled chairs out from another table, far enough away to see beneath Squires's table, with their drinks in their non-gun hands.

"Yeah," agreed Billy Earl, flanking Cora and throwing back his entire shot. "We don't intend to be here more than a *night*, ye understand."

"Here." Squires nudged the bottle toward Cora. "Fill Billy Earl's glass before it starts collecting fly shit."

As Cora refilled Billy Earl's glass, Squires said, "As you can see, there's only four of us. He glanced at the older gent on his far right and the stringbean beside him, each man strategically spaced about three feet apart in case of a dustup. "Pee-Wee Grayson here and Sonny Dark." He glanced at Chulo Alameda sharing dark stares at the bar with Heinz and Sykes. "You've met Chulo. *I* met him a couple of weeks ago, just after he delivered a passel of Chinee girls to the miners down in Palo Pinto."

"Shit," Billy Earl growled, setting his opera hat onto an empty chair and glancing over his shoulder at the big bear at the bar. "Slave tradin', huh?"

"Good money in the slave trade." Squires grinned proudly at the big Mexican. "Chulo broke out of Yuma pen a year ago, killed two guards and four of the Mojave Indians sent to track him."

"*Ate* the last one," chuckled the stringbean, Sonny Dark. "Cut him up and rock-fried him on the desert floor."

"*Mmm-hmmmm!*" said the older gent, Pee-Wee. "That's good stuff, them Mojaves!"

Both Sykes and Heinz turned toward the group at the tables. Then, as though their heads were both tied to the same string, they turned back slowly, brows mantling their eyes grimly, to Chulo Alameda regarding them cow-like as he leaned on an elbow and rested his rifle on his shoulder.

"Chulo is worth a good handful of average shooters, but even so," Squires continued, leaning back in his chair with a shot glass in his hand, "we need more men . . . and, uh, *women* . . . for a job we have planned. A job too big for only the four of us."

Cora slanted an eye at her old beau. "You're askin' us to throw in on a job with you?"

Squires squinted back at her. "When I came *down* here, I didn't know *you* were here. I came *down* here, to the Seven Devils, for a job, hopin' to pick up some help from one of the gangs in these parts . . . if there was any I could trust. I learned last week from Rippin' Robbie Price that the Three of a Kind Gang was hidin' out in these rocks. So"—Squires raised his hands— "I've been lookin' around, found out from Salinas you and your boys stopped in from time to time." He smiled. "Between jobs, I reckon."

Cora glanced at Rafe, Billy Earl, and Custer Flute. "Yeah, well, there wasn't no money in the last job, but it was right satisfyin' just the same." She removed her straw hat decorated with dry desert wildflowers, and pinched up the crown. "What kind of a job you got? Mexico, I reckon. Guns, money, or gold, and how much? Or you just wanna kill somebody?"

"It's gold." Squires raked his gaze around her men before letting it settle back on Cora. "You in? Perhaps you'd like to talk about it?"

"How much gold?" asked Rafe Flute, flicking weed seeds from an arm of his green-checked suit coat.

"If my information is right, we should each walk away

with between five and ten thousand. *Each* of us. That's a lot of walkin' *anywhere* we wanna walk for as *long* as we wanna walk."

Custer and Rafe Flute whistled at the same time. "You must be figurin' on one o' them Mex immigrant trains," said Billy Earl, his eyes lighting up and his long, thin lips shaping a smile inside his scraggly black beard. His glasses hung low on his nose.

"Or army payroll coins," Heinz grunted from the bar, for the moment taking his eyes off Chulo Alameda.

Squires shook his head. "Nope. One of the hacendados down in Sonora found gold on his hacienda. An old Franciscan digging, I hear. I got a man down there workin' for the don, and he sent word that the don will be sending a shipment of gold, almost a hundred thousand dollars' worth, to a Tucson bank."

"When and where?" asked Custer Flute.

Squires smiled, slid his eyes to Cora and the other two Flute brothers and to the men at the bar, then back to Custer. "That'll have to wait until we've gotten to know each other better." The handsome outlaw stretched his lips, showing more teeth. "Suffice it to say, we'll be hitting it soon not far from here."

Cora sat back in her chair and crossed her arms on her chest. Her stony expression belied that her heart had swelled at the prospect of riding the outlaw trail with the once repulsive and irresistible rake who still set her blood to boiling and her loins to quivering . . . and that she hated herself for it. "How many men will be guarding the shipment? How much firepower?"

"At least twenty well-armed men. My man working for the don says the old boy has a couple of Gatling guns. I doubt he'll leave them at home. But if we surprise them at the right time and place along the trail, we should be able to pull it off."

Rafe Flute bounced his sombrero on his knee. "*Two* Gatlin' guns. *Twenty* guards?"

Cora glanced at him. "You don't wanna do it, Rafe?"

Rafe flushed slightly, hiked a shoulder, and gave his hat a hard bounce. "I didn't say that." He glanced at his brothers. "If you boys are in, I reckon . . ."

Cora feigned an indifferent yawn and looked around at the others. "Well, I could stand a few thousand dollars in my pocket—I know that. I'm tired of workin' like a dog and runnin' around this desert like a fuckin' pack rat." She turned around to scowl at Jayco Squires. "My problem is you. If you think you can keep your hands off me and give me about twenty feet elbow room at all times, I'll give it some serious consideration."

Squires dropped his eyes to her blouse and the pale cleavage that the undone buttons revealed. "I'm guessin' you'll be fightin' your way under my blankets in two nights."

The others laughed.

Cora's face warmed. "I wouldn't place any bets. . . ."

She let her voice trail off as high-pitched grunts and groans rose from near the bar. It was the Apache girl. She'd donned a baggy sackcloth shirt, which hung off one slender, brown shoulder, and she was carrying a wicker basket filled with bedding. She was sidestepping toward the door around Chulo Alameda. The big man stepped back and forth in front of her, harassing her, guttural chuckles rumbling up from his chest.

Cora leaped up out of her chair, grabbed one of her pistols, and swung toward the door and fired.

The shot crashed like thunder. Chulo Alameda's hat flew off his head and bounced off the back wall to reveal his sweat-matted, louse-peppered hair.

His eyes snapped wide with shock and fury. As the Apache girl screamed and ran outside with her basket, Alameda jutted his lower jaw and stepped toward Cora while raising his rifle.

Holding her smoking revolver straight out from her shoulder, Cora thumbed back the hammer with a ratcheting click and aimed down the barrel at the center of the big Mexican's broad forehead. "You leave that girl alone, hear? Or you and me gonna dance, you shit-smelly son of a bitch!"

Alameda stopped, his rifle halfway to his chest. He blinked. His dark features turned darker. The rest of the room had fallen silent, all the men with their hands on their guns, each faction glaring at the other, wondering which way the wind was going to blow.

Alameda glanced at Squires, then flicked his enraged stare to Cora and slowly lowered his rifle.

Cora heard Squires chuckle as relieved sighs rose from his

group as well as from her own. A firefight in close quarters was never a pleasant experience.

"Girl," Squires said, "why does everything have to be so damn complicated with you?"

"Jay, you keep this big tub of rancid hog guts away from me, understand? Or I'm gonna turn his ugly hide into buzzard feed."

She holstered her revolver and hooked her thumbs in her cartridge belts. "Now, if you boys'll excuse me, I'll be seein' if that poor girl is all right." Holding the big man's stare, she backed across the room and out the door.

Behind her, Squires threw back another whiskey shot and slammed the glass on the table. Chuckling, he shook his head and stared at the door.

"Got that girl wrapped around my little finger." He switched his sparkling gaze to the Flute brothers regarding him distastefully. "Yessir, boys, I purely do!"

15

PROPHET, LOUISA, AND Big Hans were mounted up and heading south well before the sun had risen. Hans straddled a stout, surly claybank with white, shotgun-patterned spots on its muscular rump. He had his Big Fifty snugged in a saddle boot. The clay and Mean and Ugly eyed each other testily, obviously not liking each other, and Louisa tried to keep her pinto between them as much as possible.

As soon as the stars faded, the sun rose quickly—a giant rose blossoming above the eastern horizon and quickly throwing down a searing heat. Prophet was relieved when the brassy orb had vaulted high enough so that his hat shaded his face.

Ahead along the flour-white, well-used horse trail ribboning through the dusty, lemon-colored chaparral, the seven sandstone spires of the Seven Devils Range—complete with what looked like horns and forked tails—loomed a thousand feet atop bald, boulder-strewn slopes, heat waves giving them a liquid, illusory air.

The only sounds were cicadas, the rustle of jackrabbits or kangaroo rats bounding through the scrub, and the occasional screech of a hunting eagle.

When the trail pinched out or disappeared in boulder snags,

Big Hans took the lead, guiding Prophet and Louisa toward a formation called the Devil's Tail. It was a narrow, vertical opening in a near-solid rock wall.

The entrance to the deeper range bypassed the more Apache-populated areas of the Seven Devils, as well as several known outlaw lairs. Big Hans guessed aloud that there probably were a good hundred hard cases at any one time scattered across the devil's playground of pedestal rocks, mesas, caves, and deep barrancas cut eons ago by ancient rivers.

Customarily skeptical, Louisa said, "So, Hans, how is it you know your way around so well in these mountains? You said you were just a shaver when you and your uncle prospected out here."

"I was a shaver, all right—but a damn curious one," Big Hans said over his shoulder, flashing a toothy grin. "Uncle Alphonse used to make cactus wine, and every few weeks he'd go on a bender and leave me to my own devices. I'd take a knife and croaker sack of salted javelina and head out into the canyons, exploring.

"Seen all kinds of things—all different kinds of outlaw bands. Some were Mexicans mixed with Injuns. Some were white men dressed in Confederate gray mixed with Injuns and Mexicans. I run across dead men, too—some hangin', some half buried in the sand. Outlaws, most like, lockin' horns—you know, double-crossin' each other and such."

Hans spat to one side and continued with barely a pause. "I even run across an old wooden chest filled with gold and silver crosses. Even had a sword in it. Solid gold. No, really—that's bond! But when I went back to fetch it with Uncle Alphonse, I couldn't remember where it was! All those arroyos and gullies and caverns look the same. Jesus, did that piss-burn Uncle Alphonse. I reckon I should've marked the trail. We looked for it for nigh on a month, but do you think we found it? No!

"You hear things out here, too. Weird things I can't even describe, and I used to think it was the wind, but you know, I sometimes wonder if it isn't the spirits of all these murdered men haunting the Seven Devils, maybe lookin' for justice."

Big Hans hipped around in his saddle to shift his blue-eyed gaze between Prophet and Louisa. "You think that might be?

Do you believe in ghosts? I never used to, but . . ." He turned forward and let his voice trail off for only about two seconds before continuing.

"The Injuns, you know, they're the ones that named the range the Seven Devils. Legend has it—and I got this from an old Apache just sittin' out waitin' to die in a cave some years ago—the Apache gods cast seven devils out of Apache heaven or whatever they call it, and this is the range where them ogres decided to live and raise all kinds of Cain.

"You know, turn evil spirits loose to roam the earth, an' such. Each one o' them peaks, close up, looks like a devil's head complete with horns and pitchfork, and all sorts of weird storms kick up around there. You don't wanna get too close. Wind and lightnin', dust flying about."

Big Hans shook his head and sighed. "Wouldn't wanna be out here alone—I'll tell you that right now."

Louisa turned to Prophet as the kid continued riding, his broad back swaying with the clay's fleet stride, and chattering as though he hadn't spoken in months. She twisted a wry grin at Prophet. "You should feel right at home here, Lou. Might even wanna stay and shovel a little coal for those ogres."

Prophet uncorked his canteen as Mean and Ugly clomped up a low rise. He curled his lip wryly as he lifted the canteen to his mouth, only half listening to the kid's incessant chatter ahead of him. "Might enjoy the peace and quiet."

"Hey, Hans," Louisa said, raising her voice slightly, "can't you prod a little more speed out of that beast?"

"Don't get your drawers in a curl, girl," Prophet grumbled. "These're the only horses we got, and we blow 'em out, it's a long walk to anywhere."

Louisa glanced at Prophet, her exquisite upper lip curled, the flat brim of her black hat hanging low over her vivid, hazel eyes. "At this pace, we won't reach even the Devil's Tail until it's time to cut our Christmas tree." Back straight and chin lifted defiantly, she gigged the pinto ahead with a frustrated chuff, passing Hans and disappearing over a hogback, the clay-colored dust riding behind her.

"If you get lost out here, you crazy polecat," Prophet hissed, gigging Mean and Ugly up to Hans's right stirrup, "I'll leave you out here for the Apaches to tickle to death!"

Prophet cursed and shook his head.

"That's a strong-willed girl there," Hans observed. "Kinda reminds me of my sister, Ruth. Why, if it was rainin', she'd say it was snowin' just to argue! I remember one time . . ."

Prophet groaned at the prospect of another big windy blowing up and tipped his hat brim low.

Louisa didn't run ahead for long.

The deeper they rode into the hills and bluffs and arroyos of that great, scarred country flanking the mountains, the more she seemed to realize she needed Big Hans to show her the way. The trail they followed, meandering through the creosote and saguaros, disappeared for long stretches under fallen rocks or eroded shale or arroyos that had flooded in the last hard rain.

From time to time, when the trail grew doubtful, she let Prophet and Big Hans catch up to her. Prophet sensed her tension, the impatience that made her chuff and nibble her lips and balk every time they stopped to give the horses a blow or to let them drink from the rare rock tank or spring.

Prophet would let her push her horse only so long as the pinto didn't show signs of strain. If he had to, for Louisa's sake as well as the pinto's, he'd hogtie her, lash her belly down across her saddle, and lead her into the mountains behind Mean and Ugly.

Late in the day, Prophet and Big Hans crested a low, sandy bluff to find Louisa waiting in the shaded wash below, staring up at a steep jumble of adobe-colored rocks and boulders stippled with saguaros, organ-pipe cactus, and spindly mesquites. On both sides rose the steep, rocky walls of twin mesas.

Prophet and the kid headed down the bluff toward Louisa holding the pinto's reins in one hand while shading her eyes with the other. Prophet's and the kid's dust rose around them, copper-colored in the late-afternoon light.

"We best walk the horses over this," Big Hans said, swinging heavily down from the claybank. "It's the only way between these mesas. We could go around, but this is a shortcut to the Devil's Tail. Takes a good half day off the trip. Uncle Alphonse figured an earth tremor probably sealed this gap." Sweating and breathing hard, the kid grinned at Prophet, showing his big horse teeth. "There's a cantina on the other side."

Prophet chuffed skeptically. He wasn't sure how much to believe about the kid's far-fetched tales of his experiences in the Seven Devils country, but surely now he was pulling the bounty hunter's leg. "Cantina?"

"An old adobe that a rancher turned into a watering hole. It's on an east-west smuggling road that ain't used anymore, but it was still open last time I was here. Mostly used by banditos and prospectors an' such." The kid wagged his big, blond head, whistling. "Boy, Uncle Alphonse spent some time there, I tell ya!"

Prophet heard the ring of shod hooves on stone and turned to see Louisa leading her pinto up the rubble mound. "Louisa, hold on, damnit!" He'd been letting Mean and Ugly draw water from his hat. "Give your horse some water and a rest, you crazy minx."

"My pinto is better conditioned than that ugly cayuse of yours," she called without turning around. The pinto slipped and stumbled on the rocks that had apparently fallen from the ridge of the southern-looming mesa.

Prophet cursed and snugged his hat back down on his head, letting the last of the water dribble down his hot face streaked with sweat mud. He started leading Mean forward. "Rest your clay," he grumbled at Big Hans. "Looks like I gotta babysit that wooden-headed wildcat, try to keep her from pulling that pinto out of its shoes."

Prophet followed Louisa's path up the perilous slope, meandering around the steepest snags and brush clumps and around the saguaros stretching their forked shadows. She was moving faster than he was, however, so he was a good forty yards behind her when he spied a shadow moving among the rocks just above her and right.

He'd just glimpsed the movement out the corner of his eye, and he thought he'd seen a streak of red mixed with the shadow, like the red calico shirts Apaches often wore.

Not again . . .

He'd just started reaching toward his rifle scabbard when he saw the Indian leap up onto a flat-topped boulder so close to

Louisa that he could have spit on her. Prophet's heart thumped. It was too late for the rifle.

He shouted, "Louisa, down!" and jerked his Colt from its holster.

Crouching and fanning the hammer, he emptied the cylinder in what sounded like one thundering explosion, the sour-smelling smoke rising up around his face. Forty yards uphill was a tough shot for a revolver, and Prophet saw a couple of slugs bark into the rocks, but two hit home with audible plunks. One ground into the Indian's knee while the other puffed dust from his shirt.

The Apache screamed as he loosed the arrow toward Louisa. The girl dove forward, and the arrow clattered into the rocks behind her.

At the same time, the brave dropped his bow and stumbled back against another boulder behind him, grabbing at his chest as if to dislodge a knife, stretching his lips back from his teeth.

His knees bent and he fell forward off the rock, turning a somersault, limbs akimbo. Hitting the slope, he rolled toward Louisa and the whinnying pinto, and Prophet could hear the thumps and the sharp rattling cracks of his breaking bones.

Prophet holstered his Colt, grabbed his Winchester, and racked a shell into the chamber as he bolted up the slope, hopscotching boulders, breathing hard. He swung his gaze from left to right as he ran, expecting arrows to suddenly start raining down from the ridges on both sides of the rubble pile. The pinto ran awkwardly upslope, stumbling on the precarious terrain, whinnying and snorting. Prophet dropped to a knee and, holding the Winchester to his shoulder, cast quick, edgy looks along both ridges.

No flying arrows. No flitting shadows of braves scurrying about for killing positions.

Could the dead brave have been alone?

He lowered the rifle and glanced toward Louisa. Only the brave was there, lying facedown, his bloody back humped slightly.

Prophet rose and continued upslope, frowning and looking for the girl while flicking cautious looks all around.

He called softly, "Louisa?"

In the corner of his right eye, the brave moved. Prophet swung around, angling his Winchester down and pressing his finger against the trigger.

The brave wobbled from side to side, then turned onto his shoulder to reveal Louisa lying on her back atop a large, slanting boulder. She blinked dazedly, grunting with the effort of trying to heave the Indian's big body off her. A long red line had been slashed across her right cheek—by the Indian's arrow, no doubt.

"Christ!" Prophet reached down and pulled the Indian's limp carcass off Louisa's diminutive frame. She rose onto her elbows, her eyes rolling around, blood dribbling from her cut cheek. Blood from the Indian's chest wound had stained the cream shirt she wore, trimmed with green piping in the shapes of prancing horses.

Prophet knelt before her, bunching his lips and shaking his head with fury. Normally she would have smelled the Indian before she'd even started up the slope. She'd gone kill-crazy, and that's how bounty hunters ended up six feet under.

She glanced at the Indian now lying belly up beside her, the dead man's half-open eyes staring at the sky. Sleeving blood from her cheek, she glanced at Prophet with a self-righteous sneer. "Well . . . at least I wasn't distracted by a gaggle of naked women!"

16

LOUISA KNEW SHE'D made a mistake, scrambling carelessly across the rubble pile in hostile country—she was too good a bounty hunter *not* to know—but she didn't admit it.

She'd looked over the pinto thoroughly, though, with a worried expression, as the horse might have been seriously injured when it had thrashed about the rocks to escape the Chiricahua arrow as well as Prophet's crashing pistol shots.

Her mistake was no less a mistake because Prophet had made one similar. But she merely watered the frightened horse while the bounty hunter and Big Hans scouted around. She rubbed the blood from the shallow burn across her cheek, then scooped up the pinto's reins. "Well, we've wasted enough time—don't you think, boys? Let's get a move on."

"You don't mind if I take the lead this time, do you, Miss Bonnyventure?" Prophet said smartly. He'd finished hiding the dead Apache's body in the rocks, in case others came looking for him and cut his sign. He grabbed Mean's reins and shouldered his Winchester.

Louisa gave her chin another defiant lift and ticked a finger against the flat brim of her black hat. "If it'll make you feel better."

"Much obliged."

Prophet led the dun past her and the pinto, and with Louisa leading the pinto behind him and Big Hans—who was suddenly, uncharacteristically quiet in the wake of the shooting—bringing up the rear with his shifty-eyed claybank, the three continued up and over the rocky rise and down the other side. Prophet watched the terrain intently, for Apaches could meld nearly completely with their surroundings.

But no more braves showed themselves or flung arrows down from the rocks.

The dead brave must have been on his own, maybe the sole survivor of a run-in with Yaquis, also known to haunt this country, or with cavalry. His face had been painted for war, so he wasn't just out here communing with nature.

At the bottom of the rubble pile and on the far side of the gap between the mesas, Prophet, Louisa, and Big Hans mounted up once more and gigged their horses into long, loping strides. The terrain was table-flat, with few rocks and cholla snags, and they wanted to get as far away from the dead Apache as possible.

The sun was a golden orb falling fast toward the toothy western ridges behind them when they broke out of the chaparral and reined their mounts down at the edge of a hard-packed yard surrounding a low-slung white adobe. A windmill sat in the middle of the yard, towering above a stone stock tank.

Right of the adobe lay an overgrown corral, and straight east lay a long line of half-ruined mud-brick stables that had probably once served the rancho. The cracked adobe walls were bathed in the coppery light of the falling sun.

Big Hans grinned at Prophet as he pulled back hard on the mule's reins; the mule and the horses all smelled the water in the stock tank beneath the windmill. "I told you there was a canteen out here."

Prophet was sleeving sweat from his forehead and raking his eyes around the place before him, noting the two saddled horses tied before the brush-roofed gallery. "Boy, I gotta admit, finding a cantina out here is like—"

A gun exploded from inside the saloon—a hollow, tinny bark that made the two horses in front of the place jerk their heads up and skitter-hop. The report was followed by a shouted curse, a scream, three more shots, and another scream.

"Double-crossin' son of a bitch!" a man shouted.

Two more pops—*k-blam*! *K-blam!*

Both Prophet and Louisa had their revolvers out as they stared toward the adobe house. Prophet thumbed his Colt's hammer back when a man in a battered hat and bright red shirt stumbled out the door and across the porch to drop to his knees on the far side of the jittery horses.

Prophet glanced at Louisa, then spurred Mean and Ugly straight into the yard. As he pulled up about twenty feet in front of the thatch-roofed hovel, the red-shirted man pushed up off his knees and stumbled forward. He twisted around and fired two shots into the cantina's front wall though it appeared he'd been aiming for the door.

The tied horses whinnied and bucked as shards of adobe ticked around the gallery.

The red-shirted man yelled, "Bastards!" and squeezed his revolver's trigger. But the hammer hit the firing pin with a sharp ping—empty. He dropped the gun and, clutching his upper belly with both hands, continued stumbling forward as though he were trying to run through quicksand.

He looked up, saw the three newcomers sitting their mounts in the yard, and angled toward Big Hans. Falling forward, he grabbed the boy's saddle horn. The mule nickered indignantly as the man looked up at the boy, his face sweat-soaked and pain-racked, and groaned several times before, knees slowly buckling, he said, "Those . . . double-crossing bastards . . . been wantin' me *dead* fer a long fuckin' time!"

Big Hans held his frightened horse's reins taut to his chest as he looked at Prophet and Louisa as if for counsel.

The red-shirted man looked up at Big Hans and sobbed. "They killed me, didn't they?"

Big Hans's eyes were large as saucers. He swallowed and blinked. His voice was thick and low. "I reckon they did, sir."

"*Shit!*"

The red-shirted man dropped to his knees and fell facedown in the yard. Big Hans's horse whinnied horrifically and, giving

a halfhearted buck, sidled away from the man whose blood
quickly reddened the dust beneath him.

Boot thumps and spur chings rose from inside the saloon,
and Prophet ripped his gaze from the dead man to the front
door. Another man appeared, bounding forward as though to
break down an invisible door.

He was broad and unshaven, and he wore no hat on his
bullet-shaped, bald head. With one hand he clutched his upper
left chest while wielding a smoking Colt Army in the other.
Blood gushed from a bullet wound in his right temple.

"Hold it!" Prophet said as he and Louisa extended their
Colts at the man at the same time, Big Hans's clay nickering
and stomping behind them.

The man dropped to his knees before Prophet's order had
died on his lips. The man groaned and panted and pressed the
heel of his hand to the ragged hole in his chest. He held his
Colt straight down to the porch floor as he regarded Prophet
desperately, his small blue eyes pinched with pain.

"That bastard dead?"

Prophet glanced at the red-shirted man lying facedown in
the dirt. The man's right boot twitched as though with a slight
electrical charge.

"Close enough," Prophet said.

"Good!" The man on the porch fell forward, his face hitting the porch floor with a resolute smack.

Prophet glanced at the two dead men once more, then looked
at the door, half expecting another man to run out yelling and
shooting. Another man did appear, but this one—an old, stoop-
shouldered Mexican with thin gray hair and an upswept gray
mustache—merely stood in the open doorway, squinting out
into the fading sunlight at the dead men.

He looked at Prophet and Louisa and at Big Hans, who had
jumped down from his prancing claybank and stood holding
the beast's reins, a wary look in his eyes. The Mex turned and
grunted something in Spanish behind him.

Presently, a young Mexican boy scuttled out from behind
the man. Clad in soiled, torn canvas trousers, a serape, and
rope-sole sandals, his black, unevenly cut hair hanging to his
shoulders, he dashed off the porch, paused to give the three

newcomers a quick, cautious scrutiny, then knelt and began going through the pockets of the dead man on the porch.

Prophet looked at the Mexican man still standing between the batwings. "You got any more shooters in there?"

"Not alive!" In Spanish, the old Mex told the boy to make sure he removed the dead men's boots—he could make some extra pocket jingle off barefoot pilgrims—and to take their horses to the stable. Then he turned and disappeared back inside the saloon.

Prophet turned to Louisa, shrugged, holstered his .45, and swung down from the saddle.

Sitting on her pinto tensely, still holding her cocked Colt in her hand, Louisa stared at his broad, sweat-dark back. "You intend to stop here?"

"Why not?" Prophet led Mean and Ugly toward the clattering windmill and the stock tank. "They got water. Inside, they probably got whiskey."

"No time for spirituous liquids, Lou."

Prophet doffed his hat and glanced over his shoulder, grinning. "There's always time for spirituous liquids, Miss Bonnyventure." While Mean drew water, swishing his tail luxuriously, Prophet leaned over the stone-walled tank and ducked his head in the cool, refreshing fluid.

When Prophet, Louisa, and Big Hans had watered their horses, they tied the mounts to the hitchrack fronting the cantina and mounted the gallery in single file, Prophet taking the lead, Big Hans bringing up the rear. The two dead men lay where they'd fallen in the blood-splashed dirt, their pockets inside out, worthless paraphernalia like playing cards and pencil stubs littering the ground around them, their guns, knives, and boots gone, their socks half off.

Prophet rested his Winchester on his shoulder and ducked through the doorway, instinctively stepping to one side so the door didn't backlight him, and looked around. Louisa and Hans followed suit on the other side of the door.

The room was well lit by high, arched windows recessed in the thick adobe walls. The herringbone-patterned ceiling was low, with several dusty ristras hanging from it. Another dead man—a short hombre in blue denims and a black-and-white-checked shirt—lay in the middle of the room near an overturned table and broken glass. He stared unseeing at the ceiling, his hazel eyes reflecting the salmon light angling through the western windows.

His boots were gone, his pockets pulled out of his pants. A small notebook, a .36 cartridge casing, a bullet-smashed, blood-smeared pocket watch, and a rabbit's foot—all apparently deemed worthless—lay on his bloody chest.

The boy was sweeping up glass shards near the dead man's head. Hatless before, the kid now wore a stained, cream Stetson that was a couple of sizes too large for his head, a hawk feather protruding from the braided-rawhide band.

Regarding the newcomers with dark, animal-like caution, he adjusted the angle of his new hat, then swept the liquor-soaked glass and a cork into a neat pile, firming up the edges.

"Any survivors?" Prophet asked the Mexican, who stood chopping up a couple of big jackrabbits on the long bar running along the room's right wall.

The Mexican dropped a bloody leg into an iron pot. "Survivors are few and far between in these parts, amigo." He shrugged a shoulder. "It's a hell of a mess, but I don't argue with the extra *dinero*."

He chuckled, showing his silver-capped upper teeth. When his eyes had finished appreciating Louisa, they slid to Big Hans, still standing near the door, and widened.

"Hansy?" The Mexican stared, frowning. "Is that little Hansy Kleinsasser?"

Big Hans slid his gaze from the dead man on the floor to the Mexican behind the bar. His lips spread in a grin. "How ya doin', Rudolpho?"

Wiping his hands on a damp towel, the barman ducked under the bar planks, wincing against the strain in his back. He tossed the towel onto the bar behind him and ambled up to Hans, his eyes wide, lower jaw hanging. "What you do back here?" He glanced at Prophet and Louisa once more, then rose up on his toes to peer over the big younker's broad left shoulder. "Where's your uncle? He's tending the horses?"

Big Hans shook his head and pursed his lips. "Alphonse is

dead, Rudolpho. That's what brings me here with my new friends—Lou Prophet and Louisa Bonaventure."

He glanced at his companions and nodded to indicate the barman. "This here's Rudolpho Salinas. He staked me and Uncle Alphonse when our bellies were kissing our backbones. Anyway, Rudolpho, there's a gang out here, the Three of a Kind Gang. They burned Seven Devils, the town, and Alphonse burned up in the barn. I couldn't get him out. We're trackin' them vipers. These two are bounty hunters."

At the mention of the Three of a Kind Gang, a cloud had passed over Salinas's broad, dark face with its slightly off-center left eye. "*Sí, sí,*" he said quickly, looking around as if the gang were lurking nearby. "I know of this gang. Five men and a girl—if you can call her that."

The barman shook his head, frowning at Hans. "No, no, Hans. You must go back to Seven Devils!"

"There's nothing left in Seven Devils but ashes."

Salinas shook his head again. "Then go to Tucson. Or Lordsburg. Christos—I will give you a job *here* tending my horses. I have accumulated so many I could start my own ranch! But do not, I beg of you, go any farther into the mountains. Many bad men. More even than before—the Three of a Kind Gang the worst of all of them. . . ."

Big Hans just stared at the shorter man, his blue eyes bleak. Salinas sighed, shook his head again, then turned and gestured toward one of the tables.

"You sit, huh? It's been a long ride, no? I bring drinks, and I have rooms in the back." He grinned at Louisa, his eyes lustily taking the high-busted, well-armed girl's measure. "I even have the old fountain working back there. It makes a pleasant sound in the evening."

Louisa ignored the old man's lusty gaze. "You know where the Three of a Kind bunch is holed up, do you, Mr. Salinas?"

Salinas held a finger to his lips as he looked around once more. "*Sh-sh!* It is not good to speak of the outlaws."

As the newcomers sat at a table against the back wall, near an old, faded painting of a plumed-helmeted conquistador on a high-stepping white stallion, Salinas pitched his voice low. "If word got around that I spoke of them . . ."

He made a slashing motion across his throat as he looked directly at Prophet. "Besides, I do not know where any of the hideouts are. It is not something that is spread around. But I will tell you this—many lawmen and bounty hunters have passed through here over the years." Salinas shook his head sadly. "Maybe one in thirty I ever see again. Now, please, what would you like to drink?"

"Do you have sarsaparilla?" Louisa asked, tossing her hat on the table and biting her gloves off her fingers.

Salinas looked at her as though she'd spoken some alien tongue. He shook his head slowly, frowning. Prophet looked at her, too, scowling.

The girl shrugged. "Glass of cold water."

"Goat milk for me," Big Hans said.

"*Sí, sí,*" said Salinas, ruffling the boy's short, wheat-colored hair. "You always loved your goat milk! And your uncle, his pulque!"

"Water and goat milk," Prophet growled. "You two sure know how to turn your wolves loose. Make mine tequila. And bring the bottle."

As Salinas limped off, Prophet glanced at his two companions, chuffed, and dropped his hat on the table. Outside, hoofbeats rose, growing louder as riders approached the cantina. Tack squawked and men talked in what sounded like English.

Shortly, boots clomped onto the gallery and the batwings chirped. Prophet glanced toward the bar where Salinas was dribbling milk into a stone mug from a bladder flask.

Raking his eyes across the newcomers, Prophet's stomach fell and filled with bile.

Under his breath, he said, "Shit."

Frowning, Louisa glanced at the three men sauntering up to the bar, dusty chaps flapping about their denim-clad legs— three rough-garbed, unshaven hombres in battered Stetsons and with holstered six-shooters thonged low on their thighs.

Prophet kept his voice low, pitched with dry whimsy. "Just had a feelin' I might run into somebody I knew out here. . . ."

17

WHEN RUDOLPHO SALINAS had delivered their drinks and limped back to the bar, where the three new-comers milled, talking and chuckling in the languid tones of weary riders, brushing dust from their sleeves and swiping hats against chaps, Louisa sipped her water and licked her lips, regarding Prophet casually.

"Which one?"

"Tall one. With the turquoise-studded ear ring."

Prophet sipped his tequila. A veteran bounty hunter riding into an outlaw lair like the Seven Devils was like a jackrabbit hopping into a rattlesnake dance. He was bound to run into badmen he'd had run-ins with or put away or relatives or friends of such men now moldering behind bars.

"I ain't certain sure he made me, but keep in mind he's left-handed and lightning fast."

Big Hans sat across the table from Prophet, his back to the bar. The kid, who wore a thin goat-milk mustache, glanced over his shoulder. He leaned toward Prophet and said a little louder than Prophet would have liked. "You know them fellers, Lou?"

Rudolpho Salinas finished pouring out shots of tequila for

the three men at the bar. Sweeping up his shot glass, the tall hombre turned around abruptly, his turquoise earring flashing in the last saffron light angling through the window to his left. He poked his hat brim back off his forehead, leaned back on his elbows, and grinned.

"Well, if it ain't Lou Fuckin' Prophet." The outlaw laughed huskily. "What are you doin' out here, amigo—tryin' to make a pile all at once so you can retire, buy one o' them big, fancy houses in Denver?"

Prophet shaped a nervous grin as he stared over Big Hans's left shoulder. The kid's back was to the bar, between Prophet and Hawk and the other two outlaws. If the hard cases flung lead, the kid was sure to catch a pill or two.

Prophet wagged his head slowly and turned his shot glass around on the table. "Lyle Hawk—didn't the judge give you life?"

Hawk lifted his chin, laughing, and let his hands dangle down toward his two .36 revolvers positioned for the cross-draw in matching black leather holsters. A short-barreled third revolver was wedged in front of his belly. His shirt was open, revealing the greasy thong from which a sheathed Arkansas toothpick hung. "Them fancy federal sweat houses were made for breakin' out of, *amigo*."

Hawk turned his head to one side, sweeping his greasy, gray-blond hair back to reveal the grisly knots where his right ear had been. A long knife scar angled down from the knotted mess toward his shoulder. "Got this in there," he chuckled dryly, letting his hair fall back into place and turning his head forward, his eyes and jaws hardening. "A little memento of the place . . . and the man who put me there."

Prophet glanced at Big Hans, who had turned his head to regard the three outlaws over his shoulder. The kid's broad bulk fairly covered Prophet completely. Somehow, he had to get the kid out of the line of fire, or get Hawk and his cohorts to pull their horns in.

Prophet clucked and shook his head. "That had to hurt somethin' fierce, Lyle. Sure am sorry to see that—I purely am."

He lifted his head toward Salinas, who stood grimly behind the bar planks. "Senor Salinas, would you please pour my friends a drink on me? It's the least I can do, seein' as how they cut the poor bastard's ear off an' all."

The stony looks of the three outlaws didn't crack.

Prophet's smile faded as Hawk glanced at the other two men on his left, then pushed off the bar. He hooked his thumbs behind his cartridge belt as he sauntered toward Prophet's table, keeping Big Hans between him and the bounty hunter.

His boots clacked on the cracked flagstones, his ostentatious Texas spurs trilling softly. The wan evening light from the west-facing windows glinted redly off the silver discs trimming his chaps. Stopping three feet behind Big Hans, he shuttled his mild gaze from the kid to Louisa and then to Prophet.

His dark eyes acquired a sardonic gleam. "Traveling with children now, eh, Proph?" He stretched his chapped lips in a hard smile and rolled his eyes back to Louisa. "That's all right. Me an' the boys—we'll take good care of 'em *both* when you're *gone*!"

He hadn't uttered that last before his hands crossed in front of his belly and came up ratcheting the hammers of both pistols back. Before he could level the barrels, Big Hans's right hand shot up and over his head. A half a glass of goat's milk splashed into Hawk's fury-reddened face.

The outlaw grunted, snapping his eyes closed and stumbling backward as he triggered both pistols at the same time. The guns roared, stabbing smoke and flames over Big Hans. The bullets whistled over Prophet's head, each parting his hair, before one tore through a window and plunked into a wall behind him.

The outlaw screamed again, cursing shrilly, as Big Hans rolled out of his chair onto the floor. Bounding forward and kicking his chair back behind him, Prophet jerked up his cocked .45. Hawk squinted through the goat's milk dribbling off his eyelashes and jerked his guns toward Prophet once more, ratcheting back the hammers.

Prophet's Colt roared twice, leaping in his hands, two slugs plunking through Hawk's neck and chest. They punched the outlaw straight back. Falling, he triggered two shots into the ceiling over Big Hans, who lay belly down on the floor, arms crossed on his head.

"Christ!" Hawk cried a half second before he hit the stone floor with a thump and a raucous rake of his spurs, guns clattering onto the flags around him.

Behind him, the other two outlaws were palming their own pistols and lurching forward, spreading their feet and stretching their lips back from their teeth.

Having bolted up and left of the table, one of her matched Colts in her hands, Louisa fired a quarter second before Prophet did. The bounty hunter fanned three shots through his and Hawk's powder smoke. Together, his and Louisa's leaping and popping pistols sounded like the cannonade of a French firing squad as they echoed off the cantina's thick adobe walls.

Only one of the other two outlaws got a shot off, the bullet hammering into a chair back, as Prophet's and Louisa's slugs flipped him up and back onto the bar, screaming and cursing and writhing like a bug on a pin.

"Sons o' bitches!" the other man cried as three slugs tore through his chest, belly, and neck at nearly the same time, whipping him around in a complete circle.

Dropping his revolver and clutching the blood-spurting hole in his neck, he pushed off the wall, staggered two steps toward the door, and dropped to his knees.

"Sons o' bitches!" he cried once more, but softer this time, blood frothing from his lips.

Then he fell facedown, grunting and sighing and jerking, making a feeble attempt to push himself along the floor to the door. He didn't get more than six inches before he went slack and died with a fart.

Quickly thumbing fresh shells into his revolver's loading gate, Prophet raked his gaze across each of the fallen outlaws in turn, squinting against the sting of the powder smoke. The one on the bar, legs dangling toward the floor, lay unmoving, as did the one by the door. Lyle Hawk's chest was still rising and falling, blood welling from his wounds with every breath.

Prophet moved around the table, stepped over Big Hans, who still lay belly down as though he, too, were dead, and stood over the dying outlaw. Hawk stared up at him, eyes wide with shock and rage. He opened and closed his mouth, but only blood frothed across his lips.

Prophet flicked his loading gate closed, thumbed back the hammer, and aimed the Colt at Hawk's head. "Tell Ole Scratch Lou Prophet says hey." The Colt barked, and a nickel-sized hole appeared in the middle of Hawk's forehead. The man's eyes rolled up as if to inspect the hole, and his lower jaw sagged, the tip of his tongue poking out like a hairless pink mouse from its hole.

Prophet let the revolver hang slack as he turned to Louisa, who was so calmly reloading her own Colt that she might have been only target shooting to hone her aim. As he dropped his gaze to Big Hans, Prophet's heart fluttered. The boy still hadn't moved.

"Hey, kid!" Prophet nudged the boy's ribs with his boot toe.

Hans lifted his head suddenly, looking around and blinking against the smoke. When he'd seen the three dead outlaws, he twisted a glance up at Prophet and ran his tongue through the milk on his upper lip. "What'd you think o' *that*, Lou? He sure wasn't expectin' no *kid* to throw milk in his face, was he?"

"I reckon you surprised him, all right. Take any lead?"

"Not that I can tell."

Prophet glanced at Louisa. "You all right?"

"Sure." The girl twirled her Colt and dropped it into its holster. "No thanks to you and that reputation of yours."

Someone groaned. "*San Pedro* . . . are they all dead?" Salinas poked his head above the bar and glanced at the dead man draped over the planks to his left.

"I reckon you just acquired three more horses." Prophet sagged back in his chair, picked up his shot glass, and threw back the tequila.

Leaving Salinas's cantina, Prophet, Louisa, and Big Hans continued pushing westward, traversing the narrow chasm known as the Devil's Tail, and camped in a box canyon a thousand feet above the desert floor.

After a quick supper of a goat quarter, frijoles, and tortillas, which they'd purchased from Salinas, Prophet climbed to a peninsular ridge to keep the first watch of the night.

The desert stretched away on three sides like a molten ocean, the liquid-orange ball of the sun sinking off to Prophet's left. Distant bluffs and mesas were vague shadows in that vast, misty emptiness, with far-off barrancas shouldering against the horizon like the fading lines of an ancient painting. Since he'd entered this wild, rugged range, he felt as though he'd been enveloped by the giant, toothy mouth of a territory-sized dinosaur.

Above Prophet, a fresh breeze jostled the limbs of a sprawling, lightning-topped cedar.

A coyote yammered—several high-pitched yips followed by a mournful howl. Others answered.

Prophet turned to look up the slope behind him. Rocks, pinyon pines, and creosote rose gradually toward a ridge he couldn't see from here. Rock turrets and broken walls leaned out of the slope, and from the top of one such ruined-castle-like formation an owl hooted three times in quick succession.

The hair on the back of Prophet's neck pricked.

He'd heard Indians—Cheyenne as well as Apache—make the same sound when signaling others in their band.

He caressed his Winchester's trigger and ran his gaze slowly along the spindly, sun-parched brush and stone outcrops. The last light died quickly, and soon the darkness closed down around him like a burial shroud. Stars like bits of glowing steel did little to alleviate the blackness. Louisa and Hans's small fire flickered in the hollow behind him and left—the size of a match flame from this distance.

He looked around again, squinting into the darkness. Was it the cool night air or the owl that made him shiver?

Later, hunkered down in the rocks, he watched a far thunderstorm move slowly from right to left, lightning flashing like cannons, the thunder sounding little louder than distant train cars coupling.

Louisa relieved him and then Hans relieved Louisa. By dawn they were on the trail again, ghosting an ancient horse trail in which he'd spied the faint sign of recent riders. The terrain was too rough to make out how many riders had passed—at least six, he figured.

To Prophet's relief, Louisa let him ride point without argument for most of the next day. The girl knew that her partner, having traversed Apache country before, had a better chance of detecting an ambush or Indian smoke signals, which, to the chagrin and horror of many soldiers and prospectors, were often mistaken for dust devils out here.

Louisa rode her pinto about twenty yards behind Prophet while Hans brought up the rear astride his clay. The boy, who was also accustomed to Indian country, spoke little now as he rode, and he was quick to lean forward and clamp a hand over the clay's nostrils whenever Prophet, spying dust or a suspicious noise, threw up a warning hand.

They pushed deeper and deeper into the Seven Devils, with massive, bald ramparts of windblown rock rising on both sides of the trail. Prophet remembered the owl he'd heard last night. Had it been a winged raptor, or Apaches organizing an ambush?

He held his Winchester across his saddlebow, and he dug his double-barreled, sawed-off shotgun out of his saddlebags. He ran his hand across the gut shredder's oiled stock, then let it hang from its leather lanyard, attached to the walnut stock by metal swivels, down his back.

The short-barreled ten-gauge would be a handier weapon in a close-quarter shoot-out, and that's what any attack amongst these narrow, rocky defiles and twisting, snake-infested arroyos would be. The bowie knife sheathed between his shoulder blades might prove necessary if an Indian leaped off a near wall, intending to trim his wick with a tomahawk.

That night they camped in a dry arroyo sheathed by cracked, cabin-sized boulders and sparse ironwood shrubs. Prophet had seen fresh horse tracks overlaying the older trail they'd been following, maybe a day or two old. Knowing they weren't alone out here, they cold-camped, washing down jerky and wild berries with only water, and kept their conversation to a minimum.

After dark, Prophet didn't even roll his customary quirley for fear the smoke would carry and give away their position.

Out here, if the Apaches weren't a danger, banditos were. Crazy damn country. Prophet would rather fight the Sioux up north than the Indians and the black-souled breed of white man that haunted this border country.

The next afternoon, he let Mean pick his own way along the trail curving up a rocky mountain shoulder as Prophet watched a golden eagle soar high above a clump of distant pinyon pines and junipers. The eagle suddenly turned away, and a cold wind blew against Prophet's sweaty back. He looked just west of the eagle and saw that a large, low mass of swollen purple clouds was bearing down on him fast.

Thunder rumbled and the wind swirled, whistling through the crags behind him. Big Hans's clay whinnied shrilly.

"Shit!" Prophet reined Mean down to inspect the storm.

Louisa came up behind him, hipped around in the saddle, her long hair blowing in the sudden wind. "That doesn't look good!" she said, her words nearly swallowed by a gust that lifted the pinto's mane straight up and down.

"Monsoon season," Prophet said. "We're about to get hammered!"

He dropped his gaze from the angry skies to Big Hans hauling back on his reins with one hand while clinging to his saddle horn with the other. His mustang whinnied and bucked, and the kid stretched his lips back from his teeth as thunder rumbled once more, like the crash of boulders down a near slope.

"Hold on, Junior!"

Prophet looked around. Nothing more than a few large boulders offered cover within a good fifty yards. Upslope a hundred yards, the mountain appeared to level out, forming a bench stretching back to a sheer sandstone wall.

As Prophet watched, the wall went from being bathed in full golden sunshine to turning the dark purple of a ripe plumb. The storm was moving in like a Kansas cyclone, icy raindrops pelting the bounty hunter's back, lifting gooseflesh.

Mean and Ugly nickered and shook his head.

Prophet looked back at Louisa and Big Hans, who was keeping his big mustang in relative check though the beast's eyes were white-ringed, its nostrils expanding to the size of jawbreakers. The bounty hunter held his hat brim low so the wind wouldn't take it as he yelled, "Let's vamoose before this little squall turns us into firecrackers!"

Thunder rocked the earth and sky. Lightning flashed like flames licking from the maws of God's double-barreled shotgun.

Prophet turned Mean off the switchbacking trail they'd been following and gigged him straight up the slope. The dun gave a whinny and dug his front hooves into the gravelly ground, lunging off his back legs.

Behind, Prophet heard Louisa urging the pinto and Big Hans yelling in frustration at the half-wild clay, which seemed determined to turn and head back *into* the storm rather than away from it.

Rain poured from the heavens. Nickel-sized drops fell like javelin spears, instantly soaking Prophet's buckskin tunic and denims and sluicing off his funneled hat brim.

To his right, a witch's finger of lightning flashed, followed a half second later by an ear-numbing boom. Sparks flew as a sprawling cedar about fifty yards away lost its crown with a loud crunch and then a long, rattling snap of breaking limbs. Mean leaped forward with a start, and Prophet had to grab his saddle horn to keep from being thrown off the horse's ass.

Mean lunged again when the crown hit the ground with another, louder crash.

As Prophet approached the bench he glanced behind, glad to see Louisa and Big Hans in close pursuit, albeit with the clay buck-kicking, shaking its head wildly. Another lightning bolt struck close by, topping a three-armed saguaro, and a second later another blasted a large, diamond-shaped boulder, the smell of brimstone thick in Prophet's nostrils, even the hair on his arms standing on end.

It was with keen relief that he gained the bench and glanced back to see both Louisa and Big Hans moving up from behind him and swinging out to his right side, unharmed.

Her head tipped low against the rain, Louisa pointed straight ahead. "Look!"

Prophet peered over Mean's head to see a building hulking

up before them, about fifty yards away. At least, it looked like a building. With the rain coming down so hard, the image was blurred.

He urged the horse forward through cedars, pinyons, and boulders and entered a clearing cleaved by a trail angling into it from Prophet's right and left. As he continued forward across the clearing pocked with rain-splashed puddles, the structure clarified slightly behind the billowing moisture curtains, the lightning reflecting off its stout adobe facade to show large cracks and fissures and wind-jostled vines.

It was a three-story barrack-like building with what appeared to be bell towers over the doors—one at each end. Crumbling stone steps rose to each entrance. The hammering rain sluiced off the roof. As Prophet inspected the roofline, a lightning flash revealed a human-shaped figure standing atop the roof, near the bell tower over the door at the building's left end.

In that split-second flash, Prophet saw a man wearing a hooded brown robe and throwing one arm out toward the yard, making a beckoning motion. The bounty hunter could see nothing more of the face inside the hood than a dark-colored beard.

"Welcome, *amigos!*" the man shouted, barely audible above the thunder and pounding rain. "Welcome! Come in out of the *storm!*"

Prophet had slid his rifle into its sheath when he'd started up the hill. Now he wished he had it in his hands. Apprehension raking him, he glanced at Louisa, who returned the look, then, squinting skeptically, canted her head toward the barrack.

"What the hell is it?" Louisa was obviously anxious; she hardly ever cursed.

"Monastery!" Big Hans shouted above the wind. "Last time me and Uncle Alphonse was through here, no one was here 'ceptin' a family of mangy coyotes!"

"Amigos!" the man on the roof called once more, throwing an arm forward to beckon wildly. *"Hurry!* Before the lightning fries you to cinders!"

Another lightning bolt lit up the building, silhouetting the figure on the roof. The light flashed off a steel object separating from the man's robe.

Prophet palmed his revolver.

"Trap!" His shout was swallowed by a wind gust. "Let's get the hell outta here!"

18

PROPHET STEADIED HIS Colt against the wind and squeezed the trigger. The revolver belched and leaped in his hand. The man on the massive adobe's shake-shingled roof pitched back and out of sight with a scream that was drowned by the storm.

"Look!" Big Hans shouted, pointing at the building's left door.

Prophet had heard the door scrape open as he'd been looking around wildly for an escape route. Now, holding Mean's reins taut against his chest with one hand, his Colt in the other, he saw a man bolt out through the door and onto the crumbling steps, raising a rifle. Two more followed, one aiming a carbine while the other palmed a revolver.

Prophet fired two quick shots, watching one man throw his head back, wincing, while the second slug plunked into the steps with a chirp.

"*You two vamoose!*" Prophet shouted, thumbing the Colt's hammer back once more. "I ain't gonna tell ya again!"

He aimed and fired another round, pitching another bushwhacker back inside the monastery.

Louisa held one of her Colts in one hand, her skitter-hopping pinto's reins in the other as she looked around wildly. "Which way?"

Prophet ducked as a slug whined past his left ear and barked into a boulder behind him. "Does it matter?"

"Come on!" Hans shouted, hoorawing the screaming clay past both Louisa and Prophet and galloping wide around the monastery's left front corner, the clay's hooves splashing water up around its hocks.

Spying movement to the right, Prophet swung his head that way. Two more men—one in a shabby, steeple-crowned sombrero, the other hatless and wearing a red leather vest over which bandoliers were crossed—stumbled out the right-side door. The man in the vest was thumbing wads into a shotgun while the other man shouted what to Prophet's cowpen comprehension of Spanish sounded like—"Come on in out of the rain, *amigos*! Bring the girl! We have a special gift for her!"

Prophet jerked his gaze toward Louisa, who was triggering a shot toward the left door. "Follow the kid, girl! Looks like we stumbled onto some lonesome banditos!"

Louisa galloped after Hans, triggering a couple more shots at the monastery as several pistols and rifles barked back at her.

The reports sounded little louder than snapping twigs amongst the thunder and lightning, the flames stabbing through the slashing javelins of bullet-sized raindrops. More guns flashed from the broken-out windows, men shouting and whooping, and Prophet emptied his Colt as he gigged Mean into a lunging gallop after Louisa and Hans.

Bullets sizzled through the rain-slashed air around his head as he made a wide turn around the corner of the monastery. Mean flinched as a bullet creased his right hip. Prophet quickly holstered his empty revolver, grabbed his sawed-off shotgun from behind him, and hipped around in his saddle.

Several men were running after him, stumbling drunkenly and shouting in Spanish while triggering lead.

Prophet sent a thundering blast of double-aught buck through the group's center.

One man screamed and dropped while another twisted

around, triggering his pistol into the ground as he grabbed his upper left arm. The third cried *"Mierda!"* and stopped to hop around on one leg, clutching a knee.

Prophet faced forward as Mean galloped through what appeared to be an orchard of some kind. There was an eight-foot-high wall on his right, stretching into the blackness behind the monastery. Ahead, Louisa was a vague, jostling silhouette in the stormy gloom, ducking low-hanging branches.

A rifle stabbed flames from atop the wall, the flash limning a sombrero-topped, silver-trimmed figure crouching there. Louisa's horse screamed, dropped, and rolled—a vague tumbling shape in the darkness. Prophet used his second barrel to blow the man off the roof, the shotgun sounding little louder than a pistol amidst the booming thunder, and raced ahead toward Louisa.

The horse and the girl were already regaining their feet. Limping slightly, Louisa jogged forward and grabbed the horse's muddy reins.

"You all right?" Prophet yelled.

Louisa swung with characteristic ease onto the hurricane deck of the skitter-hopping pinto, which was looking around crazily, eyes bright with terror. "I'll feel better when I've dried out." She slammed her heels against the pinto's ribs, and the horse lunged forward after Hans.

As lightning forked across the sky and the rain continued hammering, Prophet glanced around him and, spying no more gun flashes or figures dashing toward him, he booted Mean after Louisa.

The girl's jostling figure swept in and out of his vision as he cut through the orchard and into the rocky bluffs beyond, rising and falling with the old cart trail he appeared to be on. Mean cut through a broad, rocky valley between thousand-foot cliffs, lightning intermittently revealing the rugged terrain spiked here and there with small tufts of brush and cactus.

As Prophet and Mean galloped up a low rise, a lightning bolt rocketed into the cliff towering on their left. Mean leaped with a start, screaming, as a cabin-sized portion of the cliff lit up like a Mexican Christmas tree, blue-green sparks dancing across the rock. Brimstone peppered the air. There was the low rumble of falling rock.

Prophet and the prancing, snorting dun topped the rise at the same time a horse screamed down the other side. Below, about forty yards beyond the base of the rise, a horse tumbled right of the trail, legs thrashing, whipping its head about furiously. The boulder that the lightning had hurled into the valley was rolling off toward a dry streambed snaking against the base of the opposite cliff.

"Louisa!" Prophet shouted, grinding his spurs into Mean's flanks.

Anxiety pinched down the corners of Prophet's mouth, and he stared unblinking through the downpour. The bouncing boulder must have swept her out of her saddle, no doubt crushed her into pudding.

Mean and Ugly whinnied as he galloped down the rise. A silent prayer tumbled through Prophet's head. *Please don't let her be dead!* Ahead Louisa's pinto rose, shaking its head as if to clear it, reins dangling, stirrups flapping like wings.

No, not Louisa's pinto. As he drew near, he saw that the horse picking itself up out of the mud before him was Big Hans's claybank.

Prophet reined Mean and Ugly to a skidding stop and leaped out of the saddle, hitting the muddy caliche at a dead run and scrambling into the rocks right of the trail. The big kid was on his back, both legs drawn up, head thrown back on his thick shoulders. He cradled his left arm across his belly, rocking to and fro and groaning as he stretched his lips, teeth flashing white in the continuing lightning bursts.

"Hans!" Prophet dropped down beside him, wincing as another lightning bolt hammered the ridge a little lower down than before.

The kid groaned through gritted teeth, his entire body quivering. "Damn rock flew a foot over my head! Scared the shit outta ole Demon! Scared the shit outta *me*!"

Prophet leaned down to inspect the kid's arm, immediately seeing what the trouble was. The kid had landed on a branch, which had ground into the underside of his arm, just before his elbow.

Prophet laid one hand on the kid's arm. With the other he grabbed the end of the branch. "Hold on, Junior. I'm gonna pull it out!"

"Pull *what* out?"

Prophet blinked, frowning. He dropped his head lower, squinting his eyes. Wrong again. It wasn't a branch sticking out of Big Hans's big arm. It was the kid's bone sticking out of his arm! Blood welled out around the splintered end of the bone and the torn, ragged flesh, thinning out in the rain.

"Ah, shit!"

Big Hans gripped his wrist, drawing the broken arm even tighter to his belly. "Look bad?"

"Junior," Prophet said, pushing off his knee and gaining his feet. "You're gonna wanna kill me for this, but there ain't no other way."

Big Hans stared up at him through narrowed, pain-racked eyes. "No other way than what?"

Prophet grabbed the kid's right wrist and forearm with both hands, and planted his right boot against the kid's chest. Quickly, before the kid had time to object, he drew the wrist sharply toward him while holding Hans's chest back with his boot.

There was a sickening crack. The kid screamed shrilly and loudly enough that, for an instant, he drowned out the storm. The scream ended abruptly. Sagging straight back, the kid's face went white as new linen. His eyelids fluttered down over his eyes. He hit the ground with a soft thud, and his head turned sideways, his chin dipping toward his shoulder.

His chest rose and fell slowly.

Prophet dropped to a knee again and lowered his head to inspect the kid's bloody arm. The bone had gone back in. Jerking his neckerchief off, he wound it lengthwise into a two-inch strip, then wrapped it around the kid's upper forearm and knotted it, hoping to keep the bone from sliding back out.

With a heavy sigh, he rose and, leaving the kid in the sopping brush, walked back out onto the trail. Both Mean and the claybank were gone, having high-tailed it uptrail.

Prophet looked both uptrail and down for Louisa, then to both sides, his eyes scouring the rain-lashed terrain. No sign of her. He was certain she'd been ahead of him. If she'd overtaken Big Hans, surely she would have returned by now, looking for the kid and Prophet.

If she was able.

Shoving his concern for the girl aside for now, he glanced at Big Hans. The kid was in shock. Prophet had to get him dry. But first he had to find the horses. Without them, they were both goners.

He moved back off the trail and pulled the unconscious kid into the relative shelter between two boulders. Then, holding his head low against the rain, which was slowing gradually, the lightning bolts growing less frequent, he stretched his legs into a jog uptrail, mud splashing up around his boots and trouser cuffs, spurs ringing softly.

He'd crested two rises when, from the second rise, he saw both horses standing hang-headed on the lee side of a black-granite dinosaur spine humping up out of the boulders to his left. The surly mounts stood side by side as if seeking shelter from each other, too scared to fight.

As Prophet approached, Mean stood where he was but the claybank whinnied angrily and sidestepped into a cleft behind it. The cleft offered him no escape, so when Prophet had mounted his hammer-headed dun, he simply rode over, swiped up the clay's reins, and put Mean and Ugly downtrail, jerking the jittery claybank along behind him.

"Come on, Junior," he said when he'd ridden back to where Big Hans lay between the boulders.

The rain had stopped but the sky was still a purple mass of low, swirling clouds. Lightning flashed in the distance. The thunder had dwindled. The surplus moisture dripped from rocks and shrubs and eddied in shallow gullies. It continued dripping from Prophet's hat.

"Hans," he said, squatting beside the kid, whose chest rose and fell slowly, head tipped to one side.

Out like a blown lamp.

Prophet cursed as he grabbed the kid's stout right arm. Rising, he set his boots beneath him, and drew a deep breath. He grunted fiercely as he pulled the kid up and, crouching, drew the boy's two-hundred-plus pounds over his right shoulder. Turning awkwardly, face creased and red from the strain, he hauled the kid over to the claybank, sucking air through his teeth, his boots making sucking sounds in the muddy clay.

It took a good bit of heavy lifting, pushing, and pulling to get the kid into his saddle, and his good wrist tied to the horn. Big Hans didn't awaken once but only grumbled and groaned and called incoherently for someone named Nancy.

When Prophet had tied the boy's mule-eared boots to his stirrups and wrapped rope around his stout waist and the saddle horn, making sure he wouldn't fall off and discombobulate that broken arm, the bounty hunter mounted Mean and Ugly, who'd been watching him with customary skepticism and downright distrust. He looked around once more for Louisa, his heart thudding heavily. Then, clucking with frustration, he put the horses up the trail. He hoped to find an old cabin or a cave in which he could build a fire and get the boy dried out and comfortable.

Then he'd ride back toward the monastery, scouring the trail for Louisa.

He'd ridden for twenty minutes, the sky clearing but the sun falling westward, when a low, adobe-brick shack appeared ahead and left of the trail, sitting at the base of a low, rocky rise stippled with creosote, greasewood, and saguaros.

Prophet stopped Mean in the trail. He rested his hand on the butt of his .45 as he stared at the cabin—a long, low, flat-roofed affair that was no doubt used as a stopover for fiddle-footing outlaw gangs. Firewood was stacked under a lean-to off the hovel's right-side wall.

Smoke wafted from the brick chimney on the shack's right side, rife with the smell of burning pinyon pine and seasoned frijoles. The windows were lit against the gathering darkness. Voices emanated from inside—the low rumble of bawdy male conversation.

Prophet cursed, glanced at Big Hans sagging sideways in his saddle, the kid's face gaunt and colorless. Prophet had seen men die from shock. The big younker desperately needed a bed and a warm fire.

No time to look for another, vacant cabin.

This one would have to do.

Prophet led the horses behind a knoll, dismounted, and tethered both to an ironwood shrub. Shucking his Winchester, he racked a fresh shell and started around the knoll, heading toward the cabin, spurs ringing crisply in the dense, post-storm silence.

"Sit tight, Junior," he growled, pausing to remove his spurs, setting them on a rock. "I'll be right back."

19

THE PINTO HAD heard the falling rock, loosed by a lightning bolt shaped like a razor-edged scythe, before Louisa had. The horse whinnied shrilly, rising off its front hooves and clawing the air. Louisa was nearly thrown straight back off the mount's butt before she got a hand on the apple.

Glancing up, she saw the black mass of boulders tumbling toward her as though thrown from heaven—bouncing off the steep, scree-covered slope right of the trail. Several broke into smaller pieces on impact with the slope, and continued careening straight toward her.

Louisa leaned forward and rammed her spurs into the pinto's flanks. *"Go!"*

The horse whinnied and, heart hammering beneath the saddle, lurched into a perilous gallop on the uncertain terrain. Louisa had dropped the reins when she'd reached for the saddle horn and now all she could do was cling to the horn, hunkered low, and hope against hope that the horse didn't slip and fall before it decided to stop.

Not a minute ago, she'd realized that she and the pinto, disoriented by the hammering storm, had gotten off the trail that Hans had been following. It was when she'd halted the pinto and begun turning around that the scythe-shaped lightning bolt had plowed into the ridge above her, loosing the rock and giving her no choice but to continue forward through the narrow, winding chasm that she and the pinto were careening through at the moment.

Behind her, the boulders loosed from above rumbled into the chasm with what sounded like two planets colliding. The rock walls to both sides appeared to shake with the violent, reverberating impact, as did the uneven floor beneath the pinto's pounding hooves, the vibrations reaching up through the saddle and into Louisa's thighs.

Thunder crashed and lightning flashed and the rain slanted down like slender spears with hammer-sized heads. The pinto's hooves splashed through puddles, slipping and sliding in the mud and slick, orange gravel.

Thunder roared like a cymbal crashing just off Louisa's right ear, and the pinto whinnied once more and veered left. Louisa gritted her teeth and flinched, expecting to be rammed against the ridge wall on that side of the trail. But as she swayed right against the horse's abrupt turn, she was surprised and relieved to find that she and the horse had not run into the wall but the horse had found another gap.

Louisa looked around through slitted lids beneath the flat brim of her man's hat. Brush and boulders swept past on both sides in a blur, and she caught a glimpse of dark gray sky intermittently lit with lightning flashes between towering mountain walls.

Holding the saddle horn with one hand, she reached toward the pinto's bridle with the other, hoping to catch a rein so she could haul the horse to a stop. She had the hand out beside the horse's head when the pinto lurched again suddenly, taking a left fork in the canyon, and Louisa was thrown right, her left foot slipping free of the stirrup.

It took her a good half minute to right herself, after several times believing she'd fall beneath the horse's pounding hooves. When she sat upright once more she hunkered down over the horn, holding the apple tight with both hands, content to relinquish her will to that of the horrified pinto.

Hazed by the storm up one canyon and down another and over a high, windy rise, lashed by rain and assaulted by thunder, then through a broad canyon once more, the pinto galloped, tireless as the storm itself. Louisa could feel its muscles expanding and contracting beneath the saddle. She could feel its heart beating like a war drum, hear its breath blowing like the wind over a cave mouth.

Suddenly, the horse lurched out from beneath her. The pinto whinnied. Louisa's arms went up as her legs plunged down with the lurching saddle below.

She gasped as cold water flew up to envelop her body with a wicked, knife-edged chill. She flung her hands toward the pinto's neck, but then her head slipped beneath the roiling, tea-colored surface of the stream. Icy, muddy water trickled down her throat and into her lungs. When her head came up, water sluicing off her face, she drew a gasping, choking breath.

Through slitted lids she saw the pinto's head with white-ringed eyes a good twenty yards downstream from her, shifting this way and that in the pounding, swirling current.

To both sides the high, willow-and-mesquite-sheathed banks rushed past. Her stomach fell as she flailed with her hands and kicked with her legs, trying to keep her head above the brutal current tugging her this way and that. She and the pinto had plunged—or had the muddy bank slipped out from beneath the horse's pounding hooves?—into a flooded arroyo churning and roaring with muddy, leaf-and-branch-strewn water from higher up in the mountains.

A branch protruding from the left bank careened toward her. Louisa twisted her body around and threw her left hand toward the branch. She grunted as she clawed at the tip of the branch, but when she got her fingers wrapped around it she was downstream from it, and the dead leaves crumpled in her hand. The branch broke with a nearly inaudible snap.

She continued twisting and turning downstream, the horse now a vague brown shadow thirty or forty yards ahead of her, between the arroyo's rising and falling banks. Several more branches swept toward her, and she tried to reach for them, but the powerful current swept her too quickly down the arroyo.

She didn't know how long she'd been in the water, fighting to keep her head above the surface and to keep from ramming boulders and half-submerged logs, when the current seemed to relent slightly. As the water followed a long bend to the right, it slowed, the banks falling away to either side.

Choking and gasping for breath, feeling mud like sandpaper in her throat, Louisa was vaguely aware that the rain and thunder had stopped and that lightning only flashed in the far distance beyond several dark peaks. But she was aware that she no longer had to try so hard to keep her head above water and that the current was no longer spinning her like a child's top.

Her right boot hit a rock on the arroyo's floor. The other scuffed sand.

The water level continued to drop until she felt both boots skidding along and snagging the bottom. When the water had dropped to the middle of her white blouse, she scrambled over to the left shore, stumbling, several times falling to her knees, her legs feeling both heavy and numb. Along the shoreline, manzanita grass grew amongst the rocks, and tall cottonwoods stood back a ways from the water, still dripping from the recent rain.

Above the cottonwoods, the sky had cleared. It had turned the light green of early evening.

The air was storm-scoured fresh and cool. Birds chirped, wings flashing silver as they wheeled over the brush.

Coughing up water and flecks of mud, Louisa stumbled onto the shore, waterlogged boots squawking beneath her. They felt like lead weights on her feet. She dropped to her knees before a large cottonwood log and, stretching both hands out onto the log, she lowered her head and vomited water, gagging and choking as she sucked air into her aching, battered lungs.

"Hey, somethin' over here!"

Louisa lifted her head. The shout had come from the darkening trees about thirty yards away. Boots thumped and spurs chinged—heavy footsteps moving toward her.

Louisa tried to quell her coughing, but her lungs refused to stop purging themselves of water. Coughing, holding the cottonwood trunk with one hand, she snatched a slippery .45 from its holster with the other and thumbed back the hammer.

The waterlogged pistol made a muffled, feeble sound, and she could feel that the action was soggy. The wet cartridges probably wouldn't detonate.

Still, her chest spasming as more water and mud burst from

her throat, she raised the revolver over the log. A shadow slid in front of her—a boot arcing up from ahead and right, slamming into the underside of her wrist. She grunted as the gun flew up out of her hand, thumping into the brush and rocks to her left.

"Goddamnit, girl—don't you *ever* draw a pistol on me!" The man leaped over the log and, crouching, wrapped a hand around Louisa's throat, driving her back against the sand and grass. "You hear me?"

The man shook her by the neck, staring down at her, stretching his thin, red-mustached lips away from his teeth, deep-set eyes flashing angrily. He wore a blue, threadbare cavalry jacket with tarnished silver captain's bars on each shoulder, two revolvers positioned for the cross-draw on his thighs. Another shoulder holster poked out from behind the jacket, and a tarnished steel saber hung down his right leg. He smelled like sweat and whiskey.

Louisa's misery was enhanced by the man's powerful hand wrapped around her throat, preventing her from either drawing air or expelling more water. Rage seared her, and she wrapped her hands around the man's wrist, trying to wrench his hand free.

As she fought to free herself, more footsteps sounded from the trees. In the corner of her eye, she saw shadows move against the tree trunks.

And she heard a woman's high, authoritative voice. "What is it, Sykes?"

The man stared down at Louisa, chuckling as she struggled against his grip. "Why, it's a girl. Purty one, too!"

Louisa wrenched the man's right thumb back across his hand.

"Ouch!" Sykes bunched his lips as he drew his hand away, eyes pinched with fury. "Little *bitch*!"

As the man drew his right hand back behind his left shoulder, preparing to loose a savage slap, Louisa palmed her other Colt.

"Hold it, Captain!" the woman ordered as she and several men approached, crunching gravel and brush beneath their boots.

Sykes did as ordered, his enraged gaze still riveted on

Louisa. Louisa left her revolver in the cross-draw holster on her right hip, as she let her own gaze wander across the woman—a tall, big-boned girl with muscular legs and broad shoulders. She didn't appear much older than Louisa. Her long, copper-red hair was relieved by thin green streaks all around her head—streaks the same green as her flashing eyes. Three of the tall, long-haired men with hawkish features, each dressed like deranged actors from the stage of some gaudy burlesque show, were near-identical copies of each other.

Triplets.

Louisa's pulse hammered in both temples as she realized, remembering how Big Hans had described the gang that had murdered her cousin, that the flooded arroyo had swallowed her up only to spit her out . . . right smack-dab in the middle of the Three of a Kind Gang.

"Well, whadoya know. . . ." muttered the triplet wearing rose-colored glasses and a shabby black opera hat. He curled a corner of his black-mustached mouth and cut his slitted eyes at the crazy-eyed redhead. "A *girl.*"

"A pretty, *young* girl," said the look-alike in a green-checked suit and straw sombrero, and puffing a fat cigar. He held a Colt Navy in his free hand, down near a savage-looking Arkansas toothpick jutting from a beaded sheath trimmed in gold. He, too, cut his eyes insinuatingly at the redhead.

"An *armed* girl," Sykes growled, reaching down and nudging Louisa's hand away from her holster. She looked down at the man's hand as he grabbed her Colt's pearl grips. Quickly, she tried to decide whether she should let him take the gun.

But even if all the cartridges had remained dry in the flooded arroyo, she wouldn't be able to trim the wick of more than two of these butchers before they turned her into a human sieve. There was no way they could know she was after them. To them, she was just a girl spit out by the arroyo.

She'd bide her time, concoct a plan for how she—all alone, with Prophet and Big Hans probably several miles behind her, on the other side of a blocked canyon—was going to send this kill-crazy crew howling off into eternity.

Sykes slid her Colt from her holster, hefted it in his hand. It was the redhead who asked with a faintly skeptical but soothing tone as she hunkered down on her heels and frowned at Louisa, "Who are you, miss? What the hell you doin' out here, anyways?"

She removed her glove and reached slowly forward to slide a lock of Louisa's wet hair away from her left eye. "How'd you end up almost drownin' to death in that arroyo? Can you tell Cora? Can you?"

Louisa dropped her head to cough, her chest and belly spasming. When she was able to suck a full breath without choking, she looked at Cora—a pretty, oval-faced redhead with the craziest green eyes Louisa had ever seen—and manufactured the most vulnerable expression she could.

"I was tryin' to get back to Uncle Lou's diggin's," she said, making her voice thin and quaking and peaches-and-cream backwoods-wholesome. "But before we could get there, the pinto got scared of the lightning and then, all of a sudden, the ground just sort of disappeared, and me and him were swimmin' for our *lives*!"

20

PROPHET DUCKED BEHIND a boulder and, doffing his hat and curving his finger through his Winchester's trigger guard, he peered around the edge of the rock.

The adobe-brick cabin squatted at the base of the rocky ridge, about fifty yards away. Smoke from its chimney curled against the twilit sky clean-scoured by the recent thunderstorm. The mass of purple clouds flashed intermittently in the far northeastern distance.

Shadows moved in the lantern-lit windows. Men's voices rose. A woman's voice sounded, too—angry, indignant. There was a light, muffled slapping sound. The woman cursed tightly.

Her voice rose slightly louder. "You are *pig*!"

A man chuckled. "If I'm pig, what are you, senorita? You were the one makin' eyes at me in Nogales!"

"I thought you were *gentleman*!"

Several guffaws rose, and the light slaps continued, with the woman cursing tightly, her speech slurred from drink.

"Sure do hate to break up a party." Prophet sighed as he moved out from behind the boulder. He jogged across the open space fronting it, meandering around mud puddles. "Especially when everybody seems to be having so much *fun*!"

He shouldered up to the shack, between the left front window

and the weathered plank door that sagged on rusty hinges,
lantern light showing through the cracks. He reached back for
the double-barreled, ten-gauge sawed-off hanging down his
back, then decided to stay with the Winchester. With the woman
in there, he'd use the barn blaster only as a backup.

He stepped up in front of the door, hearing the voices
from inside, the clink of a bottle against a tin cup, the intermittent slaps, and the woman's angry curses. Backing up,
Prophet lifted his right leg and thrust his foot forward, slamming the boot flat against the door, just right of the leather
latch.

The door burst open, the latch and slivers from the frame
flying into the room. As the door smashed against the wall,
Prophet bounded inside and stopped the door's recoil with his
left boot, raising the Winchester to his right shoulder and
scowling down the barrel.

There were five men in the low-ceilinged room in which a
couple of dusty lanterns shunted deep shadows to and fro. The
place had several bunks and cots. At the back was a table
around which three of the men sat, playing cards and drinking
whiskey from tin cups.

They were a hard-eyed, shaggy, unshaven lot, each with a
pistol or rifle near. When the door had burst open, they jumped
as one, reaching for weapons but turning still as stone when
Prophet bellowed, "Hold it right there, you mangy sons o'
bitches, or I'll blow you outta your spurs. The name's Prophet.
Bounty hunter! Any one of you so much as twitches, I'll buck
you out in a hail of hot lead! Turn ya deader'n a goddamn fence
post!"

Truth was, Prophet had no intention of wasting his time on
these gents. He had bigger fish to fry. But Prophet was no
cold-blooded killer, so he'd let this hard-eyed lot of fetid, human blowflies make the first move.

Frozen in various positions, all five men regarded him with
red-rimmed eyes hard as marbles—three from the table at the
back of the room, one crouched in front of the woodstove and
clad only in longhandles, the other on a cot against the right
wall, about ten feet from Prophet.

The gent on the cot—a half-breed with one eye—lay atop a

black-haired, round-faced woman. The man wore only a grimy undershirt while the woman was as naked as the day she was born, naked knees spread wide.

The half-breed's brown ass dimpled as he glared at Prophet, molasses-colored eyes flashing furiously. A Remington revolver jutted from a black leather holster coiled with a shell belt on the floor, within easy reach of the man's left hand.

"Lou Prophet," one of the men growled, making a face like he'd just bitten into a lemon. He was bald, clean-shaven, and even-featured. He would have been handsome if the tip of his nose wasn't missing, giving him a piggish look.

He wore a sheepskin vest over a blue denim shirt. In one hand he held playing cards; the other hand, trimmed with a giant ruby ring, lay over the silver-plated Schofield on the table before him, near a black cheroot sending pale smoke ribboning into the cloud already filling the cabin.

"Mark Diamond," Prophet growled back. "I shoulda known if Lyle Hawk was around, you wouldn't be far. There's a mangy cur ghostin' every gut wagon."

Diamond lifted a mouth corner. "You don't really think you're gonna bring us all in, do ya?"

"Not really. No."

Prophet had taken down enough owlhoots to know which of a group would move first. That's why he was ready, after having read the eyes of each of these five, for the man in the longhandles by the snapping sheet-iron stove to drop the wood he had in his left hand and to grab the Henry repeater standing against a wood box with his right.

Prophet shot him before he'd lifted the Henry a foot above the floor, the Winchester's explosion filling the entire room and causing the whore to scream, *"Maria madre de la Jesus!"*

As the man in the longhandles screamed, flying back against the woodstove, then screaming even louder, Mark Diamond snapped up his silver-plated Schofield and leaped to his feet, throwing his chair straight out behind him.

Racking a fresh shell into the Winchester breech, Prophet drew a bead on Diamond's chest, squeezed the trigger, and watched through the wafting gun smoke as the bullet drilled a quarter-sized hole through Diamond's blue denim shirt, rocking the man back on his heels and sending his triggered slug into the ceiling above the table.

Two more quick shots dispatched the other two men at the table. Aware of the man on the cot to his right, Prophet had no sooner fired his fourth round before he dove forward into the room.

The man on the cot had reached down and grabbed his Remy from its holster. The Remy roared. The slug sliced across Prophet's back and into the adobe wall to his left as he rolled off a shoulder.

The man on the cot drilled another round across Prophet's left cheek.

Rising onto his knees, the bounty hunter snapped the rifle to his shoulder once more and drilled two quick shots through the half-breed's chest and one more through his left cheek.

The man screamed and slammed against the wall behind him, triggering a slug into the ceiling, eyes snapping wide with pain and horror. Flopping around on the cot beneath him, the woman screamed and covered her head with her arms.

Prophet racked another round and swung toward the rear of the room, his cartridge casings clattering onto the earthen floor behind him. Squinting through the powder, wood, and tobacco smoke, Prophet saw that all four men at the rear of the room were down and still.

Spying movement to his right, he jerked around toward the cot. The half-breed dropped down from the wall against which Prophet's slugs had pinned him and collapsed like an oversized puppet, his hairy, naked legs slapping together, his shaggy head lolling to one side, blood welling up in a corner of his thin-lipped mouth.

His black eyes rolled toward Prophet and widened slightly just before they glazed over in death.

A long sigh rumbled up from his chest. His legs twitched before gradually falling still.

"*Mierda!*" the woman screamed, cowering against the wall, drawing her naked legs toward her chest. Her huge, brown-nippled breasts swayed as she raised her arms to her head as though to shield herself, and she turned her hands toward Prophet, palms out. "*Por favor!* Please, mister, don't *shoot!*"

"Pipe down." Prophet lowered the Winchester and kicked the half-breed's Remy under the cot. "I've never shot a woman without damn good cause."

Keeping his Winchester aimed from his hip, he stomped back into the cabin's shadows, and inspected each of the bodies. Deeming them dead, including the child killer and notorious Utah bank robber Mark Diamond, he grabbed the log that the man in the longhandles had dropped on the floor and chunked it into the stove.

He strode back to where the whore sat on the cot, one leg dangling over the edge, the other knee raised. She held her hands to her neck, half hiding her amazing, pointed breasts between her elbows, and gave Prophet a brash up-and-down, swishing a light brown foot against the floor.

Prophet looked at her. She wasn't bad-looking for a whore in this neck of the woods, but she'd known some tough years. They were written in the deep lines around her mouth and eyes, one of which was lightly bruised. She had a small, glistening cut on her chin. Her cinnamon hair curled, thick and rich, to her shoulders, giving a glimpse of two silver hoop rings dangling from her ears.

"You with this bunch by choice?" Prophet asked her.

She looked down at the half-breed bleeding onto the floor and wrinkled her nose. "They *took* me out of Nogales. Said I would entertain them out here, while they planned their next job." She spat a wad of spit onto the half-breed's ruddy cheek, then plucked a brown bottle off a nearby shelf and threw back a drink. "I'm *glad* you killed them. Now I can go back to Nogales and feed my dogs."

"Where's their horses?"

She jerked her head toward the back of the cabin. "Stable out back in the brush. If you are taking their horses, leave me one." She rolled her brown eyes up to give him a lascivious look. " 'Less you want take me with *you*, uh?"

Prophet snorted and headed for the door. "Be right back."

He ducked out of the cabin and retraced his steps back to where Big Hans sat on his claybank near Mean and Ugly. The kid was groaning and sort of whimpering in his sleep, his head thrown back on his shoulders. If not for the rope securing him to the saddle, he'd have rolled straight back off the clay's ass.

Prophet led both horses back to the cabin and tethered them to the hitchrack out front. He gently maneuvered the kid out of the saddle, but couldn't help, because of the younker's two-hundred-plus bulky pounds, a semi-rough landing. Big Hans sagged toward the clay and lifted his head, groaning.

"Wh . . . where . . . ?"

"Easy, kid," Prophet said, snaking Hans's good arm around his neck and leading him toward the open door. "Have you bedded down in no time."

"Wh . . . where the hell . . . Jesus God, my arm hurts!"

"Leave it be, boy, or . . ."

Prophet let his voice trail off. He and Hans had stopped just in front of the hovel's open door. The woman was on one naked knee at the back of the room, a blanket draped so carelessly about her shoulders that it hardly covered a thing.

She had Mark Diamond's left hand draped over her thigh and was cursing softly in Spanish as she tugged on the dead man's large ruby ring, her voluminous breasts slanting out from her chest and pillowing out over the dead, pale fingers.

Sensing Prophet's stare from across the room, the woman looked up. Her thick brows wrinkled, and her eyes grew peeved. "They paid me for only one night in Nogales. For none of the half dozen nights they have held me here like a rabid bitch in this maggot patch of a vermin-infested casa!"

Prophet continued guiding Big Hans toward the cot where the woman and the half-breed had been frolicking. "Reckon it ain't stealin' if you're stealin' from a thief . . . and a dead one, far as that goes."

He chuckled as he ruminated absently on the breed of humanity he'd discovered so far in the Seven Devils Range. He sobered quickly, however, when he considered that his estimation of humanity, based fairly or unfairly on what he'd discovered here, was only bound to worsen.

When he'd gotten Hans lying down on the cot, the kid still grumbling and holding tight to the wrist of his broken arm, Prophet reached down and started dragging the half-breed out the cabin door by his ankles.

When he'd gotten the half-breed outside and about forty

yards north along a narrowing, winding canyon and partially concealed in rocks, he went back for the others.

Ten minutes later, he returned to the cabin, breathing hard from his labors, to find the whore sitting on the edge of the cot beside Hans. She was sponging the boy's broad, sweaty forehead with a damp cloth. A basin of water rested on her near-naked thighs, and a corked canteen lay at her bare feet, beside the brown bottle from which she'd been drinking.

She turned as Prophet walked in. "What happened to your young friend?"

"Boulder rolled down a ridge, damn near took his head off." Prophet stood gazing down at the whore. Tiring of having his gaze attracted to her amazing bosoms, he drew the blanket across her chest with a sigh. "Can you tend him for an hour or two? I done lost another friend in the storm. I'm gonna ride back a ways, see if I can track her."

"I am not going anywhere until morning."

Prophet hunkered beside the kid, placed his hand on the boy's heavy shoulder. "Hans, if you can hear me, I'm gonna leave for a while. This nice lady's gonna stay with you." Prophet glanced at the woman. "What's your name?"

"Loretta."

Prophet glanced at the woman. "This is Big Hans."

The kid's eyes fluttered, and he turned his head from side to side, the very picture of misery. His skin was pasty, his blond hair sweat-matted and mud-flecked. Perspiration beaded his forehead and streamed down his cheeks. "I . . . I reckon I'll be here, Lou."

"Loretta's got some whiskey, and I reckon she'd share if you asked her real—"

Prophet stopped when the woman, who had just twisted around to stare wide-eyed toward the door, screamed, *"Mierda! Look out!"*

The bounty hunter wheeled around, swinging the sawed-off ten-gauge out from behind his back. In the doorway, the half-breed stood, stooped and pale and bloody, regarding Prophet with bloodshot, heavy-lidded eyes as he raised a .36-caliber Remington that he must have produced from a boot well. As Prophet threw his back against the cot, he raised the ten-gauge one-handed, thumbing back both rabbit-eared hammers.

Ka-boooommmm!

The resurrected half-breed was blown straight back out the door in a spray of blood and viscera, as though he'd been pulled out from behind by a log chain attached to a six-mule hitch with their tails on fire.

21

"THERE'S MY HORSE!" Louisa said, still down on her butt behind the log with the bizarre Three of a Kind Gang standing in a half circle around her in the quickly fading light. The men regarded her suspiciously, hands on their gun butts while the young woman, Cora, was a little more fawning than Louisa felt comfortable with.

Louisa stretched her gaze around the group while a burly black man with a red sash led the pinto through the trees. The man's skin was as black as his frock coat, four-in-hand tie, black hat, and canvas breeches. At times only his white shirt and red sash could be seen against the ink-black cottonwood trunks that he and the horse were passing through.

The pinto snorted and coughed as the man led him by his reins and bridle bit, the horse's saddle and Louisa's bedroll hanging down its left side, so that her two rifle sheaths flapped around up near the horse's back. Both sheaths were empty. Her saddlebags were gone.

As the black man approached, she saw that he was carrying her Winchester in the same hand as the one in which he held the reins. No sign of her Sharps.

"Oh, joy—you found him!" Louisa exclaimed, keeping up her routine of lost little babe in the desert, and hoping that the men would pull their horns in, thus making it easier for her in due time to blow their hearts out their spines in a vapor of blood and bone.

"We heard the whinnies down arroyo," Cora said.

"Well, well, well," the black man said, stopping the horse on the other side of the log and staring down at what the arroyo had washed in. "What in the pure-devil, ever-lovin' hell we got here?"

"It's a girl," said Captain Sykes, chuckling. "What's it look like, Heinz?"

Her lungs still feeling boggy, Louisa began to scramble to her feet, then did her best playacting as she dropped to her knees suddenly and convulsed in more lung spasms that were not so much feigned as exaggerated. "Thank you, sir," she croaked between coughs, lifting her head toward the black man called Heinz, twisting her face with feigned misery. "Without my horse . . . I'd truly . . . be lost out here."

Cora dropped down beside her and placed a hand on her lurching back. "Actually, I was the one who found your horse, Miss . . ."

"Louisa," Louisa croaked.

"I was the one who found your horse, Miss Louisa. But don't tell me you're thinking of getting back on him tonight!"

"Gettin' back on him and ridin' *where*—that's what I wanna know," Heinz said.

"Will you quit, Rosco?" Cora scowled up at the big black man. "She's been through a terrible ordeal. Why, she nearly drowned in the arroyo while trying to make her way back to her uncle's mine diggin's."

"Diggin's!"

This from the look-alike in the Lincoln-style top hat. He, like the others, had a singsong Southern accent even more pronounced than Prophet's. Louisa had never visited the South, but even to her ears his accent called up mossy oaks sprawled across rolling, emerald-green hills and pillared mansions adorned with Southern belles and straight-backed gentleman in impeccable beards and black, clawhammer coats.

The look-alike in the Abe Lincoln hat rolled his cigar from one side of his mouth to the other. "Who the hell's diggin' out here? The whole damn range is taken over by outlaws and 'Paches!"

"Shit, I ain't seen a prospector—at least not a *live* one—in a month of Sundays," said the look-alike in the green-checked suit. He stood out against the gathering darkness like a green spring meadow.

"You haven't seen my Uncle Lou," Louisa sniffed. "Now, if you'll excuse me . . ." She gained her knees and swooned. While she wasn't in love with the idea of taking the gang on herself, now that she was here she saw no reason to leave. But looking like she *wanted* to stay would make the gang suspicious. "I reckon I'll be back . . . on my . . . way. . . ."

She made her eyelids flutter and sagged to one side, as though about to pass out.

"Oh, no, you won't, dearie," Cora said, letting Louisa fall against her and wrapping her arm around Louisa's waist. "You're not going anywhere—not in your condition. Rafe, carry her up to my shack."

"I'll do it," the man called Sykes said, stepping forward and stretching out his hands toward Louisa.

"I want Rafe to do it," Cora said.

Sykes furled his bushy red brows. "Huh?"

Cora turned to Rafe standing with his hawk-faced, long-haired brothers—the three standing around like actors all garbed up with no lines to perform. She smiled mockingly and said with a sneer, "Because the Flute boys ain't so *willing.*"

The Flute in the top hat tossed his cigar onto the ground and bolted forward angrily, spitting out in his petal-soft, anger-edged accent, "Now, lookee here, Cora. My brothers and I are the leaders of the troupe, and we're goddamn tired of putting up with your insults against our manhood."

Rafe said, "And don't forget who's ramroddin' this group, girl! We're the ones who threw it together, and we're damn certain sure the ones who . . ."

"The ones who'd have gotten us all thrown into Yuma pen six months ago if I hadn't joined up and taught you boys the proper way to rob a bank and take down a payroll shipment!"

Cora straightened and placed a hand on the grips of one of her revolvers, leaning forward at the waist. Sagging against the

young woman's thigh, as if only half conscious, Louisa stared
at the men through slitted lids, feeling Cora's mad, defiant
fury flutter up from deep down in her heels.

"Without me, you goddamn tinhorned sons of the Rebel
South would be wobblin' and reelin' around like schoolboys
drunk on their first warm beer. And you'd best take your hand
away from your pistol there, Billy Earl, 'less you want a lead
swap, though I doubt there'd be much of a *swap*!"

Cora lowered her voice with menace, twisting and turning
her out-thrust face as she continued her tirade, her green-
streaked red hair dancing about her shoulders. "You boys fancy
yourselves fast, but you know as well as I do that there ain't one
of ya *faster* . . . or more *willin'* . . . than good ole Cora. Now,
get your hand away from that .45, ya damn peckerwood, or fill
it, and fill it *now*. This is the last damn argument I'm ever gonna
have with you."

Billy Earl stood, hand still draped over the butt of his .45,
staring through the semidarkness at Cora. It was too dark to
see his face clearly, but Louisa saw that his eyes were as
white-ringed as those of an enraged bronc, and his long,
slender legs were quivering. His skinny chest rose and fell
heavily beneath the ruffled white shirt he wore under a bur-
gundy vest trimmed with silver piping. His cavernous cheeks
dimpled, and Louisa thought she could even hear his molars
grinding.

The others had fallen silent and as still as stone statues.

Cora's leg against Louisa's cheek did not shake or flutter in
the least. Her blood ran calmly through her veins as she waited
for Billy Earl to make the first move. This girl, Louisa thought
with a vague apprehensive air while waiting for lead to fly,
might even be nervier than she, Louisa, was.

"Oh, for Christ's sakes," muttered the look-alike in the
brown-checked suit, bulling up between Billy Earl and Sykes.
"Lower your tails, both of you. I'll give the damn girl a tow."

He chuffed as he leaned down toward Louisa. She let herself go limp as the man snaked his arms beneath her, straightened, and started to carry her through the group still standing
around the log, toward the rustling cottonwoods. Fires glowed
ahead through the trees, and Louisa could see several ancient
stone huts huddled amongst rocks and cactus along the base

of a steep slope rising into shadows toward a ridge over which stars were kindling.

Behind her, the others followed, spurs trilling and heels grinding gravel. The pinto clomped, shod hooves ringing off stones. A couple of the men—it sounded like Sykes and the black man, Heinz—spoke in hushed tones, chuckling.

"What ya got there, Custer?"

Louisa, flopping like a dead fish in Custer's arms, let her eyes roll to the right. Three men slowly materialized from the shadows, two leading three horses while the third, striding ahead of the others, batwing chaps fluttering about his denim-clad legs, moved toward her and Rafe.

One of the men flanking the man approaching appeared nearly as large and hairy as a grizzly bear. He wore Mexican-cut clothes and a steeple-crowned sombrero. It was from this man, moving up behind the leader, that a sickly sweet smell seemed to emanate, making Louisa's nose constrict.

"Caught us a fish in the creek, we did," Custer said, letting his words roll with an accented flourish over his velvet tongue. "A little blond fish, purty as a speckled pup, and half drowned."

"Cora wants to tend her her own self," said Sykes, coming up behind Custer with the others, his own voice teeming with a sneer, "in her own shack . . . of course. . . ."

Cora told Sykes to diddle himself as she walked up beside Rafe and Louisa. The newcomer approached from the left—a tall, slender gent in a crisp black Stetson and black vest over a ruffled white shirt. He wore two guns in holsters, and had another pistol wedged over his belly, behind his cartridge belt.

The flickering firelight showed a rakishly handsome face, tanned by the sun, with a clean jawline and straight nose above a trimmed, cherry-blond mustache. Blond hair of the same hue curled down over his ears. On his feet he wore beaded Indian boot moccasins.

"What the hell are you talkin' about, Custer?" The newcomer chuckled.

Custer stopped and turned to the man. He jostled Louisa in his arms. Louisa fluttered her eyes and groaned a little, wagging her head from side to side as if to clear it. "Sure enough," Custer said. "Ain't she purty as a rose petal, Squires? You'd prob'ly rather I took her to your shack, but you'll have to take that up with Miss Cora."

The man called Squires slitted his blue eyes, which flashed in the crimson fires' glow, as he ran his gaze back and forth along Louisa's body sprawled across Rafe's arms. He whistled and poked his hat back from his broad, tan forehead. "Damn. You're tellin' me the arroyo just up and spit that out?"

The big, bearlike Mexican pushed his round, scarred face over Squires's left shoulder, his broad nostrils expanding and contracting, letting his black-eyed gaze roam across Louisa. He grunted and sniffed. Louisa's eyes burned from his stench—the fetor of several dead men staked out in the sun—but the others didn't seem to notice.

"Keep movin', Custer," Cora ordered. "I don't have time to palaver with snakes."

"Hold on." Squires pulled Custer back by his arm and stared down at Louisa once more. He chuckled, shook his head, and slid a conspiratorial glance at the big Mexican. "Don't know as I've ever seen a girl like that out here—aside from Miss Cora her own self, of course." His tone grew skeptical, suspicious, and he canted his head to one side, squinting an eye at the pretty blond in Custer's arms. "Who is she and where'd she come from? Anyone with her?"

"If they is," said the top-hatted Billy Earl, smoking a cigar off Custer's left flank, "they done washed up farther down the arroyo."

Squires held his gaze on Louisa, who gave a little cough. He growled, "Someone cut her tongue out?"

"She damn near drowned in the flood," Cora said. "I'm puttin' her to bed. You can make all your inquiries tomorrow, Jay."

Cora jerked her head forward, and Custer continued walking ahead, toward a gap between two of the ancient stone shacks that looked little more than window- and doorless shells, a couple with half-collapsed brush roofs, all surrounded by boulders and grown up with chaparral.

Behind, Jay said, "You want me to join you two tonight, Kitten, just toss a rock my way."

"I'll toss a rock, all right, you fork-tongued son of a bitch!"

Cora grunted and continued striding along with Custer and Louisa, back into the shadows away from the fires. "I'd rather you sent that big, stinking bean eater of yours."

"Don't go gettin' overly distracted now, Cora," Sykes called, angling off in another direction. "Remember—we got us a little job day after tomorrow."

He and Heinz chuckled. Cora told them to diddle each other. Heinz cursed.

As Custer walked back into the brush, Cora strode ahead, heading for a shack set back from the others. The windows were lit with lantern light.

The place had a brush roof and a narrow porch that appeared to have been recently repaired with new boards. There was a timbered door. Cora strode onto the porch, threw the door open, and stepped aside as Custer carried Louisa over the threshold, sidestepping through the narrow opening.

Cora pointed toward a bed in a far, dark corner that the light shed by a single lamp hanging from a ceiling beam did not reach. "Put her there and vamoose."

Custer chuckled as he set Louisa on the bed covered with a bobcat hide. As he turned back toward the tall redhead standing by the open door, he gave a lavish bow. He strode toward her and stopped a foot away from her, then slid his face to within six inches of hers.

"Don't talk to us like that again, Cora. Not Rafe, Billy Earl, or me. You might be faster an' more willin' than my brothers, but you and I both know you ain't faster nor more willin' than *me*."

Custer glanced back at Louisa, who lay on the bed, hands on her belly as she continued pretending that her swim in the river had taken a higher toll than it had. As the sombrero-hatted outlaw turned back to Cora, he said, "And your tastes ain't no *purer* than ours, neither. So save your venom for Jay an' his boys . . . once we get our hands on that gold."

Custer kissed his index finger, pressed the finger to Cora's forehead, and strode out the door and into the night.

"Faggot!" Cora slammed the door.

Running the sleeve of her flowered blouse across her forehead and bunching her lips with revulsion, she strode over to the bed and stared down at Louisa.

"You're pretty." She ran the back of her hand across Louisa's mud-streaked cheek. "Damn purty."

She hunkered low, shoved her face to within inches of Louisa's, and smiled. The smile did not extend to her green, cat-like eyes. Saliva crackled as she stretched her lips back from her teeth.

"Now, suppose you tell me what you're *really* doing here, Pretty Girl."

22

FOR THE SECOND time that night, Prophet dragged the half-breed out to the edge of the yard and rolled him up onto the other four dead men. Prophet had no doubt the man was really dead this time, as there were nearly two separate halves of the man to drag off, such was the size of the wound that the ten-gauge gut shredder had carved through his middle.

That task completed, the bounty hunter wiped the blood off his hands in some Mormon tea growing near the cabin, then turned Big Hans's claybank into the well-concealed brush corral in which the outlaws' horses milled. Mounting Mean and Ugly, he headed back the way he'd come, scouring the thickening, still-dripping darkness for Louisa, thoroughly baffled and anxious and wondering what had become of his hot-blooded, headstrong partner.

He doubted that the banditos they'd fought off at the monastery had taken her, because she'd been ahead of Prophet, and he would have seen any banditos overtaking them. Of course, Apaches were always a threat out here, but in a raging desert gully washer?

Most likely her horse had fallen, and she was lying along the trail somewhere, injured, possibly dead.

When he came to the scuffed area marking where Big Hans had been dislodged from his claybank, he continued moving north, staring at the terrain even more closely, keeping his Winchester's butt handy beneath his right thigh while holding the sawed-off ten-gauge straight out from his belly. The banditos from the monastery were no doubt twanging guitars in front of a warm fire by now, but he wasn't taking any chances.

The farther he rode without seeing any sign of Louisa or her pinto, the heavier and sharper the frustration grew inside him.

Between two hogbacks, he drew back on Mean and Ugly's reins and frowned down at the ground just left of the trail. Hoofprints, nearly obliterated by the wind and rain and darkness, angled off to the west.

If Louisa had gotten off the trail here, between these hills, Prophet wouldn't have seen her. The terrain being a mess of rocks, brush, and several fallen saguaro skeletons, it would have been easy for Louisa to mistake the forking game trail for the trail Big Hans had been following. Especially during the height of the storm.

Prophet followed the game trail meandering through the scrub and into a dark defile in the canyon wall. He'd ridden only a few minutes when a black earthen mass rose up before him—a good two-hundred-foot-high pile of broken boulders that completely blocked the passageway. The faint, sporadically washed-out prints Prophet had been following disappeared at the base of the slide.

The jagged mass loomed before him, wedged tight between the defile's steep walls and capped with stars flickering down from a black velvet sky. The muddy earth around it was scuffed and scraped from the recently fallen rock, several saguaros and ironwood shrubs flattened beneath wagon- and barrel-sized slabs. Many chunks had rolled several yards out behind Prophet, leaving scuffed, water-filled troughs in their wake.

Again, Prophet looked at the tracks that disappeared at the rock pile's base. He rose up in his saddle, his heart thudding. If Louisa had ridden this way—and it looked like she had— either she lay crushed at the bottom of the slide, or she'd made it through before the defile had been sealed and was wandering around on the other side.

"Louisa, goddamnit . . ."

Prophet's own voice startled him. It sounded unnaturally loud and forlorn in the quiet desert night relieved occasionally by the scuffs of some burrowing critter, the distant bugling of a wild mustang, and the soft hoof thuds of a foraging javelina.

Finally, convinced that there was no way through the massive snag, and that to find Louisa he'd have to locate another route back behind the mountain walls on either side of it, he reined Mean and Ugly around and jogged back the way he'd come, his hoof clomps echoing in the stony silence.

When the defile fell back behind him, he took a sharp right and rode along the base of the steep western ridge humping up blackly in the darkness, searching desperately for another passage south.

He rode for a good hour, finding nothing but occasional clefts and box canyons, a few more fresh rock slides, what appeared to be an ancient prospector's dilapidated fieldstone cabin at the bottom of a cactus-choked arroyo, and a pile of fresh bobcat plop. No more defiles or passages into the next canyon.

Tired and weary, he realized that his fevered following of the ridge base had gotten him perilously disoriented; it took him another hour to find his way back to the cabin.

He took the time to rub Mean and Ugly down thoroughly before feeding and watering the mount, then turning him into the brush corral with the claybank and the outlaws' horses. Inside the cabin, he found Big Hans snoring raucously and smelling like a whiskey vat.

The whore, Loretta, sat on a nearby cot with a couple of blankets wrapped around her shoulders, her whiskey bottle propped against a hip. She strummed a beat-up guitar—a sad, lonely Mexican ballad that complemented Prophet's dark mood and his worry over Louisa.

He went over and picked up the bottle. Loretta continued singing, eyes on some spot in the low ceiling on the other side of the room, as if at the man or the lost, lamented years she was

singing about. Prophet took a couple of pulls of the busthead,
corked the bottle, returned it to Loretta's hip, then sagged down
to the first cot he came to.

Pensive, his thoughts on Louisa, he pulled off his boots. He
doubted he'd sleep, but he needed some rest if he was going to
do more than a half-assed job of looking for the girl in the
morning.

He pulled his blankets up to his neck, closed his eyes, and
as Loretta continued keening and plucking the solemn guitar
strings, he drifted faster than he'd thought possible into a
deep, warm pool of healing darkness.

"Come on, Pretty Girl. You can tell Cora. What're you *really*
doing here?"

Cora stretched out on the bed beside Louisa. Her lips
widened into a smile, but the skin above the bridge of her nose
was furled, a dark cast in her crazy, green eyes. Her left hand had
disappeared under the bed, and now, as she rolled toward Louisa,
until Cora's breasts were mashing into Louisa's, she lifted a
bone-handled stiletto up high so that the wan lantern light
flashed off the round, pointed steel blade.

Louisa's blood rushed to her face—a toxic mixture of fear
and fury. Mostly fury. She remembered Big Hans's story
about the gang including Cora chasing Louisa's cousin into
the rocky desert north of Seven Devils. Her cousin had either
been thrown off the cliff, or she'd jumped off to save herself
from more of the same torture she'd no doubt suffered in the
brothel. To save herself from the kind of deaths suffered by
her son and her husband.

Despite her boiling blood, Louisa kept her face implacable
as she watched the stiletto drop slowly toward her face. Cora
laid the tip against Louisa's nose. Nibbling her lower lip, the
redheaded killer slid the stiletto tip across Louisa's lips to her
chin. The sharp blade, not quite tearing the skin, traced a
straight line down Louisa's neck.

"Sooo purty." Cora swallowed, her pale cheeks flushing
slightly, as she followed the blade's trail with her eyes. "Such
soft skin."

As she slid the blade down between Louisa's breasts, which

her wet shirt conformed to like a second skin, Cora lowered her head and pressed her lips to Louisa's left cheek.

"Gotta tell me," she said in a strange singsong. " 'Cause, ya see, I don't believe that story about you and your old, prospectin' Uncle Lou. Uh-huh. Not in the least bit." She stopped the stiletto halfway down Louisa's chest and pressed the tip against Louisa's left breast. It barely pierced the surface, feeling about like a mosquito bite.

Louisa didn't wince. She gazed coldly into the crazy, murdering woman's face.

Holding the blade still against Louisa's breast, keeping a firm pressure, Cora pressed her lips to Louisa's other cheek— a warm, lingering, diabolical kiss. "No siree, girl. When I first saw your eyes, you know what I saw?"

She drew her lips back from her teeth, the spittle crackling softly as she opened her mouth slightly, lifting her chin to stare down both sides of her nose. "I saw myself."

For a half second, Louisa felt as though the stiletto blade had slipped through her skin to pierce her heart. Though she kept a level stare, the young woman seemed to sense her reaction. Cora lifted her chin slightly and pursed her lips. "Now," she said, "you gonna tell me what you're doin' in the Seven Devils?"

Louisa let a stretched second pass. Then she nodded once and, clicking back the hammer of the double-barreled, silver-chased derringer that she'd slipped out of her boot when Custer had laid her on the bed, she said, "I'm here to blow your vile brains all over that wall over there, see?" She hardened her jaws as she angled the popper's upper and lower barrels toward Cora's left temple. "Because you killed my cousin and her son and husband, and then you burnt her town. Remember?"

Cora's eyes grew glassy with shock and caution as they slid toward the derringer in Louisa's fist.

Louisa's voice grew taut as she said softly, "I rather figured you would."

Louisa's fury was a wild mustang inside of her. There was no taming it, no reining it in despite her knowing that the shot would alert the other gang members and no doubt get her killed.

Still, her index finger tightened against the trigger. As it did, Cora jerked her left elbow up and twisted her head sideways, lifting her chin and snarling like a bobcat.

Louisa's derringer popped loudly. Cora squealed as the bullet carved a bloody gash across the nub of her right cheek and a bloody notch across the top of her right ear. As she flew sideways off the bed and hit the floor with a loud, tearing shriek of pain and fury, Louisa dropped her legs to the floor and lowered the derringer toward Cora scrambling on all fours toward the little shack's opposite wall.

Louisa had vaguely heard, beneath the hammering fury in her ears, the thud of loudening footsteps as men approached the cabin. Now a sharp exclamation rose from outside. As the door burst open and the handsome gent, Squires, bolted into the room clawing a revolver from a low-thonged holster, Louisa rose to her feet and, hair flying about her head, teeth gritted, swung the peashooter toward the door.

The derringer popped.

At the same time, Squires threw himself sideways, tripping over his own boots and piling up at the base of the far wall with a pained grunt and a curse. Louisa's .32-caliber slug had slammed into the chest of the tall, skinny gent rushing in behind Squires.

He groaned and, throwing his arms up and wincing as dust puffed from the hole in his soiled duck shirt and dusty, sun-faded vest, stumbled back out the cabin's open doorway.

Cora was kneeling at the base of the far wall, in front of Squires. The handsome blond outlaw, bunching his lips and slitting his eyes, raised his revolver toward Louisa, who bolted to her left.

The revolver roared, the slug slamming into the stone wall above the bed.

Louisa took two long, running strides and dove through one of the room's two windows, hearing the bark of Squires's six-shooter once more and feeling a bullet nip her boot heel as it cleared the window ledge.

"Get that little bitch!" Cora squealed.

Squires fired two more quick, hammering shots as Louisa hit the ground outside—a violent landing on the stony, prickly ground still wet from the rain—then rolled down a slight grade to the base of a gnarled cedar.

Back inside the shack, Squires shouted, "I'm not shooting at rats, my heart!"

There was the rake of soft leather heels as Squires scrambled to his feet inside the shack. Outside, heart hammering, Louisa gained her own feet.

Clawing at the ground with her hands and digging her heels into the sand and gravel, she bolted out from under the cedar and headed up the grade toward cover in the form of rocks, shrubs, and boulders rising blackly against the starlit sky.

"Get back here, little one!"

Squires's mocking, echoing shout was drowned by two more loud revolver barks. The slugs plunked into the gravel just inches off Louisa's pounding, raking heels as she half crawled and half ran up the rocky slope toward the towering northern ridge a good two hundred yards away.

When the echoes of Squires's last two shots had dwindled, he shouted, "Got us a crazed polecat, fellas! Better come hither and pronto. I mean, *vamoose!*"

The voice, muffled by the growing distance Louisa was putting between herself and the cabin, echoed ominously in the silent, clean, pine-scented night. She hadn't run far amongst the ruined shacks cropping up out of the chaparral, looking as though they'd been here as long as the rocks, when she realized the flooded arroyo had taken more out of her than she'd thought.

Her feet and legs grew heavy, her breath short. Her lungs felt little larger than prunes. Her chest ached.

Behind her, the outlaws were calling back and forth. A couple whooped and yowled like wolves on the blood scent. Cora continued screaming so shrilly that Louisa couldn't make out her words, though she was sure the crazed she-bitch was demanding Louisa's head.

Boots thumped, gravel crunched, and spurs rang. Louisa could hear labored breaths raking in and out of her pursuers' lungs as they stormed up the grade behind her and fanned out across the slope, stalking her. She could sense their bloodlust, the thrill of the chase, the fevered anticipation of what they'd do once they caught her.

If they caught her, she knew what they'd do. And without her weapons and ammunition for the derringer, there'd be nothing she could do about it.

23

WHEN LOUISA HAD run a good hundred yards up the slope from Cora's cabin, she stopped near what appeared to be an old mine yawning blackly in the slope before her, surrounded with cracked rocks, weathered lumber, and a rusted, overturned wheelbarrow overgrown with buckbrush and junipers.

She dropped to a knee, breathing hard.

Down the slope behind her, the killers were flitting shadows amongst the rocks and cactus. Upslope, another two or three hundred yards away—it was hard to judge in the darkness—the sheer northern ridge loomed. One of the devil-shaped spires giving the range its name rose from the ridge's mantel-like crest, climbing another three or four hundred feet skyward from the rest of the ridge.

Looking around the broad, deep canyon in which the ancient village nestled, Louisa saw that the other surrounding ridges were capped with similarly shaped devil-like spires complete with tails and eroded horn-shaped stones protruding from their elongated tips. A couple even wielded what looked like pitchforks.

The devil-like formations surrounding her didn't so much heighten her fear as make her wish the big, Georgian saddle tramp who'd sold his soul to the Devil, Lou Prophet, were here. Armed with his mean and ugly horse and his sawed-off, double-barreled barn blaster, he'd find a way to save her in his clumsy, awkward way and blow out the lamps of the howling demons moving in on her now.

But Prophet was no doubt somewhere on the other side of the devil-capped, star-shrouded northern ridge, miles away in the darkness, and wondering where she was but too far away to save her.

Downslope, something flashed, and then the gun's roar reached Louisa's ears. There was a shrill, animal shriek and the muffled thrashing of trampled brush.

"You git her?" one of the men yelled about fifty yards downslope and right.

"Javelina," called another, a wry pitch to his voice.

Louisa quickly considered her options and decided that she couldn't continue moving. Unable to outdistance the gang, and without the means to fight them, she'd be overtaken in minutes. She had to hide.

Remaining crouched, she swiveled her head, looking around. On the other side of the gaping mine hole, three low stone walls rose from the scrub. Part of the old brush roof remained, partly attached to one of the vine-covered walls.

Louisa scrambled over to what remained of the shack, circled, and stepped over the remaining wall, quietly shoving aside the slender, sun-bleached ironwood poles composing the roof.

Stooping, she climbed beneath the low-slung poles and, hoping she'd run into no rattlesnakes or black widow spiders, scuttled in beneath the sagging roof and pressed her back to the cool, stone wall as far from view from the outside as possible.

She hunkered down, drew her knees to her chest, and listened as her pursuers continued shouting back and forth across the slope on both sides and below her.

"Goddamnit!" Cora screamed like a wounded she-grizzly, somewhere above Louisa now, stumbling around in the brush. "I *want* that little bitch. *Find her!*"

"We are, Cora," one of the men said placatingly, barely loudly enough for Louisa to hear. "It's dark out here. . . ."

Cora said something else but she must have turned her back to Louisa, for Louisa couldn't make it out above the thumps of boots moving toward her from below and left.

Louisa pressed her back harder against the stone wall as the footsteps and spur chings grew louder, with the occasional rattle of a kicked stone or the crunch of cactus spines. She could hear a man breathing hard. To her right, through a small gap between the fallen roof and the crumbling wall, a shadow moved. Louisa opened her mouth to breathe more quietly as the man stopped beside the hovel. He was probably only about six or seven feet away from her. Probably scrutinizing the fallen roof.

Louisa's heart beat with hard, measured strokes. The man stood frozen beside her. She could tell he was looking around, shifting his weight; gravel ground dully beneath his boots.

"Hey, Little Bitch, you in there?"

It was the voice of the black man, Heinz. In the night's heavy silence, his voice was almost bizarrely clear, as though he'd spoken from only inches away.

Silence.

Heinz's breath raked evenly in and out of his lungs. Suddenly, there was the low groan of boot leather. The man grunted softly. Louisa jumped as something struck the branches over her head with a loud, wooden thump. A stone slipped through a crack between the branches and plopped into the dust just inches in front of her boots.

Louisa opened her mouth wider, drawing a deep, silent breath. Her heart thumped painfully against her ribs.

The black man's bulky shadow moved toward her, and Louisa steeled herself, prepared to fight. If he found her, she would jump him, claw his eyes out, and try to wrestle a gun away. . . .

An owl screamed from up the slope—an eerie, rasping cry shattering the night's dense quiet. There was a windy flapping of wings. Heinz stopped and turned to stare upslope.

Louisa waited, listening to the owl's distressed cry as it faded off toward the ridge.

Heinz muttered something, turned away, and began striding up the slope, his shadow disappearing amongst the pinyons and boulders. When she could no longer hear his footsteps, Louisa let her head sag back against the wall and let out a long, slow, relieved breath.

She'd wait here until they gave up looking for her. They'd no doubt quit soon, go back to their fires and their liquor bottles. Besides, that wound her bullet had sliced across Cora's cheek and ear needed tending. Louisa had to bide her time. She'd never been much for patience, bulling headlong into bailiwicks with her horns out, but if she tried to make a run for it too soon, before the entire gang had slinked back down into the canyon, she wouldn't make it.

Patience, Prophet had told her more times than she could count, was the key to a bounty hunter not pushing up sage from a wooden overcoat before his time.

Snickering in spite of herself at the remembered advice, Louisa settled back against the wall and hugged her knees, shivering as the night's chill penetrated her wet, muddy clothes. What she wouldn't give for a warm blanket and a hot fire, maybe even a rare nip from Prophet's bottle. . . .

She waited for what must have been about two hours, watching the stars through the slats of the weathered ironwood logs and listening as the sounds of the searching gang ebbed and flowed around her. Several times the angry, inquiring voices and the thumping footsteps and crashing brush died, and Louisa thought they were retreating. But then more scuffling rose maybe thirty or forty yards away, upslope or down, and she settled back against the cold wall, shivering, waiting. . . .

It went on like that all night.

Louisa would find herself almost in a doze, sliding down against the wall. Then some bird or animal sound would rouse her, and she'd lift her head to listen. Just when she thought the slope was clear and she began moving her stiff limbs to crawl out from under the roof, she'd hear a voice or the unmistakable sound of a kicked stone or someone clearing his throat.

The gang might have been named for the three bizarre look-alikes, but obviously Cora was the one in charge. She kept the men out there, kicking around for the girl who'd no doubt disfigured her permanently, all night long.

Again, Louisa awoke from a doze, roused by her own rasping breath. She jerked her head up and peered through the roof slats. The sky was lightening, the stars fading. Birds chirped in the brush all around her.

She listened intently for about five minutes.

Only the bird sounds and the distant, frenzied yapping of ridge-sitting coyotes. Had the outlaws finally drifted back to their cabins?

Louisa couldn't hide here forever. She'd need water soon or she'd shrivel up and die like a mouse at the bottom of a dry well pit. It had gotten lighter than she would have liked, but she had to make a run for it, find a way through, around, or up and over that ridge, somehow make her way back to Prophet.

She winced as she stretched out her legs, hearing her stiff muscles and bones snapping and popping. She turned onto her hands and knees and crawled slowly out from beneath the shack's slanting roof, then lifted her head above the low, stone wall, looking around and listening.

Except for the birds and the yammering of the coyotes, nothing. She picked up a brick-sized, jagged-edged stone— she felt too naked without any weapon at all—and, continuing to look around, began walking slowly up the slope. Meandering around the rocks and cactus, she also avoided the mine holes and tailings pocking the terrain.

She stopped suddenly, drew a shallow breath through her nose, detecting the smell of tobacco. Frozen, she looked around, heart quickening once more. Smoke wafted in the predawn shadows, a couple of thin, weblike lines rising from her left.

Louisa swung her head around, and her stomach leaped into her throat. The man called Sykes stood about seven feet away from her, in front of a boulder and a juniper shrub, bringing a quirley to his lips as he stared up the slope, slightly away from Louisa. The tip of the quirley glowed brightly in the purple shadows.

Louisa's mind reeled as her stomach continued churning, her ears screaming. Before she could make up her mind about what to do, Sykes turned toward her suddenly, as though he'd spied her in the periphery of his vision. His eyes beneath the brim of his blue cavalry hat snapped wide. His fingers opened, and the quirley dropped, spraying orange sparks along the ground.

As he reached for the revolver jutting from his shoulder holster, he shouted, *"Heyyy!"*

Louisa bolted toward him, cocking her arm, then slamming her rock against Sykes's temple so hard that she could feel the impact all the way up her arm and into her shoulder.

"Uhh!" The man stumbled back and sideways, tripping over his own boots and bringing a hand to his forehead.

Louisa stepped toward him once more, swinging her arm back behind her. Bunching her lips, she swung it forward with even more power than before. The rock struck the side of Sykes's head with another resolute, cracking thump. He groaned as his hat flew off his head and into the cedar behind him.

"Here!" Sykes bellowed, falling to a knee against the cedar, his voice cracking with misery. "Bitch's heeeere!"

From downslope rose the unmistakable shriek of Cora. Cursing and bellowing like a bull trapped in a wildfire, Sykes again reached for his shoulder-holstered six-shooter. Louisa wheeled and, hearing footsteps and snapping brush all around her—she must have been moving right up through the killers stationed around her hiding place—she sprinted up the slope.

Sykes triggered shots behind her, the slugs screeching off rocks around her scissoring heels.

Leaping rocks and small shrubs, breath rasping in and out of her still-boggy lungs, Louisa ran hard, pumping her arms and lifting her knees. More shouts and shrieks rose behind her, and Sykes continued yammering and triggering errant rounds.

"I can't see!" the man bellowed. "Bitch *blinded* me!"

"Shut up!" Cora's cracking wail lifted the hair on the back of Louisa's neck. *"Where is she?"*

To Louisa's left, a man's voice boomed. "I got her!"

"Bitch blinded—!" Sykes shouted again, his voice clipped by another scream from Cora and a pistol blast.

There was a blue flash and a pop from maybe twenty yards away. The slug whistled inches in front of Louisa's face and barked into a boulder ahead and right.

Louisa offered a rare curse and continued running, tripping over obstacles in the uncertain light, hearing her own wheezing breaths and involuntary groans like some creature keeping pace beside her.

Boots thudded behind her, a man's labored breath growing louder.

He triggered another thundering shot, and the slug sliced across Louisa's left shoulder to smack the ground ahead with a whining thud. Louisa lurched to her right. Her boot clipped a stone, and she stumbled, flew forward, sliding and skidding along on her hands and knees.

She whipped around to cast a look behind her. The handsome blond-haired outlaw materialized from the shadows, a revolver smoking in his right hand. White teeth shone as he stretched his mustache in a broad grin, then turned his head sideways.

"Over here!"

The others, including the big, grunting Mexican, running up the slope behind and around him, closed on him and Louisa.

She looked around for a branch or a rock—anything she could use for a weapon. Her heart hammered, raging fury seething inside her. She'd wanted to get away from this bunch only so she could confront them again on her own terms and with the help of Prophet.

The need to avenge her cousin and her cousin's boy and husband, and the whole burned town of Seven Devils, was a roaring explosion inside her head. The sob that slipped from her lips was one of frustration only slightly tinged with the fear and terror at seeing her own end reflected in the faces of the gun wolves closing on her now from the shadow-obscured brush.

Squires continued toward her, angling his smoking revolver toward Louisa's head. The other men had run up to either side, breathing hard, the look-alike called Rafe stooped over and wheezing while he grinned down at Louisa. The big Mexican's fetor reached Louisa like a palpable wave as he approached on her right, his shoulders sloped, eyes glistening with goatish lust and fury beneath the brim of his steeple-crowned sombrero. His big Chihuahua spurs rang with each slow, purposeful step, dust puffing up around his steel-tipped boots.

Coming up behind Rafe and his brother in the opera hat and rose-colored glasses, Cora pushed between them. She continued forward, shoved Squires's gun hand aside, rammed a shoulder against the Mexican called Chulo, wrinkling her nose, and took one more step toward Louisa before she stopped and stared down, crazy eyes flashing gold sparks in the shadows.

She'd wrapped a white cloth around her head at an angle, so that it covered her ear and bullet-nicked cheek. Knotted just under her opposite ear, it was heavily bloodstained. The white parts glowed in the gradually lightening darkness.

"She's mine."

Cora's voice was eerily calm. Her chest rose and fell heavily, slowly. She holstered her revolver, then reached up and behind her head. When she lowered her right hand again, gray dawn light flashed off the bone-handled stiletto jutting toward Louisa. "When I'm done with her, the rest of you can have her . . . if there's anything left."

She giggled her insane, high-pitched, little-girl giggle, and started forward.

Propelled by hot, swirling fury, Louisa scrambled to her feet and ran stumbling forward over rocks and brush, bulling through low cedar branches. Her left boot dropped over the edge of a hole she hadn't seen in the murky light, and she gasped, panic overtaking her.

She flung her arms out to stay the fall, but she grabbed only mine tailings and a juniper branch that broke off in her hand.

Before she knew it, both her legs were in the hole and she plunged down the steep trough angling into darkness, her stomach hurling into her throat.

The pick-and-chisel-gouged side of the hole scraped her arms and legs, and her chin bounced painfully against it before her feet struck bottom. The air left her lungs in a rush. She fell backward and rolled several more feet before piling up against a wall buried in heavy darkness.

Sand and gravel rattled down behind her.

She lifted her head from the sandy floor and looked around. She heard voices above, but she couldn't see the killers, for the hole angled back beneath the ledge, and she was as far under the ledge as she could have fallen. Lilac light hung before, but now she was shrouded in shadow.

Louisa's ears rang. Her heart pounded. Her vision swam. She felt the cool, searing pain of the scraped undersides of her arms and her knees. She groaned as she heaved herself into a sitting position against the low-ceilinged pit's back wall and shook her head to clear the cobwebs.

Along the wall to her left, something moved—a vague,

serpentine shadow. Two small, pellet-sized lights glowed like tarnished pennies. There was the hair-raising rasp of quivering rattles.

Louisa sucked a sharp breath and had just begun to recoil from the flat, diamond-shaped head slithering out from a crack in the wall when the eyes shot toward her.

A burning ache filled her as the snake buried its teeth in her upper left arm, holding on for a good two or three seconds while Louisa sucked a sharp breath through gritted teeth, feeling the toxic, black venom pumping into her arm.

The last thing she heard before passing out was Cora's insane laughter from above, and the outlaw woman's strange, little girl's jubilant singsong. "She done found the rattlesnake pit. That oughta do her . . . reeeeel slowwww!"

24

PROPHET REINED MEAN and Ugly down and stared over the horse's bobbing, snorting head at the three men—or what remained of the three men—staked out on the ground before him.

A couple of buzzards that had not fled into the cedars and cottonwoods as he'd ridden up, following the stench and the raucous quarreling of the feeding carrion eaters, lingered proprietarily atop the bloody, eviscerated corpses.

They continued to peck and prod as they regarded Prophet angrily, strings of bloody sinew dangling from their colorless beaks, the little eyes in their bald heads flashing in the brassy, late-morning light like miniature ball bearings.

It was hard to tell much of anything about the three men beneath the birds—aside from the fact that they were white men, that they were naked, and that they'd had their eyelids cut off no doubt soon after they were staked. The long crosses hacked across their torsos marked them as double-crossing outlaws, left here to season in the sun as they died, ruminating on the dark impulses that had brought them to such an undignified, painful end.

Doubtful they'd been much given to shame or regret. The

grimaces frozen upon their beak-pecked faces, showing wide gaps of bloodstained teeth and gums, told of unbearable suffering.

His eyes watering against the sweet, rancid death stench, Prophet rose up in his saddle and looked back toward the fold in the high, brown hills that had brought him here to the southern Seven Devils, searching for his wayward partner's lost trail.

He'd left the Mexican whore and Big Hans still sawing logs in the outlaw shack and ridden out well before dawn, finding the gap in the southern hills only an hour or so later, as the sun had blossomed in the east.

That had been three hours ago and, while he'd been angling back toward where he figured Louisa had entered the southern range, he'd found no sign of her in the still-soggy, washed-out chaparral and semi-flooded canyons. He stretched his gaze farther west and downslope, over the canyons and arroyos and gullies meandering around pointed buttes and rolling up toward distant, saffron mesas and pedestal rocks.

No telling where she was. This half of the Seven Devils was as large as the largest western county. Trying to find one blond-headed, pious, kill-hungry, Yanqui senorita out here was like trying to pluck a single porcupine quill from the brasada of southern Texas.

Prophet gigged Mean on past the dead outlaws, and the buzzards once again flopped down out of the trees, their din growing louder in celebration of his passing. Looking around for any sign of Apaches or outlaws of any stripe, he continued south, following a slender horse trail up and over several ridges and canyons, before something caught his eye in the brush lining a broad, ancient watercourse to his right.

He checked Mean down, then swung out of the saddle and, pausing to look around for rattlesnakes or Gila monsters, he pushed through the ironwood and willows. Along the bank of the muddy arroyo, mud-crusted saddlebags were hung up on a root protruding into the cut, about three feet up from the recently flooded floor.

The small of his back loosened hopefully as, grabbing a slender willow trunk with one hand, he reached down to pluck the saddlebags off the root with the other. He hauled the bags back through the scratching, grabbing brush, then held them up for inspection.

Each flap was fastened to the pouch with a diamond-shaped, silver-chased buckle trimmed with wang strings. The style of the buckle told him the bags were Louisa's, but he rummaged around inside and found a couple of shirts he recognized, as well as a small, hide-bound diary in which she kept a record of the men she'd taken down.

The bags were Louisa's, all right. Since they'd been in the arroyo, it was safe to assume the girl had been in the canyon, too, no doubt swept away by last night's flood waters.

His heartbeat quickening, eager to get moving, Prophet draped the bags over his own on Mean's back, then bulled back through the brush. He dropped into the arroyo, and when the scalloped sand told him which way to ride, he climbed back aboard Mean and Ugly and spurred the horse into a slow jog. He remained on the bank beside the cut, as the arroyo's floor was still too muddy for fast travel, and the higher ground gave him a better view of the surrounding terrain.

The old watercourse dried in the hot sun even as Prophet followed it, having to cross back and forth when the ground on either side became blocked by boulders or brush snags, or when a butte cropped up in front of him.

After a half hour of hard travel, steep, rocky slopes dropped down to either side of his trail, and he dropped onto the arroyo's floor itself. It was while tracing a long, slow bend, Mean's hooves moving almost soundlessly in the still-damp sand, that a female voice rose from somewhere ahead and on the ravine's right side.

Prophet jerked back on Mean's reins and lifted his head, listening.

The voice sounded again—a girl's voice, from the pitch. Muffled by distance and swirling slightly on the hot, dry breeze, it rose and fell sharply, as though the girl were running or digging hard, working up a sweat. The voice didn't sound like Louisa's, but Prophet had to check it out.

He dismounted, swung his ten-gauge around to his back, and shucked his Winchester from the saddle boot. When he'd tied Mean and Ugly to one of the larger willows, he looked around. Ahead and right, a low, rocky shelf angled up out of the arroyo, running perpendicular to it.

Deciding the shelf would give him a good vantage, Prophet racked a shell into his Winchester's breech, off-cocked the hammer, and tramped across the arroyo and up the opposite bank, digging his boots into the damp clay and pulling at willow shrubs for leverage.

Where the willows and catclaw petered out, the shelf rose, and he climbed slowly, meandering around large rocks, cedars, and junipers, with occasional Spanish bayonet and ironwood shrubs. He gained the top of the shelf, breathing hard, sweat basting his buckskin tunic to his back and chest and troughing the dust on his cheeks.

The perspiration dried quickly when he hunkered down at the shelf's crest and the warm breeze slid against him, tanged with sage and the smoke of a distant cook fire.

He'd been hearing the girl's strange, passionate cries off and on while he'd been climbing. Now, crouched between two boulders, he stared into the cut on the other side, where two people were milling.

No, not milling.

The man—a lean, well-put-together gent with a full head of straight, strawberry-blond hair—had a tall, solidly built red-headed girl backed up against a stout cottonwood. She wore a bloody bandage at an angle across her face. Her hair was streaked with lime-green dye like that which pleasure girls often used, though Prophet had rarely, if ever, seen it worn outside of a whorehouse.

The girl's blouse was open, and her pants were bunched around her ankles. She sat back against a rock at the cottonwood's base, her bare legs spread wide, both her hands curled around a low-slung branch just above her head.

A saddle blanket lay between her bare bottom and the rock. She was bracing herself, jerking violently to and fro, hair flying, as the man pistoned his pale, narrow hips against her, pawing her breasts with one hand and tugging at her hair with the other.

Obviously, he was tugging with a little more vigor than the girl would have liked. She cursed him between grunts while the man retorted in words Prophet couldn't distinguish from this distance, because the man's back was to him and they were about fifty yards away, at the broadest stretch in a short, crooked box canyon.

"Squires!" the girl mewled, gritting her teeth and throwing her head back on her shoulders, the bandage falling away from her face, and careening groundward. "Ah . . . *goddamn* you, Squires . . . !"

Prophet remembered that Big Hans had said that the only female in the Three of a Kind Gang had red, green-streaked hair and a "funny" voice. Pondering the information, Prophet saw something move farther up the canyon.

He slid his gaze from the coupling pair to where a pinto was tied to a long rope running along the cut's brick-like rock wall, where several other horses had obviously been tied recently, judging by all the apples and the trampled manzanita grass lifting up around a spring bubbling out of the wall itself.

Prophet stared at the pinto, his eyes tracing the brown spots sharply contrasting the dusty, mud-streaked cream.

Louisa's mount. No doubt about it.

Had the vengeance-crazed polecat waltzed—or floated— right into the Three of a Kind Gang's bailiwick? Or had she drowned in the arroyo, and only the horse had made it? Or . . . maybe she was wandering around afoot out here, trying to get a bead on one of the gang members?

Prophet chewed his lower lip and glanced back at the pair now going at it with even more abandon than before, the blond gent throwing his head far back on his shoulders and thrusting crazily, his hip bones appearing about to bust out of his pale, hairless ass.

Lifting his gaze over the canyon, the bounty hunter picked out a handful of men and horses moving around several low, stone ruins. Men and dwellings were nearly lost amongst the massive boulders that had spilled down from the high, southern ridge.

Prophet hadn't taken a good look at the formations surrounding the canyon, and studying them now, he ran a pensive thumbnail along his unshaven jaw. Each of the range's notorious seven devils hovered over him—vast monoliths of sun-blasted, wind-carved stone rising a good two or three thousand feet above the canyon floor, sprouting from steep, rock-littered, andosite cliffs.

If the formations didn't look like the demons that had haunted Prophet's dreams in the first few months following the War—and which still cropped up every few months or so, howling and grinning and dancing around in smoky shadows, flicking their forked tails—his name wasn't Prophet and he hadn't sold his soul to the real thing.

As his eyes ranged across the formations, dull and brassy in the noon light, he felt some invisible crawling thing under his shirt and stifled a chill of revulsion.

The two lovers—if you could call them that—were fairly screaming now, as though they were both being carved up slow by stone-faced Apache squaws.

"Christ, Jay," the girl moaned, panting and slumping forward against the handsome gent's strawberry-blond head, her voice carrying cleanly in the high, dry air, "no . . . nobody does it like *you* do."

"Ah, hell." The man laughed. "Cora, girl, you're just all steamed up over that little bitch in the snake pit. Hell, the next purty little filly that comes along, you're gonna forget all about me . . . again!"

The man chuckled as he stumbled back from between the redhead's legs. Prophet stared down at him, his eyes spoked with deep lines, his mouth a knife slash across his broad, tan face. "That little bitch in the snake pit" echoed around inside his skull.

Louisa.

He looked around quickly for a way down into the canyon, his brain reeling, heart pounding. He had to get to Louisa, and the two lovebirds knew where she was.

Backing away from the lip of the shelf, he dropped down the slope several yards, then scrambled northward, up canyon.

When he figured he'd run about forty yards beyond where the girl and the man had been coupling like rabid minks, he moved back to the canyon's lip. Finding an eroded trough in the brittle sandstone, he took his Winchester in one hand and scrambled down through the jagged-edged trough.

He half slid on his butt, trying to break as little of the shell-like rock as possible, ignoring a Gila monster regarding him blandly from the sage of a nearby dwarf cedar, its striped sides contracting and expanding as it breathed.

Prophet landed in the narrow, shaded cut with less grace than he'd intended, the air pushing out of his lungs in a hard grunt. He froze, knees bent, rifle held high in his right hand, breathing through his mouth, ears pricked.

The man and the girl were about thirty yards down the crooked canyon, bantering now in jeering tones, both still breathing as though they'd run a long way across a hot desert. Taking the rifle in both hands, resting his thumb on the hammer, Prophet moved slowly down canyon, toward the gradually loudening voices. His sawed-off ten-gauge swung back and forth across his sweaty back—the old gut shredder always a reassuring presence.

The pinto appeared just ahead and left. Prophet slowed, held out a reassuring hand as if to quiet the beast. The pinto watched him, ears pricked. It rippled a wither and stomped a foot, but otherwise made no sounds that would betray his presence.

The man and the girl continued talking in their mocking tones. Prophet heard a lucifer scratch to life, and then the smell of tobacco smoke touched his nostrils.

The bounty hunter moved far right of the tied mount and continued down canyon along the cut's right wall from which water bubbled, seeping out from the moss-lined cracks between the shelving, adobe-colored stones. He moved maybe twenty more feet before stepping even closer to the canyon's right wall, trying to keep a thumb of sandstone, which jutted into the canyon just ahead, between him and the wider dogleg in which the girl and the man had been playing their wild game of slap 'n' tickle.

Prophet moved up behind the sandstone thumb and pressed his right shoulder against it, edging up toward the gap. He set his gloved thumb firmly on his Winchester's hammer, the words of the loving couple reaching him clearly, the girl asking the man if, despite the notch in her ear, he still thought she was pretty.

"I mean, my cheek'll heal," she said, her voice quivering slightly as she moved around, gathering her clothes. "But that notch outta my ear—that's gone for good."

"Darlin'," the man said, tobacco smoke wafting back through the opening ahead of Prophet, "nuthin' could take away that somethin' extra you got and all the other gals—even them without a scar anywhere on 'em—could only *want* for."

The girl giggled—the high-pitched squeal of a child laughing uncontrollably in church—and said, "Jay, how come you always know just what . . ."

Her voice trailed off as Prophet stepped into the gap and raised the Winchester to his shoulder, loudly cocking the hammer back and aiming the rifle at the girl crouched before the rock she'd been sitting on a few minutes ago.

She wore only silver-trimmed, blue-denim trousers, a funnel-brimmed straw hat adorned with a dried-up desert rose, and one boot. A big-boned but well-proportioned girl, she was naked from the waist up though she wore her double pistol rig, both holsters thonged to her shapely thighs. She'd been stepping into the other boot when her eyes had slid to Prophet.

The man called Jay sat on another boulder in the middle of the narrow canyon, his back facing Prophet, between the bounty hunter and Cora.

He was fully dressed except for his feet and, beaded moccasin boots lying nearby, he was pulling on his right sock when, following Cora's startled glance, he turned to peer over his shoulder. When his blue eyes found Prophet, vague surprise widened them slightly, made them sparkle like gold flecks in a shallow stream. His loosely rolled quirley dangled from between his perfect, white teeth.

He dropped his sock and stood, barefoot, making no sudden movements. Stretching a rakish, self-satisfied grin, he stepped back away from the rock and held his hands out away from his waist—he had only one revolver visible—and chuckled.

"Well, well, look what the cat dragged in."

Cora straightened, seeming unaware of the fact that her breasts were bare. A small tobacco pouch dangled between them by a braided rawhide cord. Eyes flashing ironically, she, too, smiled with calm confidence and, giving Prophet the quick up-and-down, said in her nasal, high-pitched child's voice, "Can we help you, sir?"

"Not havin' to listen to anymore of your stupid banter is almost enough. *Almost*, but not quite."

Prophet's eyes and jaws were hard, and his nostrils flared as he slid the rifle back and forth between Cora and Jay.

"I'm here for the little, blond polecat that floated or rode or wandered in here with her horns out. Now, she's purty as a speckled pup, though like most women I've noted of late she's sadly lacking in charm. Just the same, I've grown right fond of the little filly, and if you don't tell me where she is pronto, I'm gonna give both you tiresome alley cats nowhere to set your hats."

Jay furled his shaggy, strawberry-blond brows and glanced at Cora. "Girl? You got any idea what he's talkin' about, Co—?"

He stopped and swung his head quickly back to Prophet as the big bounty hunter, who stood a good three inches taller than the handsome blond gent and had about forty pounds on him, strode straight toward the outlaw, lowering the Winchester slightly. Jay replaced his complacent expression with one of unabashed fear as Prophet flipped the Winchester around in his hands and, gripping the rifle by its barrel, swung it back behind his shoulder, then swiped it forward so quickly that air whistled over it shrilly.

"*Hey!*" Jay cried.

The outlaw had only started raising his hands toward his head when Prophet smashed the rifle's stout, scarred butt against the side of Jay's handsome head with a resounding, bone-cracking smack.

25

JAY PILED UP at the base of the canyon wall like a long slab of venison thrown down from the bed of a market hunter's rolling wagon. Lying belly down, nose buried in mud from the springs, the man gave a gurgling sigh and fell silent.

Prophet snapped the Winchester to his shoulder again, and stayed the girl's hands, which, taking advantage of his momentary distraction, had dropped over the handles of her holstered six-guns. Seeing the Winchester's maw yawning at her once more, however, she raised her hands shoulder high, palms out.

"Keep 'em there," Prophet growled. He hated dealing with women. But the way he saw it, bare-breasted as she was, this was no woman but a cold-blooded killer. He'd have no more trouble killing her than he'd had trimming her wrestling partner's wick.

At least, he didn't think he would.

Aiming the Winchester at the crazy-looking redhead's parted lips, he sidled over to the unconscious, barefoot outlaw, whose chest rose and fell ever so slightly. He held the Winchester in one hand as he crouched, ripped Jay's revolvers from their holsters, and tossed them up and over the canyon wall above his head. They hit the brush with barely audible thuds.

Jay's slow, shallow breath gurgled softly in the mud. He groaned.

Straightening, continuing to aim the Winchester one-handed at the redhead's wide mouth, Prophet strode over to Cora quickly, pressed the rifle barrel against her dimpled chin, and ripped her revolvers from their holsters. She flinched with each violent thrust of Prophet's hands, her breasts and the makings sack bouncing slightly.

Blood trickled down from the long bullet burn across her cheek and from the painful-looking notch in her ear. When he'd tossed both guns up onto the canyon's lip with Jay's, he pressed the Winchester harder against her dimpled chin.

Fear had flashed in her eyes as Prophet had strode over to her. It flashed again now—stronger, darker. Prophet could tell from her expression that she wasn't accustomed to feeling such an emotion, and her fear mixed with indignation and downright murderous rage. He could feel her passion rippling up through his rifle.

"You give me a bullshit answer, you're gonna end up like your sweetheart over there." Prophet stared at her hard, his own broad chest rising and falling behind his sweat-soaked tunic. "Where's Louisa?"

Cora dropped her eyes to the rifle pressed against her chin. "An old mine diggin' upslope a ways." She swallowed and lifted her eyes to Prophet's. "If you'll let me put my blouse on, I'll show you."

Prophet rolled his eyes around. When he saw the woman's blouse, he backed away, keeping his rifle aimed at her face, and scooped it up off a cedar sapling.

He tossed it against her, then grabbed her bare arm and jerked her forward. She groaned indignantly as she stumbled forward, holding the blouse to her chest, Prophet shoving up to where the pinto stood, regarding him and the girl wonderingly in the corner of its right eye.

Prophet cleared his throat as dread buckled his insides, but his voice was even as he asked, "She alive?"

"She was. Couldn't tell you about now. There's snakes in that pit."

Prodding with the Winchester's barrel, Prophet backed her

up against the canyon wall, just up canyon from the pinto. "Stay there. Any sudden moves, I'll drill you."

Her voice was low and faintly sneering as she continued holding her blouse against her chest. "Do you know how many men are less than a hundred yards away? Men, I might add, who are well armed and always ready and willing to kill."

"Just shy of a dozen, I'd say." Keeping an eye on the girl, Prophet set the rifle against the canyon's opposite wall, then grabbed the pinto's saddle blanket off the juniper upon which it and the rest of the horse's tack had been tossed.

He tossed the blanket onto the pinto, glancing every now and then at the lip of the ridge behind the girl, faintly hearing the voices of the rest of the gang.

Cora shook the blouse out in front of her. "Who're you? I mean, besides being a dead man."

"Name's Prophet. Bounty hunter."

The girl froze with one arm in the blouse, seemingly completely uncaring that both her breasts were exposed, and blinked at him in shock. "You came in here aimin' to collect the *bounties* on us?"

Prophet had thrown the saddle over the pinto's back and moved over to the horse's left side to buckle the latigo. He glanced over his right shoulder at the girl, who continued donning the blouse. "Nope. Came here to kill ya." He gritted his teeth as he punched the pinto's side, trying to get the horse to let its breath out. "Every last stinkin' one of you kill-crazy sons o' bitches."

The girl stared at him, wrinkling the skin above her nose, her eyes regaining that wary cast she'd acquired after Prophet had all but decapitated Jay. "That's a mighty tall order. You're a big, ornery-lookin' son of a bitch, but there's nigh on a dozen of us, like you said."

She buttoned the shirt's last bone button and looked down her chest. As if in afterthought, she freed one of the top buttons, exposing a good bit of her deep cleavage, and sauntered forward, stuffing her hands in her back pockets and throwing her shoulders back, breasts out.

"Why don't you quit this foolishness and throw in with us?

Me and the fellas—even the queers, or, I should say, *especially* the queers—would be pleased as punch to sign up the gent who cleaned Jay Squires's clock."

"Squires, huh?" Prophet chuckled dryly as he stooped to pluck the bit and bridle off the juniper. "Thought he looked familiar. Seen paper on him up in Wyoming, a few months back. Thousand dollars, dead or alive."

She sidled up against Prophet as he draped the bridle over the pinto's twitching ears and slipped the bit through its teeth.

"Have you cleaned the dust out of your ears lately? Did you hear what I *said?* Me an' the boys are fixin' to ride out for a job that would set us up—you and *me* up, if'n you like big-titted redheads with every man-pleasin' skill you can think of and several you can't!—for a good ten years in Mexico. Hell, we could buy our own island!" She rubbed a firm, pointed breast against Prophet's shoulder. "Come on—let's ride on over and say hello."

With the pinto saddled, bridled, and ready to go, Prophet moved around behind the girl. "Sounds right enticin'. Let me mull it over." She gave a startled gasp as he wrapped his big hands around her waist and threw her up onto the pinto's back.

He grabbed the Winchester and led the pinto out from the wall. He was about to mount up behind Cora when a grunt sounded from down canyon.

Jay Squires was bringing a .32-caliber hideout gun up from an ankle sheath. His handsome, pain-racked face was lifted toward Prophet, the side of his head bloody and swollen, his lower jaw hanging askew. Lips bunched, eyes bright with malice, Squires thumbed the .32's hammer back and began raising the gun from the mud.

Prophet dropped the Winchester. His .45 was in his hand almost instantly. He cursed as the gun's roar filled the canyon, echoing like one of last evening's thunderclaps and no doubt clearly heard by the rest of the gang.

The bullet careened through Squires's forehead, snapping his chin up sharply. Squires's mouth formed a small, round O as his chin dropped into the mud. The back of his shirt and vest shone with a red blood spray stippled with bone slivers that had been blown out the back of his head.

"Damn," Cora exclaimed when the Colt's roar had finally ceased reverberating about the narrow canyon, "I've been wantin' to do that for years!"

Prophet growled another curse, then holstered the .45, grabbed his Winchester, and swung up behind Cora.

"Only problem is," the girl said with a smug, jubilant air, "the other fellas done heard it, and they'll be here in three shakes of a mule's tail. I don't see how you got any *choice* but to throw in with us now . . . or get your fool hide tossed to the same snakes as that cute little blond."

Holding the reins in his left hand, Prophet reached forward to slide the Winchester into the saddle boot. He palmed his .45, snugged the barrel against Cora's back, and gigged the horse up canyon, hoping to find a trail up one of the ridges.

"You're gonna lead me to that cute little blond, and you're gonna do it fast," Prophet snarled, his voice quaking as the pinto trotted up the crooked canyon, his heart pounding in hard, even thumps, "or you're gonna be the one snugglin' snakes—*comprende*?"

"I don't know," Cora said, shaking her head as she and Prophet continued up the boulder-and-brush-littered cut, "I don't take you for a man who'd kill a woman. Leastways, not one who'd shoot a girl in the back!"

Prophet spied a narrow trough in the canyon wall, twisting up into shale and cedars, and swung the pinto into it, prodding the horse hard with his spurs. "There was a time I would have agreed," Prophet said. As the horse lunged up the trough, snorting, hooves clomping loudly, he rammed the gun hard into the girl's right kidney. "But, girl, if you don't lead me to that snake pit without further bullshit, I'm gonna show you just how wrong you are!"

"*Ouch! Christ!*" Cora recoiled against the gun stabbing into her. "Damnit, you're *hurting* me!"

When the horse had lunged up out of the trough and stood amidst giant rock slivers and cracked boulders shaded by pines, Prophet stopped the horse and peered behind and right. Voices sounded down the rocky shoulder of the slope, growing louder as the girl's compadres moved toward the cut to see about the gunshot. Prophet couldn't see them from this angle, which meant they couldn't see him either.

He kept his voice down as he turned to the girl, still writhing, groaning, and cursing against the .45's barrel buried in her kidney. "Which way?"

"Up the slope!"

"Straight?" Prophet said, grinding his spurs into the pinto's flanks and grabbing the horn in front of the girl to keep from being thrown back over the horse's lunging hindquarters.

"I think so! I don't remember exactly! I'll have to see once we're farther up the mountain!" She glanced over her shoulder, her eyes pain-racked and indignant. "That gun in my back ain't helpin' my memory none, you big, mean bastard!"

Prophet put the pinto straight up the slope, looking around and spying several mine tailings and pits either dug straight into the rocky soil or angled back under massive boulders—none of which the squealing redhead claimed was the right pit.

"Left," the girl groaned.

"How far?"

"I don't know—I'm lookin' around for it, damn you!"

Prophet reined the pinto left across the slope, meandering around pines, cedars, talus slides, and boulders of every shape and size while two of the monolithic devils stared down from the steep southern ridge. The westward-sliding sun hit the tops of the devil heads and appeared to stretch toothy grins across their stony, red faces.

Prophet looked down the slope, catching glimpses of men moving along the base of the slope, between several ruined hovels and the brush-sheathed arroyo, toward the canyon in which they'd soon find Squires with a bullet through his bashed-in head. Prophet glanced farther back behind him, at the thick, clay-colored dust rising from beneath the pinto's scissoring hooves.

Too much dirt. One of the Three of a Kind Gang needed only to glance up the slope, and they'd see the dust if not Prophet himself weaving amongst the rocks and trees.

He turned his head forward, anxiety surging through him. "Where is she, damnit? If you're jerkin' my picket pin, I'm gonna—"

Prophet cut himself off as something flashed in the brush straight ahead.

The girl groaned and leaned forward. "We're close, damnit. You got me so rattled—!"

"Shut up." Prophet put the pinto slightly upslope toward the reflection continuing to flash through the branches of a squat, dusty cedar.

He reined the horse to a halt over a man in cavalry blues sprawled dead in the dirt. He had a red beard and mustache, and his small, deep-set eyes stared straight up at the sky. Blood dribbled from a hole over his right ear, the nearby ground splattered with blood and brain tissue. The sun glanced off the gold-chased pocket watch lying in the dirt near the man's coat pocket.

"I drilled Captain Sykes not far from the pit." The girl pointed upslope. "We're close!"

Hearing voices rising from the direction of the arroyo, Prophet put the horse up the slope until a slag pile appeared, sheathed in cedars. Prophet jerked back on the pinto's reins and slid back off the horse's rump, hitting the ground on both feet. He lunged toward the black hole yawning on the other side of the slag pile, stopped suddenly, and turned back toward the pinto.

Cora was sliding the Winchester from the boot on the pinto's right side. Prophet reached for it. Cora squealed and racked a shell. Prophet wrapped his hand around the barrel, and as he started to jerk the gun from the girl's grip, she pulled the trigger.

The ripping crack flatted out over the canyon, the slug flying skyward.

Prophet pulled the rifle forward. Cora screamed again, her finger caught in the trigger guard, and tumbled down the horse's left wither and hit the rocky ground headfirst at Prophet's feet. Groaning, she lifted her head feebly, pushing off her hands. Blood dribbled onto the rocks beneath her. She groaned again, her muscles went slack, and she fell flat against the ground, unconscious.

Prophet swung around and jogged up and over the slag heap, dropping down on his hands and knees beside the hole. Below he saw little but a few feet of steep, gravelly slope dropping into blackness. The air smelled of rock and soil and trapped air.

"Louisa?"

His voice echoed, then an eerie, grave-like silence.

"Louisa, you down there?"

26

SILENCE ROSE UP from the musty hole, and Prophet's pulse throbbed in his temples as a strange voice from deep in his heart screamed the girl's name while he stared, blank-faced, into the yawning darkness.

He licked his taut lips and was about to call again when, from below, he heard a muffled grunt and the scrape of a boot heel. Louisa's voice rose up from the dark pit like a soothing balm to a deep burn. "Lou? . . . Where've you *been?*"

Prophet choked back a relieved sob and chuckled. "I take it you're down there."

"Very funny." Her voice sounded a little pinched.

"You all right?"

"Not exactly. A viper chomped into my shoulder and I took a pretty good rap to my head."

Prophet felt apprehension nip him once more. Just because he'd found her didn't mean everything was roses. "I'll be down."

He leaned the rifle in the rocks, scrambled up and over the tailing pile once more, and jogged back to where the pinto stood where he'd left it, beside Cora, who still lay facedown in the gravel, unmoving. Down the slope he could hear voices, but he didn't have time to worry about the killers now. He had to get Louisa out of the snake pit.

He led the pinto up near a gap in the tailing pile, grabbed Louisa's rope coil from the saddle horn, and tied one end to the horn itself before turning the horse away from the hole.

"You stay here till I tell you, boy," Prophet said, slapping the pinto's shoulder and, breathing hard with anxiety and the need to hurry, he uncoiled the rope through the gap in the tailing pile.

Prophet glanced into the hole once more. "Louisa, you still with me?"

"No, I've gone to the Larimer Hotel in Denver for sarsaparilla and ginger snaps."

Prophet adjusted the position of the ten-gauge hanging down his back, wrapped the rope around his waist, slipknotted it, turned his back to the hole, and, keeping the rope taut between himself and the pinto, dropped over the edge, starting down.

The pit's walls were steep though not sheer, and he descended quickly, the daylight drifting up over his head and his breath beginning to echo in the stony, cavernous silence. His boots scuffed along the wall, loosing occasional shards of orange shale. He winced as he heard them clatter to the pit's floor maybe thirty feet below, possibly hitting his partner crouched in the shadows.

Semi-level ground rose beneath him, and a wall pushed up from behind to scrape against the double-barreled gut shredder. He set his boots, released the rope, and looked around in the dark gray light.

Louisa's voice trilled under the low wall behind him, like water in a sepulcher. "Under here. Watch out for the snakes."

Prophet ducked under the low-angling ceiling and peered farther back into the cave. Louisa's booted feet and riding denims stretched toward him, her upper body, obscured by the cave's inner dark, resting against a four-foot-high wall. As if to give credence to Louisa's warning, a snake rasped to her left. Along the base of the wall, left of the girl, a slender shadow moved. The penny-colored, pellet-sized eyes shone in the dimness.

"Shit!" Prophet slipped his .45 from its holster, thumbed

back the hammer, and fired. The rocketing blast felt like two cupped palms slapped hard over Prophet's ears. Louisa gave an irritated grunt.

The rattling died abruptly, and the two cold eyes winked out like distant railroad lanterns. The slender, coiled shadow continued to jerk and quiver.

Keeping his revolver unholstered, Prophet scuttled under the low-angled ceiling, looking all around for more vipers, and knelt beside Louisa. "How in the *hell* did you end up in *here*?"

"Don't ask stupid questions. Is the gang dead?"

Prophet laughed dryly as he snaked his arms beneath Louisa's back and legs. "Talk about stupid questions—no, they sure as hell ain't!"

"Good. I'd like to handle that job myself."

Kneeling and sort of sidestepping while remaining crouched beneath the ceiling, Prophet slid the girl out from the wall. "I don't doubt it, Miss Bonnyventure. I don't doubt that one damn bit."

"Ouch! My head hurts."

"Where'd the snake bite you?"

"Shoulder. Another bit me in the leg."

Prophet looked at her sharply, brows beetled with concern. He'd never seen anyone recover from two rattlesnake bites. In fact, they'd both died long, painful deaths, begging him and the other men present to drill slugs through their heads.

Louisa stared at him, tightening her grip about his thick neck. "Don't fret, Lou."

Prophet glanced at her as, hauling his blond partner out from beneath the low ceiling, he straightened in the light falling from the circle of blue sky overhead. The light found Louisa's half-open hazel eyes and sparkled. "How's that? You just done told me you been snakebit twice. Do you know what that means, you crazy polecat?"

"I'm immune to rattlesnake venom."

Prophet froze, staring at her. The bland way she frequently reported important information always took him aback, and he was never sure she wasn't joking. The two hazel orbs staring at him now were totally lacking in irony, however.

Prophet laughed with newfound relief and genuine humor as he set her feet on the stony ground before him, propped her against him, and reached for the rope. "You know that doesn't surprise me?" He laughed again, louder, the laughter echoing around them. "No, sir, that doesn't surprise me one damn bit!"

That she herself believed she was immune didn't mean that he believed it, for he'd never heard of anyone being immune from rattlesnake venom. But just the possibility that he might not lose her made him feel better. She certainly didn't *seem* to have one foot in the grave.

With her wrapped in his arms before him, the rope's loop encircling them both, he chuckled again and clucked to the pinto at the top of the hole.

The rope grew taut, pinching Prophet's sides, holding Louisa firmly against him, and the loop began lifting them up the hole's steep wall, the shotgun swinging back and forth across his back. Prophet ground his boots into the wall as they rose, walking up the steep incline while holding the rope firm in his gloved hands.

He chuckled again. "Nope. Doesn't surprise me one damn bit. In fact, I'm beginnin' to feel sorry for the snake that bit ya!"

"Ha-ha."

Prophet stared at the blue opening growing before him, listening for voices or boot scuffs—anything to indicate the gang was closing on the mine pit. There was only a thin mare's tail of sun-bright dust blowing on the dry breeze.

The rope creaked to a stop. Prophet and Louisa stopped moving. The bounty hunter looked at the rope bending down over the hole, creaking slightly from the strain as it ground into the dirt and rock.

"Damn horse." Prophet grabbed a chunk of shale protruding from the side of the hole and threw it up out of the hole, aiming for where he figured the horse was probably standing.

"Get a move on, boy!"

The last word hadn't died on his lips before a hawkish face with rose-colored spectacles slid out from the hole's right side, staring down. The man held a revolver in his right hand. He snapped his eyes wide, jerking the glasses down his nose, as the stone sailed past his cheek, barely missing it and ticking against the brim of his opera hat.

The hawk-faced hombre bunched his lips with anger and cocked the pistol. "Hey, ole son," he raged in a Southern accent even thick to Prophet's Georgian ears, "you damn neah knawcked my *block* off!"

Prophet winced as the man angled the revolver's barrel over the lip of the hole. Throwing his head over Louisa slumped before him, Prophet gritted his teeth and sucked a sharp breath as he awaited the bullet that would no doubt splatter his brains all around the mine pit's floor below.

No bullet came. Instead, another, more distant gun barked.

Prophet looked up. The bespectacled, hawk-faced hombre who'd been about to shoot Prophet was gone. Along the edge of the sphere of skylight, other hatted heads and mustached faces bobbed and jerked while men shouted and screamed.

Louisa said thinly, barely audible beneath the din from above, "What's going on?"

A horse whinnied.

The loop around Prophet and Louisa drew torturously taut, both grunting as it pinched the air from their lungs. With a violent jerk they were propelled up the side of the hole, the ascension so quick and unexpected that Prophet's boots slipped off the stone ridge, and he and Louisa slammed the jagged rock wall so hard that Prophet felt as though his shoulders had been fused together. Twisting around, he put his back to the jagged stone incline, his back and shotgun taking the brunt of the scrapes and bruises from the pick-and-shovel-carved sides of the hole.

Louisa groaned, bunching her cheeks and slitting her eyes as she stared straight up at the opening growing wider and wider above.

Prophet gritted his teeth as, gripping the taut rope in both his gloved hands, daylight and the acrid smell of powder smoke washed over them and the hole shot back behind them.

Louisa gave an anguished cry as she and Prophet blew up out of the pit like sudden-struck oil and slammed back to the shale-littered ground. With the girl's back snugged against Prophet's chest and belly, they were dragged forward together as if drawn by a team of runaway horses along the rocky ground away from the hole, the ground searing and cutting into Prophet's left shoulder. Rocks flew to either side as he and Louisa, lashed together like Siamese twins, fishtailed through the gap in the tailing pile.

Gritting his teeth against the ground hammering and raking him, Prophet caught a quick, blurred glimpse of men around him falling or crouching or shooting up toward the devil-capped southern ridge, powder smoke wafting as flames stabbed from gun barrels.

Ahead, the pinto was running and buck-kicking at an angle across the slope, dust spitting up from its hooves. The horse jerked sharply right, loose shale flying up around it. The horse went down and rolled in a thick dust cloud, wrenching Prophet and Louisa sharply sideways.

As the horse screamed and lifted its head, hooves scissoring as it tried to regain its feet, the rope slackened, and Prophet and Louisa, propelled by their previous momentum, skidded down a rocky, brushy bench, dust flying up around them. They piled up together against a low knoll, Louisa squirming and groaning on top of Prophet, her dust-caked hair in his face.

Prophet felt the rope jerking at his waist and turned to see the pinto starting to draw its feet under it. Holding Louisa's shoulders with one arm, he reached back behind his head with his other hand and slipped his bowie knife from the thong between his shoulder blades.

Quickly, as the rope began jerking him and Louisa ahead once more, he flung his arm out, slashing the razor-edged blade through the quivering hemp. He and his partner bounded back from the suddenly released tension, one of the cut ends recoiling like a viper striking him while the other bounced and leaped behind the pinto, which was once again screaming and galloping off across the slope, away from the guns still cracking and popping in the rocks and cedars behind it.

Prophet wrapped his arms around Louisa and lay his head back in the sand. He sucked a long breath, vaguely taking reconnaissance of his battered body, trying to ascertain if anything was broken. Gently, he rolled Louisa to one side and brushed her hair away from her face with his forearm. Her cheeks were scraped and dusty. Her eyelids fluttered.

Prophet's gut was in a knot. He couldn't believe she'd survived the two snakebites as well as the pummeling they'd both just taken. "Hey . . . you still kickin'?"

She rolled back onto her elbows, looking around like a

drunk just waking up in an alley. "What happened? Who's shooting?"

Prophet chuffed at the girl's sand once more. He groaned as he pulled a boot beneath him and began pushing himself to his feet. Once standing, dizzy and battered but still operable, he reached for his .45, relieved to find the revolver still secured to his holster by the hammer thong. "I don't know." He thumbed open the loading gate, plucked out the one spent shell, and replaced it with a fresh shell from his dust-caked cartridge belt. "Reckon I'd better go find out. You stay here."

He'd taken only one step forward, toward the din rising upslope and left, when a gun barked closer than the others. The slug whistled over Prophet's right shoulder and screeched off a boulder behind him.

Prophet dropped to a knee, every bone in his big frame squawking in protest of the sudden movement, and raised the .45.

He hammered three quick rounds at the figure peering at him through cedar branches, snapping branches, tearing bark, and puffing dust from the man's chest.

The bushwhacker screamed and jerked back. He stumbled out from the other side of the tree, dropped to a knee—a scrawny gent in a funnel-brimmed Stetson and with bandoliers crossed on a deer-hide vest—and Prophet fanned two more shots.

Both slugs took the man through his forehead, blood and bone spraying as he flew straight back, hit the ground, and lay spread-eagle, as though dropped from the moon.

Quickly, looking around for more shooters moving in on him, Prophet opened the smoking .45's loading gate and began plucking out the spent casings. The gunfire around the snake pit had grown sporadic, and several men were shouting angrily. Beside Prophet, Louisa leaned back against the knoll and shook her hair from her eyes.

"Give me your pistol, Lou."

Prophet thumbed a shell into an empty chamber and narrowed an incredulous eye at the dusty, rumpled, snakebit girl.

She jerked her hand toward him, furrowed her brows impatiently. "Give me your pistol. You still have your barn blaster.

We'll circle those fork-tailed demons and send them to their rewards in a hail of hot lead."

Prophet snorted. "You oughta write them pulp yarns with yellow-backed covers."

He flicked the revolver's loading gate closed and looked around once more. "Forget it. Stay here."

He started forward, stopped, and turned back to where she flung pitchforks at him with her sparkling hazel gaze between breeze-buffeting wings of dusty blond hair. "And for once in your ornery, pea-pickin' life, sit tight!"

27

PROPHET HELD HIS barn blaster in his left hand, the Colt in his right, and crept forward slowly, heading away from Louisa, making his way around the boulders, and swinging his hatless head from left to right.

The sporadic shots now rose from ahead and to his right, from upslope, and they all seemed to be aimed toward the ridge from which purple shade was slowly bleeding into the canyon.

He moved around a boulder and stopped. A long-haired gent in a green-checked suit coat and brown trousers lay facedown, blood staining the orange caliche around his head. Prophet kicked him over. From Big Hans's description, the hawk-faced corpse glaring up at him, lips stretched with shock and horror, was one of the triplets the gang had been named for. A big-caliber bullet had smashed a silver cartwheel-sized hole through one side of his head and had left a fist-sized, gaping cavern in the other side upon its exit.

Squeezing the barn blaster in one hand, his Colt .45 in the other, Prophet continued forward until the snake pit sheathed in mine tailings appeared just ahead. The redhead, Cora, was no longer here, but her blood marked where she'd lain.

Three more bodies lay around the pit, blood like red paint

splashed from a bucket. Another triplet lay beside the hole—
this one dressed in a brown-checked coat and fawn vest, the pistol with which he'd been about to clean Prophet's clock lying a few yards from his pale, long-fingered, outstretched hand.

A big black man lay draped belly up over a small boulder, a hole the size of a wheel hub gushing blood from his chest.

A few yards farther up the slope sprawled a tall gent with long, sandy hair and a handlebar mustache. He held two Buntline Specials in his fists, one cocked and splashed with blood from the hole in his throat. His eyes stared glassily at the rocks beneath him, one cheek and a black boot twitching in death spasms.

Men's voices drifted from upslope. A boot clipped a rock. Prophet glanced around more, then, sleeving sweat and dust from his eyelids and hefting his Colt and his barn blaster, began striding upslope, moving quickly but quietly.

He tramped between the rocks and dwarf pines, keying on the voices continuing to drift down from the rocks just ahead. He couldn't hear what the men were saying, as they were forty or fifty yards away, facing the ridge, but he could tell from their conspiratorial tones they were setting up an ambush.

As he moved, Prophet glanced at a large, flat-topped boulder leaning slightly to one side and snugged up to the ridge wall behind it. Several smaller boulders and pinyons lay around it. The boulder seemed to be the point the two killers—he could tell there were two by their tracks and voices—were heading for.

When the boulder was about thirty yards away, the crown of a black opera hat appeared, shifting around behind rocks and brush ahead of him. Prophet hurried forward, sidled up to a boulder shaped like a cracked eyetooth, and edged a look around it. A man with a black braid falling down the back of his salmon-checked suit coat knelt, facing the ridge from behind a wagon-sized chunk of black granite.

Breathing hard from the climb, Prophet sucked a deep breath and stole slowly out from behind the boulder. He'd set his left boot down softly in the dry gravel, when his quarry swung his head around sharply, black eyes snapping wide and lifting two saddle-ring Schofields in his black-gloved fists.

Prophet froze and, with an implacable expression on his

scraped, dusty, sunburned face, tripped his ten-gauge's left trigger. At the same time, he fired the .45 in his right hand.

The .45's crack was drowned by the short-barreled barn blaster's cannon-like explosion, which made the ground shudder beneath the bounty hunter's boots.

If he'd hit the man with the .45, he'd hit him in the same place that the double-aught buck punched a pumpkin-sized hole through his lower chest, lifting him violently off his feet and throwing him straight back over several rocks to finally disappear in a deadly patch of spiked catclaw and ocotillo, dust rising in his wake.

One of the Schofields, which he'd thrown into the air unfired, dropped to the gravelly caliche only a few feet from the man's boot and spur prints, the soft, baleful plunk of iron against earth fittingly punctuating a wasted life.

Prophet holstered his .45 and, jogging forward, knowing the other killer would be headed in his direction, dropped down behind another boulder in the shade of the mammoth stone devil capping the looming southern ridge. He breeched the ten-gauge, plucked the spent wad from the left barrel, and replaced it with a fresh shell from his cartridge belt.

He dug a boot heel into the gravel and started to push himself up. Smelling a sweet, cloying odor—the stench of an overfilled privy doused with hog slop—he froze. Staring straight ahead, keeping his ears pricked but hearing nothing, he sat with his back to the boulder. The stench grew more intense, stinging his eyes like the devil's own supper.

Behind the boulder lifted the rasp of an indrawn breath. Prophet winced against the pain in his aching bones as he heaved himself quietly to his feet and, crouching and holding the barn blaster straight out from his waist, cat-footed around the side of the rock and edged a look behind it.

A huge figure—a good four inches taller than Prophet—clad in a short charro jacket and bull-hide chaps over bell-bottomed deerskin slacks—was turning around the boulder's other end, his back facing the bounty hunter. The stench emanating from the man was now so thick that tears squeezed out from Prophet's eyes to dribble through the dust down his cheeks.

The bounty hunter began raising the shotgun. Behind him a squeal rose sharply, freezing the blood in his veins and jerking him around suddenly, eyes popping wide, his right index finger drawn taut against the ten-gauge's curved triggers.

Something dog-sized and dark moved in the brush, snorting and grunting. The javelina pulled its pink snout back, wheeled, squealed loudly, and burrowed off through the scrub. At the same time, the smell of the man Prophet had been stalking became so strong it was like an actual dead thing in his nose.

A spur trilled softly. Sensing a target drawn on his back, Prophet twisted around, grinding his heels into the gravel and diving back the way he'd come.

Behind him, a rifle barked—two quick shots flatting out over the canyon followed by the mad, frenzied yowl of the shooter.

As Prophet hit the ground on his belly, his barn blaster tumbled out ahead of him. Spurs rang and boots thumped behind him. He turned to look over his right shoulder as his heart rattled in his chest and blood rushed to his cheeks.

The big Mexican, with a suety face shadowed by four-day stubble and a thick mustache, grinned with delight and, stalking toward Prophet lying helpless on his side, raised his Winchester to his shoulder.

He narrowed one eye as he drew a bead on Prophet's chest with the other. His mouth was a near-toothless cavern crusted with long-seasoned chaw.

Prophet's legs turned to putty as the man bore down on him. He didn't have a hope in hell of reaching either his .45 or the shotgun before the big, stinking demon looming in front of him sent him to Ole Scratch in a smoking, smelly cloud of glowing lead. He mused vaguely that at least he'd come to an appropriate place, a hot canyon ringed with massive red devils, to receive his send-off to El Diablo.

The Mexican slammed the cocking mechanism home with an angry, metallic rasp. Unexpectedly, he lowered the rifle to glare down at the silver-chased breech. As though the long gun had just insulted him, his grin dissolved, replaced by a face-crumpling, exasperated frown.

Prophet's chest fairly imploded.

The Mex's rifle was empty!

The bounty hunter threw his right arm out in front of his

head, curled his fingers around the barn blaster's stock, and brought it back toward him. At the same time, the Mexican threw his empty Winchester down as though it had suddenly turned hot.

Knowing it was now himself who didn't have time to reach for one of his holstered six-shooters or knives, he bolted forward and sprang off the heels of his high-topped, mule-eared boots, bellowing as he dived toward Prophet, arms stretched out in front of him, hands spread wide, thumbs forward.

He landed atop Prophet just as Prophet drew the rear stock of his sawed-off ten-gauge down against his right rib cage and, raising the barrel up in front of him, curled his index finger over both triggers shaped like a pretty girl's long eyelashes.

The Mex wrapped his big hands around Prophet's neck and, half rising on his knees for leverage, his stubbled, dusty cheeks puffing, his black eyes popping wide with fury, began to sink his thumbs into Prophet's throat.

The man dropped his gaze suddenly to the stout barrels of the barn blaster snugged up under his chin. Just as suddenly, he pulled his thumbs back from Prophet's neck, crumpling his cheeks and slitting his eyes, throwing his head back on his shoulders.

Prophet lifted his head from the ground, hardening his jaws, tears dribbling down his cheeks from his stinging eyes. "Goddamn, old son—you ever heard of a *bath*?"

The hammering explosion of both detonated shotgun barrels drowned out the last word of his sentence, and he stared up as the Mexican's head turned to red jelly and flew in pieces from his shoulders.

The thundering boom continued echoing off the southern ridge, as though several cannons were being fired in the far distance, one after another. Finding himself staring at the bloody, ragged hole where the Mexican's head had been, Prophet kicked the man off him and rolled away.

Resting on one elbow and staring at the remains of the Mexican's head painting the catclaw and ocotillo and rocks beyond, a few strands of hair and one big eyeball clinging to a bloody boulder, a contemplative expression brushed Prophet's dusty, haggard features.

"Chulo Alameda." The bounty hunter rammed a fist into the dirt beside him. "Goddamnit!"

"What is it, Lou? He get ya?"

Prophet turned to see Big Hans ambling across the rocks from the direction of the large, flat-topped boulder hulking against the base of the ridge. The kid's arm rested in the sling Prophet had fashioned for it. In his other hand he carried his Big Fifty. His blond head was shaded by his shabby sombrero while his dusty coveralls flapped around the tops of his lace-up boots.

"Nah," Prophet said, shaking his head and gaining his knees. "It just came to me who he was. Chulo Alameda. Army payroll thief, rustler, and regulator. Even done some slave tradin' back and forth across the border. If I remember right, the U.S. government has two thousand big shiny ones on his head." The bounty hunter cursed again as he breeched his blood-splattered barn blaster. "Shit, not even ole *Jesus'd* recognize that son of a bitch now."

"Pee-*ewe*!" Big Hans exclaimed, stepping wide of the headless corpse whose knees continued bending slightly, as though in some bizarre, half-remembered death dance. "That's one rotten-smelling son of a bitch!"

"They included that description on his wanted dodger. 'Stinks to High Heaven.'" Prophet cursed as he plucked the spent wads from his shotgun's breech and tossed them back over his shoulder. "You shadowed me, I reckon."

Big Hans nodded. "Damn arm wouldn't let me sleep. I figured you might need a hand."

"Much obliged."

"Ran out of cartridges about fifteen minutes ago. Thought for sure these fellas were gonna smoke me out of my hidin' place and grease me up for the fryin' pan." Big Hans looked around, stretching his thick lips back from his white teeth. "Where's Louisa?"

As if in response, a shrill scream rose—a high, keening cry like that of a grief-stricken squaw. Prophet's pulse jumped. "What's that high-headed filly gotten herself into now?"

He snapped his shotgun together as he leaped to his feet and, with Big Hans ambling along behind, ran back down the slope, wending his way through the scrub.

Prophet leaped atop a flat-topped rock and stared into the canyon below, filled now with angling, wheat-colored light slanting shadows out from the sage clumps and rocks. The copper-headed outlaw girl was running across the canyon toward the brush-sheathed arroyo, to the left of a dozen or so saddled, waiting horses.

As she ran, stumbling and yowling, she twisted around to look at the slender blond striding purposefully behind her, a pistol in Louisa's outstretched right hand.

"Noooo!" Cora begged, stumbling over her own feet and dropping to one knee, throwing her arms toward Louisa with prayer-like beseeching. "Please, don't. I don't *wanna* die!"

If Louisa said anything, Prophet didn't pick it up. The pistol in her hand belched smoke and flames, and the red-head flinched, brushing a hand across her right temple a half second before the pistol's report and Cora's cry reached Prophet's ears.

The outlaw girl twisted forward, fell, scrambled back to her feet, and stumbled into the brush along the arroyo. Louisa followed, striding stiffly, with grim purpose, keeping about ten feet between herself and her hapless quarry.

"Jeepers," Big Hans said, breathing hard as he stood to Prophet's right, staring skeptically into the canyon. "Think we should go help her?"

Prophet shouldered his shotgun and laughed.

EPILOGUE

PROPHET, LOUISA, AND Big Hans didn't linger in the death-drenched canyon after Louisa had finally finished off Cora, stifling those eerie squeals that chilled Prophet even in the high heat of the desert day.

When silence finally descended, the buzzards weren't long behind.

The unlikely trio gathered their horses and weapons, mounted up, and headed back through the narrow fault in the northern wall that Big Hans had discovered several years ago during his boyish explorations. The defile's west-side opening was concealed amongst pinyons and boulders so that you had to know the country as either an Apache or an adventurous boy would know it to find it.

Even in the defile they could hear the raucous barks, growls, and squawks of the feeding buzzards that had nearly darkened the sky behind them.

No one said anything as they filed out of the fault and made their way back to the flat-roofed owlhoot hut. Prophet watched Louisa for the effects of the diamondback venom. Most men would have been writhing around in near-death agony, screaming like a bobcat in labor and begging for a bullet.

Louisa just looked tired and pensive as she straddled the

pinto, her clear, somehow still-innocent eyes scanning the terrain around her, no doubt thinking about those graves they'd left back in Seven Devils, and the life she might have had after so many years of wandering and trying to right the world's wrongs, if it hadn't been for the Three of a Kind Gang.

In the early afternoon, Prophet spied the long, low, flat-roofed cabin at the base of the cactus-studded ridge. The hovel shifted amongst the saguaros and boulders ahead as Mean and Ugly wended his own way through the chaparral, Big Hans and Louisa clomping along beside him.

As the side of the cabin dropped away to their right flank and the front wall slid up before them, so did a saddled horse with two well-stuffed burlap sacks hanging from a long rope across the pommel. The horse was tied to the hitchrack and stock tank fronting the cabin's open door. A guitar leaned against the cabin's front wall.

The chesty whore, Loretta, stood on the sorrel's far side, tightening the latigo strap. She wore a ratty, low-crowned straw sombrero, which bobbed and pitched as she worked at the saddle. A couple of phony flowers protruded from a band around the crown.

"Well, I'll be jiggered," Big Hans muttered. "She's still here."

Loretta lifted her gaze over the saddle, frowning owlishly and setting a hand on the stock of a Henry rifle jutting from the saddle boot. She studied the approaching riders for a moment, and then her eyes snapped wide beneath the sombrero's brim and she dropped her hand from the rifle.

"Hansy!"

Prophet looked at Big Hans skeptically as he drew Mean to a halt off the cabin's front corner. "Hansy?"

"Hello, Loretta!" the big kid said with a toothy grin and a wave. "You're still here?"

Big Hans swung down from the saddle with more speed and grace than he'd shown even before he'd broken his left arm. Clumsily doffing his own sombrero, he dropped his reins and strode over to where Loretta stood near the sorrel's tail, holding one hand to her hat brim and planting the other fist on her hip like an admonishing schoolmarm.

She wore a gaudy, frilly red dress exposing her shoulders

and arms and her legs below her knees as well as a pair of
pink, bow-trimmed, high-heeled shoes. The dress was cut so
low that those magnificent brown breasts were nearly as naked
as they'd been last night.

"I woke this morning, and you were *gone*," Loretta scolded
in her heavy Spanish accent. "Where did you go, bad gringo
boy? You were supposed to stay in bed. I was going to change
your bandage and fix you *breakfast*!"

Big Hans flushed like a sunset as he cut his gaze at Prophet
and Louisa still sitting their horses behind him. He muttered
a few phrases to Loretta in a boyish, beseeching tone, then,
glancing once more with chagrin at his two mounted partners,
took Loretta by the arm and led her a few yards away.

"Who's she?" Louisa asked Prophet, regarding the pair
with one arched brow.

"That's Loretta."

"Who's Loretta?"

"Hans's nursemaid." Prophet thumbed his hat back off his
forehead. "But I'm startin' to think I maybe shouldn't have
left the kid alone with ole Loretta. Or," he added, snorting rue-
fully, "maybe I shouldn't have left Loretta alone with Big
Hans."

Loretta and Hans spoke in hushed tones, arguing a little at
first in a cow-pen amalgam of English mixed with Spanish.
The grave tone of the conversation turned gradually lighter
until Loretta burst out laughing, throwing her head back on
her shoulders and wrapping her arms around Big Hans's big
neck, then rising up on her toes to kiss the beefy lad on the
lips.

Big Hans, flushing all over again, sheepishly glanced at
Prophet and Louisa, both of whom were regarding him now
skeptically. Chuckling happily, Loretta wheeled, the hem of her
red dress flying out around her bare, brown legs, and strode toward the cabin and the guitar leaning against the wall beside the
front door.

At the same time, Big Hans donned his hat and, with that
same shit-eating expression on his red-mottled face, strolled
back over to Prophet and Louisa.

He hemmed and hawed a few seconds, casting his eyes
downward and prodding a sage clump with a boot toe, before

he finally lifted his chin and blurted, "I reckon I'm gonna ride on over to Nogales with Miss Loretta. She's gonna tend my wing for me, and I'm gonna tend her dogs and chickens. She's got a milk cow, too, and you know how I like milk."

He seemed to be waiting for either Prophet or Louisa to say something. When neither said anything, he shrugged and glanced around at the sun-blasted hills and mountains.

"I reckon I don't have nowhere else to go, so . . . so I reckon I'll do that, then. Loretta's got amazin' healing abilities. She said she's descended from Injun witches . . . mestizo witches, you know . . . but the good kind, the doctorin' kind . . . not the ones that put evil hexes on a fella an' such . . ."

Leaning forward on his saddle horn, Prophet cut a sidelong glance at Louisa, who returned it. Then he shuttled his gaze back to the big kid standing before him looking as happy as a kid with a new Colt pistol.

Loretta had hung her guitar over her saddle horn and was climbing onto the claybank's back, grunting and cursing in Spanish with the effort, her heavy breasts swishing this way and that and up and down in her skimpy dress.

Prophet narrowed his eyes and tongued a tobacco fleck from between his two front teeth. "I reckon you could do worse than shackin' up with a good witch with a milk cow." He leaned forward, extending his hand to the boy. "Luck to ya, Junior."

"Luck, Hans," Louisa said, extending her arm out around her horse's neck.

When Big Hans had shaken both hands, he stepped back and hooked the thumb of his good hand behind his coverall straps, grinning. "Much obliged to both of ya. We ran 'em down, didn't we?"

"I reckon we did," Prophet allowed.

"You two know the way back out of the mountains, right?"

Louisa said, "It won't be easy without your guidance, Hans, but I reckon we'll manage."

Big Hans climbed awkwardly into his saddle, wincing slightly at the pain in his broken arm. Loretta had reined her own mount southward and held up, turning the horse sideways to the lodge as she waited for the boy.

"Bye, now."

Big Hans pinched his hat brim at Louisa and Prophet as he

urged his horse up beside Loretta's clay, then, side by side, they put their mounts into a southwestward trot, kicking up a screen of adobe-colored dust behind them.

Prophet watched until the two had disappeared over the other side of a low, cactus-studded hill. Shaking his head, he chuckled. "That boy's gonna have one hell of a time. But I reckon he ain't a boy no more. At least, he won't be a boy after, say, good dark tonight!"

Prophet looked at Louisa beside him. She stared after Hans and Loretta, but her mind was elsewhere.

"What do you say we head back north?" Prophet said quickly, intending to break the ominous train of her thoughts. "Find you another nice, quiet town with some good folks in it. Maybe a sarsaparilla-swillin' boy . . ."

Louisa turned to him and blinked as though swimming up through a thick fog. Finally, she lifted the corners of her bee-stung lips, leaned toward him, and wrapped an arm around his neck.

She kissed him, holding him tight for a long time.

"See you around, Lou."

"Ah, doggone it, Louisa!"

She held his gaze as she backed her pinto away from him. "It wouldn't work, Lou. You and I both know it wouldn't."

"Give it a chance."

Louisa's eyes flashed indignantly. "I did." She reined the horse around, put him onto a faint, west-angling trail, and heeled him into a ground-eating lope.

Her hoof thuds dwindled gradually.

And then she was gone.

Prophet stared after her for a long time.

"Come on, Mean and Ugly," he grumbled, reining the hammer-headed dun southeastward. His broad face was grim beneath the funneled brim of his battered Stetson, his wind-burned lips set with frustration. "I'm with Big Hans. Let's go to Mexico. I've always said you can never go wrong headed for Mexico."

Mean and Ugly stepped into a trot, shaking his ugly, can-tankerous head.

Prophet glanced back into Louisa's still-sifting dust. He thought he could make out her long-haired silhouette bobbing up another distant rise. He'd probably never see her again, but hell, you never knew about Louisa.

Hell, he never knew about *him*. He'd probably get himself knifed or shot or both down in Monterrey.

The big bounty hunter turned forward in his saddle and tipped his hat against the sun.

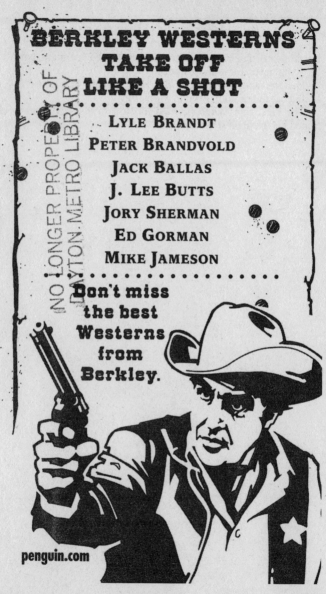

BERKLEY WESTERNS TAKE OFF LIKE A SHOT

LYLE BRANDT
PETER BRANDVOLD
JACK BALLAS
J. LEE BUTTS
JORY SHERMAN
ED GORMAN
MIKE JAMESON

Don't miss the best Westerns from Berkley.

penguin.com

M10G0907